PIGS

PIGS

DANIEL JAMES

To my family and friends for their support. A huge thanks to Ethan Ellenberg for giving me a chance. And of course, to whoever reads this, thank you.

PROLOGUE

The big bad wolf wore a navy single-breasted suit and black tie. His line of work tended to get messy, so he avoided the more formal double-breasted suits in favor of off-the-rack tailoring. The disposable surgical gloves stretched taut over his strong, slender fingers had originally been white; now they were stained with red and black poppies. One hand wielded a pair of fiendishly painful pliers, the other daintily held the freshly pulled fingernail of Lou MacKinnon's right ring finger.

"Give me the names," the wolf repeated, his deep baritone voice patient and neutral behind the mask of latex and black faux fur. "Who else was involved in that job? Who set it up?"

Huffing and panting from the ongoing ordeal, MacKinnon watched his brutaliser stand there in the harsh light of the barn through two swollen eyes, and once again attempted to dodge the question by feigning confusion and ignorance. He was now down to seven fingernails, or so he guessed. It had become difficult to distinguish the blistering heat of each sensory outrage at this point, and he had become lost in a confusing, pulsing throb of pain, the current tally of misery consisting of two plier-pried incisors, his right canine, multiple bodily contusions and various shallow, stinging cuts that cried out with every thump of his stressed heart. Behind this stranger with the rubbery snarl stood a line of similarly cheap-suited men, wearing rubber pig masks with some truly gruesome detail, a militant army of slaughtered swine led by their toothy apex executioner.

The wolf-headed inquisitor, unsatisfied with his subject's stubbornness, leaned in close, his shoulder blocking MacKinnon's view. MacKinnon's uncooperative attitude was crumbling proportionately with the systematic ravaging of his body, and yet his blood-engorged tongue, quivering behind his remaining crimson teeth, only surrendered an indeterminate plea which morphed into another screech of agony, bouncing off the weathered brick walls and timber beams of the empty cattle barn.

Silently, the wolf backed away softly, and through tear-filled eyes MacKinnon noticed that he held something up like it was some important clue. It was his own right index finger, severed at the first knuckle. It would never pull another trigger, never caress a hot piece of ass or skim through a bundle of green backs. Unsurprisingly, he noted, there were some physical traumas which could still rise above his more comparatively trifling wounds, his missing nails and teeth briefly forgotten whilst his stump gushed. The wolf tossed the crooked digit into the bucket of slowly accumulating bloody pieces.

McKinnon thrashed against the coarse ropes binding him to the rough wooden chair's armrests, blanching a shade below bleached bone as he watched another warm, rhythmic jet spritz from his knuckle stump, barely missing the wolf's polished black leather shoes. He was done—he couldn't hold out any longer macabrely wondering how much of him would fit in that pail. It was amazing he had lasted this long. He was a part-time thief, not one of the hardened leg-breakers he regularly rubbed shoulders with, but when the only true deterrent against spilling secrets is the threat of violence, it quickly loses its power in the presence of actual violence.

"Okay," he begged, his naked body hot and sweating profusely in its agonies, so much so that the nightly chill sinking deep into his bones was incapable of offering any further discomfort. Gagging on his own copper-zinged blood, he gobbed it out like thick red wine. "I'll give you the names." Between his racking sobs and pouring tooth sockets, speech was messy work. "I'm dead either way."

The wolf nodded quietly, dispassionately, at the captive's accurate assessment of his situation.

Afterward, he speed-dialled a number whilst one of the slain pigs in suits placed the cold muzzle of a semi-automatic pistol against the base of MacKinnon's skull and splashed his dreams, fears and any other secrets he harbored across the hay-strewn muddy concrete.

"He sang, sir. We have the names." The wolf obediently listened to his following orders then hung up.

It was feeding time.

Free Bird

It was going to be a long ride north to Chicago. Five and a half hours. But it couldn't possibly feel as long as the ride down here to the Menard Correctional Center of Randolph County, Illinois. Isaac Reid leaned his head against the cool glass of the Grayhound's window, feeling the prison transport bus lurch and roll on with the hydraulic hiss of a giant silver snake. With the prison and the muddy Mississippi River at his back, Isaac listened to the conversations of the jubilant passengers overlap into a susurrus of good cheer and excitement. Some of the men talked about their cravings for cigarettes, booze, food, female companionship, and, in less salty instances, their eagerness to be reacquainted with their relatives. Good for them, was all Isaac thought. Outside his window, the rambling farm lands looked gray, matching the sky and making the whole horizon resemble flesh on life support.

He was nervous. Nervous about the coming reunion. Nervous about letting Maggie and Will down. Nervous about ruining this fresh start.

Yeah, it was going to be a long five and a half hours to the last stop.

A heroin-thin Latino with an impoverished black caterpillar over his top lip gave Isaac a friendly nudge. Isaac turned to look at the young banger beside him, bristling with energy, his gray sweater draped over his bony frame like a tent. "You know what else, we're all freezin' our nuts off in these prison-issue rags, broke, but I'm not seein' that as a reason to be pissed." Isaac glanced down at his own prison-issue black sweatpants and not-nearly-thick-enough sweatshirt, garments which would be of little use once autumn shrivelled and died under the imperialist frown of winter, and looked back up at Hector 'Hex' Bermudez. "To me it's a push in the right direction. It's telling me that I fucked up once before and I ain't ever goin' back to that place. No way, dog. No way. I'm out of that life, not wasting my time with that bullshit." The young reformer's voice was gaining traction and speed as he worked to convince himself with his pumped-up pep talk. "Lost enough vatos already, know'msayin'." He was holding tight to his manila envelope packed tight with family photos and letters which had seen him through the hard parts of his stint.

Isaac's own hands were empty, but his trouser pocket did carry the standard Bureau of Prisons pay-out. Twenty dollars. Barely enough for a bus ticket once he reached Chicago. He could have called Maggie for a pick-up. His release wasn't a surprise for her and Will, but he didn't want them driving to pick him up from the bus depot. Call it pride, or most likely shame.

"That's cool, Hex." Isaac gave him a supportive smile. "Sounds like you got yourself some big game-changing ideas." Hex was one of the few allies cool with Isaac. Squealing on others was a strict no-no, even if it was purely out of vengeful spite. It tended to leave a mark on one's rep, fortunately for Isaac, his rep could boast of associations with enough powerful names to balance out his one act of finger-pointing.

"You're a sarcastic pinche cabrona." Hex smirked, exposing a few gold teeth.

""Fucking bitch"?" Isaac cocked one eyebrow, wondering if any of the gutter Spanish he'd picked up had stuck.

Hex flashed a bit more of his polished grill, his wide grin accentuating his gaunt cheeks and deep, cadaverous eye sockets. It was some kind of miracle that he had managed to kick his habit in the joint of all places. "Pretty smart, blanco. So, phase one is—" He framed an idyllic picture with his inked hands. "Get the fuck away from my block."

"How do you manage that with only that change in your pocket? You'll spend most of that on smokes."

"Well, that's phase two. Remember when I told you my cuz was looking to hook me up with a job at the car wash?"

Isaac did, vaguely. "And who said getting that diploma wouldn't pay off?"

Hex nudged him again, the both of them trading survivor's smiles, and the young Hispanic flitted off to try to bum a smoke and further conversation from one of the other dozen ex-cons. Last night's lack of sleep snuck up on Isaac, covering his eyes with its heavy hands. It wasn't excitement which had kept him awake. He wasn't too surprised to accept it as fear. A crawling sensation, marching its century of centipede legs around his neck and guts. Did the other guys on this transport feel the same way? Isaac splayed his right hand, the dirty slush-colored sun glinting off his wedding band. They had just hit St. Louis.

Only four hours to go.

He clenched his right hand into a fist and allowed the sleepy thief of time to take him under, the vibrations and the ocean noise of chatter washing him away to an uneasy sleep.

Isaac snapped awake to the buzz of excitement in his ears. The antiseptic white lights of the bus were on. Isaac squinted away the poor excuse for slumber and noticed the cause of the celebration. The bright skyline of Chicago was a large electrical etching against the amber dusk.

The bus finally wheezed to a stop outside the Greyhound station on West Harrison Street. Stepping off the bus into the chilly scrape of the Windy City, Isaac tried to work out the kink in his lower back, lightly stamping his feet to get the blood pumping again. He watched the other fifty-fifty make-or-break cons hug and kiss emotional relatives and friends. He eased through the affectionate gatherings unnoticed. A few of the other loners were slinking off in the direction of halfway houses, down unreachable rungs of a slippery economic ladder. A few more of the doomed group would be strolling off toward their next relapse or the grave.

He was about to step off the curb when a hand gripped his shoulder. It was Hex, teeth already chattering from the cold but his smile broader than ever. "This is it, man. The future starts here." A tricked-out ocean blue Cadillac was prowling along the curb toward them, subwoofers decimating the paving with Cypress Hill or some such. Isaac wasn't too clued up on rap music, Latino or otherwise. Hex cocked his head to his ride. "Drop you someplace?"

"I'm good. Been away for a dime, I could use the walk. Figure out what I'm going to say to them."

Hex clapped Isaac's right hand and pulled him in shoulder to shoulder, slapping him on the back. "You take care of yourself out here, amigo."

"You too. Be good."

Hex slid around to the passenger side. "Hey, if you ever need your car washed, look me up."

Isaac smiled and watched him vanish into the probable cause on wheels. He hoped Hex made it, he sincerely did, but he was a realist.

There wasn't much chance of anybody making it with only $20 in their pocket. They were all left to fend for themselves now in this cold world without tools or fire.

Nests and Broken Wings

Isaac stood on the wooden porch of Maggie and Will's home. A lovely four-bedroom detached property of hardwood and brick on North Hermitage Avenue. It was a quiet suburb in Uptown. A place with history and lots of aesthetic appeal. Picket fences, lots of green spaces, illuminated by soft street lights. Peaceful neighbors. Isaac felt like he was on an alien planet. His palms were greased, his heart was going into overdrive. He paced back and forth a little and became paranoid a neighbor might spot him looking guilty in undesirable sweatpants and top, on a dark porch, and decide to call the police. He knocked, tentatively at first, then with more confidence for the final few raps. What if she doesn't take me back? Maybe Will wants nothing to do with me. What if they only visited me out of some strange sense of obligation? Like a burden they couldn't quite cut loose. Isaac couldn't answer so many rising voices of discontent.

The door opened. Isaac froze. The doubtful voices were about to get their answers.

Maggie stood there and smiled, but it looked awkward and uncertain. She was dressed comfortably in dark lounge slacks and a white zip-up top, her long, black, curly hair framing her angelic but troubled face. Isaac's heart was in his throat, blocking his words. After a horribly difficult pause she beckoned him in and embraced him tightly.

Isaac broke through his panicked stall and held her tight. "I missed you."

She held a hand to his face, feeling the light cheek stubble she hadn't felt in so long, its blond fuzz the same color as his short hair. Her brown eyes were tearful with relief, triggering a reactive leak in Isaac's own dark eyes. Movement on the stairs caught Isaac's attention. Will, in his jeans and t-shirt, slowly descending the beige carpeted steps, not racing down them to meet his dad for the first time without a toughened window between them.

"Will, hey buddy." Isaac moved a step further into the hallway to make the first move, then hesitated and looked at Maggie for permission, still unsure of where they currently existed as a family. Was that too strong a word at this juncture?

Maggie pressed him on, her hand on his shoulder, helping to slowly build the courage up in Isaac. Will remained at the bottom of the stairs, a cautious smile, much like his father's, settling into place. Having never hugged each other before, the pair of familial males seemed unprepared for the custom, and struggled through a painful handshake.

"How are you, kiddo?" Isaac squatted before him, needing some form of close connection.

Will nodded quietly. His shyness had never been this pronounced during the prison visits. Then, mercifully: 'I'm okay." He glanced to his mom, perhaps for some practised cue, then back to Isaac. "I'm glad you're home."

Isaac draped a large hand on Will's shoulder. "Me too, kid."

Isaac sat on the softly swinging bench hanging on the back deck, enjoying the peaceful view of silvery moonlit flowers and the company of his family. It still felt like that at any moment he might make some error, say something or do something which might implode this whole dream. Wrapped in a thick, warm blanket, he and Maggie drank hot coffee whilst Will, sat at the opposite end of the bench, keeping Maggie as a buffer between himself and Isaac, sipped a glass of juice. Isaac was a little hurt by Will's distance at first but he could understand. If he hadn't messed up so spectacularly in life he wouldn't have spent the past decade watching his boy grow up from behind glass or in photos. As it was, he felt a quiet but deep contentment he hadn't thought, or dreamt, possible. The slow, stumbling process of forging a rapport with Will, and perhaps rekindling the spark of trust with Maggie, was beginning to feel tenable. Will had politely indulged Isaac with talk of his friends, his school, and even updating him on his ongoing love of science fiction. Isaac had loved every moment of it, but now, half-in and half-out of the bonding session, Will was entertaining himself with his phone.

Maggie tousled Will's black hair, a physical trait he received from her. "It's getting a little late now, hon. School night. Say goodnight to your dad."

Will obediently crawled out from under the warmth of the blanket and stood there looking like a third wheel. Isaac felt agitated, not knowing whether he should try to hug him now, or would that be overstepping a boundary? And he didn't want another formal handshake with his young son. His actions seemed to be issued by signals from a confused brain. He put his mug of coffee down on the wooden boards and made to get up.

Will had made the decision for him, slowly inching toward the French doors. "Goodnight, Dad."

Isaac was afraid his voice might break. "Goodnight, son. I love you."

Will nodded and smiled pitifully, like Isaac was a wounded animal needing to be put out of his misery. He paused at the doors and looked back at his father. "Grandpa said you're a really bad guy. That still true?"

Isaac felt like the air had been stolen from him.

Maggie didn't glare at Will, but looked pained, her hand going to her forehead.

"I made some dumb choices in the past. I hope I'm not a bad guy any more. I don't want to be. I just want to be with you and your mom."

Will's face was unreadable. "Goodnight." He went in and closed the patio doors behind him.

"I'm sorry –' Maggie started to apologise, but Isaac swept it away.

"No, I'm the one who should be sorry. I'm the one who screwed everything up. Nearly lost you both." The silence stretched a moment, each second weaving a fine thread of fear through him. He quickly tried to find a lighter note. "I like the new place. It's very…neighborly," he said, trying out a grin he might soon be able to impress the suburbanites with at BBQs and such.

"It is that. I wanted to move while Will was young enough not to lose any good friends or have to change schools. Must be hard for a kid to have their life uprooted." Maggie exhaled. "I didn't have to move. I know I was safe, your friends watching out for me."

"They owed me."

"I think it was a sense of cleansing. A fresh start. Leave the bad stuff behind."

"Have I been left behind?" His eyes pleaded.

Maggie shook her head softly, her black, twisty bangs banded with shimmering moonlight. "No. We can work through this. If I can trust you."

"I'll never lie to you again," he vowed. "That old life, it's a closed book." She sipped her milky coffee and huddled against him beneath the blanket, finding his hand and holding it tight. "I'll find work. I'll start looking tomorrow."

"I could talk to my dad about maybe getting you a job at the dealership?" Maggie voiced the suggestion with such little enthusiasm it didn't really warrant an answer.

Isaac shook his head gently. "Did that sound as bad in your head as it did out loud?"

She snickered and slapped his chest. "Not really."

"I doubt Hank has gotten over what I said to him last time."

"That he's as big a crook as you?" Maggie was utterly deadpan. She could have been reading a transcript.

Isaac hummed deeply in affirmation. "And then there's the whole ten years in prison thing. You broke your daddy's heart when you fell for me. Then I broke yours."

"Yeah, well, I'm a big girl and I can make my own choices. He never could understand that, though. I got seduced by your whole bullshit bad-boy charm."

"You just didn't know how bad."

Isaac tried to smile at the rosy memory of their younger selves but found it tarnished by blood and deceit. He remembered the first time he'd laid eyes on her at the Rocket, one of those 1950s-themed throwback restaurants which, unfortunately for the owner, was thrown right back by the forces of disinterest and ailing revenue. Before the Rocket went under, Isaac had spent one late morning nursing a hangover and an accidental black eye after celebrating a successful heist with his crew. The BBQ chicken, aspirin and several refills of water had moderated his throbbing skull, but the black-haired waitress with the sparkling hazel eyes and well-fitting pink uniform had been better than any hair of the dog. He never had been one to fall for any of that star-crossed lovers mush, and it later turned out that neither was Maggie, which was a boon—but he always remembered how she practically knocked him out when he first laid eyes on her. His panda eye and dishevelled, beer-reeking clothes provided an easy icebreaker for the pair of them, and as luck would have it, their chemistry clicked. More than that, it burned. And just like that, they became inseparable.

Isaac had never thought he would want to settle down by the time he was twenty-four, but being around her seemed to fill a yearning emptiness he hadn't even known was there. An emptiness he had previously filled with bouts of wild drinking and, of course, plotting his next score. She made him want to do better, to be better. And it didn't require any form of subterfuge or conniving intent on her behalf. On the contrary, it was his splintery edges which had attracted her to him. So she fled the crashing Rocket and landed a job at the Lakeside Bank. And Isaac, he really did try to change his ways for her, wanted to step back from his outlaw friends and lifestyle and find genuine employment. But the rush and his loyalty stayed his hand, causing his good intentions to quickly dissolve within the morally toxic environment he had been raised in. So he continued to be a "bar manager" at his boss's various establishments. Isaac didn't think he'd ever stop hating himself for lying to her for so long. Making her feel the fool.

"You were no saint. And you know I'm not going to bullshit you or mollycoddle you. But you've changed." It wasn't a question; she trusted him, against all odds. "I know you have. That last job…you tried to stop that monster. Tried to do right." She rubbed her hand over the old scarring on his stomach. "You've done your penance. That's the whole point of the system. Reformative, right? Now you need to do right by Will."

Isaac was prepared to spend his entire life making it up to his son. To be the father he'd never had. "I will, I promise. I'm going to do right by both of you."

The motion sensor light popped on, illuminating the bright autumn flowering: borders of starry purple asters and orange heleniums. It lit up a number of clay bird ornaments hanging from tree branches or perched on the rockery. LeConte's sparrow.

Isaac wasn't any wildlife buff—with the exception of a few nature documentaries he'd caught in prison—but he remembered those little sculptures well. "Hey, you kept them?"

"Course I did."

The light went off.

"I'll be honest, I mean, I think it's pretty clear I was pissing myself about getting out and seeing you and Will tonight. It's hard to tell how much love will be left over after all our time apart. Strain, distance…I wouldn't have played the pity card if I had found out you had burned everything from our past."

The light went on again. Maggie quietly watched the tree branches undulate in the breeze. "Can we go inside yet? It's colder than a witch's tit out here."

Isaac laughed quietly. "I just needed my fill of fresh air." He exaggerated an inhalation. "That's the breath of a free man."

Maggie kissed him on the cheek. An intimate moment which seemed to promise more. The light went out. "Does the free man want to do anything else?" She pulled him up off the bench and led him toward the patio doors.

REST

Something wet on his face. And warm, like a summer rain. It jarred Isaac out of the first good night's sleep he'd had in a long time.

Stirring and confused, he opened his eyes to Maggie thrashing beside him in the dark, her hands jammed against the savage wound in her throat, eyes wide and beseeching, movements already diminishing their fight. Isaac tasted his wife's blood; it ran down his face in rivulets. Shocked, trying to make sense of what he was seeing, he froze in delirious panic, wanting to act but not knowing how. A nebulous figure obtruded in the darkness to his left, a stab of meagre light catching the bloody butcher's blade in his hand.

The knife came down.

Isaac rolled off the bed as the knife skewered the mattress. In blind survival mode, he threw himself against the dark, featureless attacker, slamming the pair of them into the wardrobe. The intruder was slim but strong, several inches taller than Isaac, and was beginning to get the upper hand in their contest of strength. All Isaac wanted to do was call an ambulance and hold Maggie. He knew she was dying at his back. Scared and alone. Isaac brought his knee up, smashing the attacker's testicles, and rushed him into the wall opposite the bed, splintering the flat screen TV on the wall. The knifeman, hunched over, arm bleeding from some shallow glass lacerations, sliced toward Isaac, the blade whistling through the dark. Isaac's eyes adjusted to the soft moonlight spilling through the window, revealing the butcher to him.

Incredible. After all this time, he had actually returned. Michael Wyndorf. He'd had a haircut and lost the beard, but Isaac could never forget him. There was no mistaking that sick son of a bitch.

Wyndorf cracked a mean smile. "Welcome home, Isaac."

Thunder and lightning struck the room, and both combatants jumped on the spot, startled by the boom. Two wild gunshots had punched through the wall near Wyndorf's left shoulder. Maggie, in her dying moments, had pulled a small revolver from the nightstand. Isaac had forgotten all about it. He had encouraged—no— implored her to get a licence and a piece for this exact scenario, sick to his stomach with worry, knowing that this bastard might crop up and get back at him by hurting her or Will whilst he was trapped in a concrete box miles away.

Maggie's arm started to droop, the arterial spray slowing down. She slumped over on the bed. Isaac bolted for her, screaming her name and taking her gently in his arms as he grabbed the Smith & Wesson from her blood-soaked grip. Taking aim across the room, he saw that Wyndorf had fled onto the dark landing. Isaac kissed Maggie on the lips, hoping she had enough consciousness left to experience it, to know he was there at the end with her. He felt something awful happening inside of himself. He could swear he had abandoned his body to this nightmare, his higher thinking locked in blind panic and leaving his anatomy to fend for itself. A frostbitten chill of despair solidifying blood vessel and organ, the gangrene killing him not only physically but spiritually.

Then a terrible notion entered Isaac's head, mooring him at the edge of the abyss. Still naked, he raced out of the room onto the carpeted landing, heading straight for Will's bedroom, six-shooter pointing at shadows. He had to fight his natural urge to sprint to his son for fear of running onto the edge of a sneaky blade, Wyndorf grinning as he sprang out of a dark doorway. Downstairs, the front door bashed against the wall, loud enough to rattle the whole street. He looked over the wooden railing to the shadowed hallway below, seeing only the door reeling back. Wyndorf was gone.

Isaac rushed into Will's room, hearing a car engine start up on the quiet street outside and tearing off at a mad clip. The car noise, and that of neighbors slowly opening their windows or front doors, seemed to be coming from a world away. All sound was filtered through a wall of white noise, the pounding of a heart, the surf beneath the skin.

Isaac remained at the threshold of Will's room. He didn't need to go any further. Will was half-in and half-out of bed, sheets splayed and drenched with blood, his staring eyes half-lidded between sleep and death. Isaac wasn't aware he was moving, but he was. He was padding slowly further into Will's domain of robots and spaceships, solar systems and aliens, the eradication of innocence and promise.

The stark white security light snapped on in the garden again, drawing Isaac's stunned attention to the bedroom window. There, at the rear of the perimeter, stood a wolf in a suit, stock still like he was sniffing for danger or vulnerable meat. Isaac sensed the surreal presence watching him, its giant shadow clawing toward the exposed innards of his destroyed home. The wolf slowly backed away toward several other indiscernible forms concealed in the thick shade beyond tree and bush.

The light blinked off, and the dark closed in.

Death on Repeat

Isaac had been cleaned of the blood but the internal carnage would never be wiped away. The crime scene officers had graciously allowed him to change into some of his old clothing, which Maggie had kept in a drawer. Black socks, underwear, jeans, a faded blue and black plaid shirt, and an old pair of brown Timberland boots. He finished recounting the events of the attack in monotone, flicking the occasional flat look at the female detective opposite him in the diner's booth. This was an interview, not an interrogation, which apparently was why Detective McGowan had picked this diner to talk in. Isaac hadn't even caught the name of the place. McGowan had had to guide him, like a beaten dog, toward the brightly lit, red and white chequered locale. A "safe, comfortable and proximate" location, she had explained to Isaac in the back of her car. The place was quiet at this late hour, with only a few white-uniformed staff members, and a couple of dozy night owl types wasting away at the counter, perhaps waiting for something they weren't sure of to whisk in and change their lives for the better.

Isaac stared at the booth's laminated table, his coffee cold and untouched. He felt her studious attention on him, analysing his account, his history and character, specifically the fact that he had just finished a ten year time-out at the Menard Correctional Facility for his part in a crime that had made national news. But he knew the neighbors who had witnessed Wyndorf's escape would help with any residual doubt Detective McGowan might be filing away. She had remained calm and quiet during his recount, keeping her body language passive and allowing him to talk at his own pace.

It was standard technique, and for a detective it was probably as natural and automatic as blinking.

McGowan switched off her small digital recorder and adjusted her posture. She was in her forties with short auburn hair, sallow-skinned and dogged from working too many nights and being privy to too many reprehensible acts of inhumanity. "Michael Wyndorf." She spoke as if she was trying the name out. "From what I know, nobody in law enforcement has seen him since—" She half-extended her hand to Isaac. "What transpired at the Jensen place."

Isaac thought it was mighty classy of her to bring that up in such a diplomatic manner. "I had hoped life would have done us all a favor and taken care of him by now." He knew he was mumbling but didn't have the energy to speak up.

"Resurfacing after ten years. You're certain beyond any reasonable doubt it was him?" Isaac rubbed his red eyes, stretching his cheeks gaunt, and nodded. She solemnly accepted this as a hard fact of life. "Some people have long memories," she added.

Isaac was vanishing into a great depression, his absent mind oblivious to the actions of his hands and their slow twisting of his wedding band. He nodded. "He's a proven fucking lunatic and I helped slap a federal bullseye to his back."

"DEA are still looking to nail his cousin Cameron Beech, but he's a ghost too. If Wyndorf is still part of his cousin's meth network, he might have help. People housing him. Maybe this wolf character you saw."

Isaac looked blankly out the window, staring through his sickly reflection at the parking lot.

McGowan's fingernail clinked against the ceramic cup. "Mrs Reid and William moved house shortly after your incarceration. Since Wyndorf knew the address, it's possible he's been stalking her. Biding his time. Which means he's likely to be hiding out somewhere within the state lines."

"What does this matter?" Isaac finally gave her his undivided attention. McGowan tilted her head a few degrees. "Here, out of state, wherever. The guy's a fucking dyed-in-the-wool psychopath. He waited ten years for tonight. He'll try again. Sooner or later."

Isaac's mind was a tangle, venomous thoughts shifting sinuously and seeking out the fresh kill memories of Maggie and Will's corpses like they were warm-blooded prey. It was pointless to resist these grievances his mind relished harming itself with. His left thumb and index finger had hastened their revolutions of his gold band, now twisting it rapidly, adroitly.

McGowan might be objective in her duty but she wasn't about to give any special treatment to an ex-con like him. "Wyndorf is on the database, and then some. I guess you have our gratitude for that. But until forensics confirm the DNA from the blood on the television glass, some of the department will be keeping an eye on you. They won't be willing to accept your reputable word."

Who fucking cares, was all Isaac thought about that. He knew that even when the blood results proved it was Wyndorf, the only likely way he would get caught by the cops or feds would be due to good fucking luck. A lifetime of criminality tended to blunt any unrealistic expectations of the capabilities of the police force.

I'll have a better chance of stopping him myself.

"We'll notify Mrs Reid's family."

Isaac's hand slid across the table to halt her. "I should do it. Can I do it?"

McGowan studied him again, considering his request. Her impenetrable street-tough gaze softened just enough. "You got a phone?"

Isaac shook his head. He hadn't even thought about that until now. Fresh off the bus and far removed from the 21st century grid. Detective McGowan produced a few quarters and slid them across the table. Isaac scraped them into his palm, dreading this call, but knowing it was his job to break this to Hank.

"You got a place to stay tonight?"

"I'll find a hotel." Isaac knew there was no chance of sleep tonight.

"Stay within the city limits, Mr. Reid." McGowan slid out of the booth and adjusted her coal black blazer.

"I'm not going anywhere." His voice was as dull as the grimy coins.

"Do I need to warn you about pulling any stupid cowboy vigilante shit?"

Isaac looked at her without really seeing her, looking far beyond to something else, something bleak.

Business concluded, the wheels of justice now in motion, the detective marched out of the empty diner. Isaac shuffled toward the phone on the wall, hoping some freak accident might kill him before he made it there. It was solid, retro; it might have offered some comfort if Isaac hadn't known the voice on the other end was about to peel away his last shreds of self-worth. He held onto the phone for dear life. Recounting the events again was akin to death on repeat.

Isaac jiggled the loose change and considered ignoring Hank—he didn't care about the man one way or the other, it was only his daughter who mattered, and now that she was gone he didn't anticipate any great and wonderful future blossoming between the shattered men. Isaac thought of calling Roach instead, or the main man Ludlow. Warn them that Wyndorf, patient fucking madman that he is, had resurfaced and the years hadn't calmed him any. They could help Isaac stop him.

Isaac stuck the receiver to his ear and slid the coin into the slot. His finger fluttered over the keypad, undecided on who would receive the news.

Father-in-law. Or his friends.

No. Wyndorf is mine.

Isaac dialled Hank and braced for another emotional reckoning.

LAKESIDE MOURNING

Isaac didn't know what to do with himself. He had spent most of his life on a clock. The stopwatch of a big heist. The restless wait between scores. And the interminable counting down of days until he was out of prison and with his family. Now, for the first time in his life, time had ceased to matter.

Hank's tearful rage still rang in his ears. Maggie's father had forbidden him to attend the funeral. He'd left the diner at some point after that, head full of white noise, and picked a random direction to walk. He had ended up in Logan Square without really noticing. A middle-class neighborhood, over an hour's walk southwest of the diner, past the river and I-90.

Logan was the middle-class neighborhood he had grown up in. Isaac was hardly even aware he had returned, as if some homing instinct had drawn him here. Some folks in Isaac's shoes might have been tempted to explore that little bit further, and do a walk-by of their childhood home and neighborhood. Full wistful immersion. Isaac wasn't wistful. He had enough demons and confusion clattering about in his head right now, and refused to shine any light on his gnarled and twisted roots. The old homestead likely belonged to another family now anyway, and he could only hope that it was less dysfunctional than his own had been.

His mother Angela had been a nurse and a long-suffering victim of her own depression, her little pick-me-up pills and a neglectful, criminal husband, Stan. Stan had been the antithesis of Isaac in criminality. Where Stan was reckless and impulsive, jumping into any quick-fix burglaries and hold-ups which would keep the lights on, Isaac felt such jobs were amateurish, mere learning curves for young, more adept thieves with the discipline and confidence to handle more rewarding scores. Angela had packed her bags and left her law-breaker husband and bad apple son without so much as a goodbye note when Isaac was twelve, shortly after his first few run-ins with the local PD. Isaac didn't recall many tears being shed for his spaced-out placeholder of a mother. Didn't recall many tears for poor old dismissive Stanley either, who had been gunned down sticking up a 7-Eleven like a hot-headed amateur when Isaac was sixteen.

It didn't really matter, though, for he had a new family by then.

The further Isaac ventured, the more he realised he was spoiling for a fight. A mugging. A blessed reprieve from this void he couldn't scramble out of. Hell, a fatal drive-by of his person would do nicely.

Maybe Wyndorf and the wolf were circling.

His whole world might have changed but these old streets remained the same. Some new stores, a renovation here and a paint job there, but largely unaltered. The wind picked up, rattling an old bottle and some desiccated leaves down the sidewalk, but it wasn't sharp enough to cut through the warmth of his thick flannel shirt. A glimmer of an idea formed inside him. A desperate fool's hope, clinging on to what he'd lost. He knew where he would go. He continued rambling in his fugue state, angling north-east.

By the time he reached West Montrose Ave, the gradual ascent into dawn was underway, slowly spinning gold thread into the sparse cloud cover, the sky shining like expensive silverware. With sore feet he shuffled through the fresh scenic parklands of Montrose Fields. It was quiet at this early hour, but he still pictured happy couples and families riding their bikes along the trails, or lounging around in no great hurry to get anywhere, the carefree laughter of a bunch of children capering about Cricket Hill, tearing down the grassy slope with devil-may-care delight. He continued east, past the Corinthian Yacht Dock, Montrose Harbor Office and the Dry Dock with their backdrop of yachts bobbing gently at the jetties in the pink tentativeness of morning.

A little bit further.

He reached his final destination, decided on by the unspoken agreement he had made with his looming despair. The Montrose Point Bird Sanctuary. A peaceful haven which played host to over 300 different species across the seasonal cycles, the pleasant unspoilt meadow spreading toward the placid immensity of Lake Michigan.

Maggie always loved coming here when they were younger.

And now Isaac sought his solace here. Hoping to capture and bottle some sense of her departed spirit. She had been so fond of this place that it had even started to rub off on him. Him, Isaac Reid, urban lout through and through. It used to be that the only birds he ever liked were plucked, cooked and served on a plate, but Maggie always found comfort in watching them, and before long he had too.

A white-crowned sparrow swooped down to the meadow to sing in a choir of chirps with its troupe of feathery musicians. A small group of adoring and borderline obsessive birdwatchers and pho-tographers observed the passerines call to one another from shrub and tree. It was a beautiful melody, but without Maggie next to him, their birdsong was simply music out of key.

No more than five yards from where he stood, a brisk wind lifted the low stems of a shrub, revealing a secretive and delicate little yellow bird with black stripes. Isaac had the feeling life was openly mocking him now. Or rewarding him? It was a LeConte's sparrow. Maggie's favorite. The whistling wind passed and the shrub dropped its limb back to the grassy ground, ferrying Maggie's tiny messenger away from him. Isaac's throat felt raw and dry, choking back the tears.

With a parting glance, he left the birdwatchers to their hobby, their shadows slowly shrinking under the mauve sky. He followed the short trail to Montrose Beach, treading the sandy planks past parasols and strewn lanterns, and slumped on an outdoor table at the Dock. The restaurant wouldn't be open for hours yet, filling the air with smells of grilled fish and tacos, the sounds of conversation and laughter of happy people. For now, he had solitude to watch several sailing boats slowly drift along the water like models which had escaped their bottle prisons. He dug his thumb and index finger into his eyes, massaging them to the point of pain.

Coming here had been a mistake. Dredging the past only served to evoke more hurt, like cutting one's fingers on the broken frame glass of a treasured photograph. If only he had changed course earlier like he had intended, he could have prevented this. It would have spared him the shame of having to watch his son grow up from blanket-swaddled newborn to fresh-faced, shy boy, with his mother's eyes and his father's chin, from the other side of a glass partition. Every time they had left the visitation room he'd wanted nothing more than to be walking out of there with them, Maggie on his arm and his free hand on Will's shoulder. If he'd eschewed his criminal leanings it would have spared him, and them, from ever meeting Michael Wyndorf.

Was he himself prepared to seek out and settle the score with Wyndorf? How far was he willing to go? Violence? Murder? Killing never came easy to him. At most he would get rough, but only if absolutely necessary. He was a professional thief, not some cruel thug. But one way or another, through his own actions or those of the obsessive Wyndorf, he knew they would cross paths again. *Could I kill again?* Breaking the oath he'd made to Maggie to live by society's rules. Proving that Hank was right about him. That he was nothing but bad news. Burning his second chance.

But he had already done all the harm he could to them. Being a pacifist at this stage could only result in his own death and the continued existence of Wyndorf.

A flash of Wyndorf's sadistic glee scorched Isaac's temper.

Welcome home, Isaac.

"I'm sorry Maggie … Will," he whispered in lament. "I can't let him get away with this. I can't. He needs to die. Please, please forgive me."

Fatigue was pulling him down. He pushed himself off the bench and started to retrace his steps.

Another LeConte sparrow took flight overhead, her song guiding him back to the cold, hard city.

JUNKYARD DIAMONDS

The dark blue Mazda gently dropped its speed on the approach to the corner of East 47th and South Michigan Avenue, easing to a stop opposite the Laurent Boutique jewellery store. The vehicle's soft and exact movements during the parallel parking were an exercise in restrained calm. Inside, though, two men and a woman sat quietly in a static fizz of tension, readying themselves for what came next. The hit and run.

That's where Fitzy came in. A precise and skilled getaway driver, he had a pretty good résumé of heists and favorable recommendations from hardened bank robbers and others who travelled the secret byways of the criminal underworld. That was why Roach had snapped him up in the first place, despite his garrulous tendencies.

Fitzy's burly frame huddled behind the wheel, his short, fiery copper hair stuffed beneath a baseball cap, his trim ginger beard flashing like gold fibres from the sunlight. He chewed a fat wad of gum like a cow chewing cud, using it as a pacifier, keeping his loquacious manner in check whilst letting him operate on autopilot, attentive to their street surroundings and the police scanner chatter coming from the dashboard. The nearest Chicago PD building lay only a mile and a half north of their current position, so it paid to monitor every nearby twitch of the tautly strained blue line of law and order.

Roach spared a fleeting glance at the boutique. It was an attractive mark. All faux-gold lettering and elegant cursive script in frost-white decals upon spotless glass. Inside, a couple of smartly dressed clerks fussed about, restocking merchandise cases or wiping away imaginary imperfections on the glass cases.

Roach's big hands flexed in their black leather gloves. This was old hat to him, a 41-year-old veteran of armed robberies and occasional leg-breaking. His pulse was smoothly thumping away, experienced and primed for this, keeping his head clear and composed. "Same old story. You both ready?"

Fitzy nodded once, his fingers slowly undulating like jellyfish limbs on the wheel.

"Yeah-yeah, let's go," the younger female voice railed impatiently. Having grown up in the Englewood district, Grace was no stranger to rough stuff, for much of it was a necessary evil, a means to stay alive. At twenty-three, she would be considered young in some parts of the world. In Englewood, no birthdays could be taken for granted. Yet despite a harsh, gang-blighted upbringing, she hadn't lost her animated exuberance before a big job. Grace grabbed the ski mask bundled atop her braids like a beanie and yanked it down over her youthful, almond complexion.

Roach did the same, and flipped his dark hood over his head to hide his short, knotted ponytail. "Go."

Fitzy watched the both of them spring from the vehicle and rapidly pace toward the boutique, leaving him in the company of the squawking garble of the police scanner.

Roach pushed through the shimmering glass door, hearing the startled gasps of the two staff members. He was a big man, six-two and wide in the shoulders. And now he had a black balaclava and a concealing coat. He charged straight toward the dark-suited security guard. Roach whipped out a small bottle of pepper spray, quicker on the drawer than the guard, neutralising him with its eye-burning toxic stink.

Grace had already pulled her semi-automatic pistol and allowed it to take charge of a man she assumed to be the manager. He must have been in his sixties, with a loose neck wattle and a nest of ivory hair. "Please, pops, let's all go home without regrets." Grace guided him and his co-worker, a thirty-something dark-skinned woman, away from the counter and any potential—likely—silent alarms. Her barrel shepherded the pair to the corner of the store's entrance, opposite the purple-faced, coughing guard.

"No heroes, no bodies," Roach decreed, pulling a resin-coated lump hammer from his bulky coat. "It's that simple."

"Face down," Grace added to the shaking staff, sounding thankful that neither of them had tried anything stupid, which would have in turn made her do something stupid. She heard the first splitting shatter of glass behind her. Convinced by their timidity and terror-stricken stares that neither of them was going to test her marksmanship, she carefully backed away, slipping her gun down the back of her jeans and pulling out her own hammer and sack from the deep front pocket of her gray hoodie.

Roach and Grace swept through the place like emaciated vultures stripping the flesh from a carcass, their loot sacks bulging with precious metals and stones. The watch on Roach's arm beeped. Their window had just closed.

Fitzy quickly shot out of his parking spot and spun half a donut, aiming the nose of their ride south and away from the police station now at his back between East 35th and 36th. Roach and Grace sped out of the boutique like the building had caught fire and flung themselves into the Mazda. Fitzy stamped down on the pedal and sent them southbound like a bullet, the police scanner now alight with an urgent dispatch to Laurent Boutique.

"Some good-hearted citizen called it in." Fitzy waved to the street, where a gaggle of concerned pedestrians were cautiously watching the events unfold. His jaw muscles rapidly working on the tasteless mound of gum, he cut into openings in the traffic before sliding into the fast lane and hitting 50mph.

Roach decided to keep his mask on. "Then you need to get us six miles without getting shot." He placed his tied bag of swag in the passenger footwell and kept a firm hold on his gun.

Grace's eyes thrummed with electrical tension behind her mask, constantly bouncing from side windows to rear in anticipation of flashing lights.

"Keep your head down," Fitzy snapped at Grace, wanting to glimpse more in his rear mirror than her swivelling neck. He had cleared a mile so far without incident, but could hear the threat of the sirens rising and falling somewhere close by. "S'long as we don't get picked up by a bird we got this."

"Shit's goin' easier than the last one," Grace said naively.

Fitzy swung the car onto East Garfield Boulevard, the rear tyres smoking on the asphalt, and made to charge headlong across the busy intersection. A responding police cruiser heading in the opposite direction found itself on a bumper-to-bumper collision course with them. Roach took a sharp breath, tensing up in his seat. Just as he made eye contact with the surprised cops, Fitzy wrenched the steering wheel, narrowly sliding them out of the cruiser's path and then boosting them across the fresh stop light, barely missing the sweep of traffic. A blaring honk admonished in their wake, followed quickly by the unmistakable bang and crunch of car on car. Roach and Grace both turned. The front end of a bus had crumpled the side of the police cruiser like a beer can, both vehicles choking the grid of traffic in a streak of skid marks and broken glass.

The scanner continued to issue urgent updates to the pursuit, the situation quickly catching fire. Fitzy made the engine work overtime, screaming the vehicle westbound at 80mph. They tore like a rocket past the Schulze Baking Company, toward the junction of Garfield and South State, when another cruiser skidded in behind them, almost barging them onto the grassy central embankment.

"What's the play, boss?" Grace asked Roach, shooter in hand, the wailing cop car enthusiastically trying to force them off the road and onto the tree-lined grass.

"Do it," Roach acquiesced. Opening fire on the police was strictly a last resort.

Grace leaned across the back seat and aimed through the rear window at the cop car's front tyre. She waited a moment, taking a breath, allowing the high-speed slalom to level out. She squeezed the trigger. The cruiser's tyre blew out with a shriek of rubber, the loss of traction incapacitating the driver, who was powerless to stop the runaway car from colliding with the steep concrete curb of a railway bridge, wrecking the bumper in a shower of paint flakes and sparks. Grace kept a keen eye on the car and its occupants. They'd both live.

"Ha-ha," she cackled in jest. "So long, po-po."

"Nice shot, kid." Roach kept listening to the scanner and checking the sky, praying that no police chopper was in the vicinity. So far the sky was clear and the safe zone was near.

"You know I earn my paper." Grace was enjoying the ride.

"Ah, shit." Fitzy punched the wheel. The next intersection of West Garfield and Wentworth was a small blockade of stalled traffic and pulsing red and blues, three cruisers circling into position to block the six lanes.

Roach and Grace's knuckles were turning white but they had faith in Fitzy. He zigged and zagged through the bottleneck, cars and vans angrily skidding aside at the sound of the mechanical banshee wail of the Mazda. Fitzy found his alternative route and jumped the central reservation, tearing up grass and dodging skinny trees. The defensive wall of squad cars was already disbanding, reacting to their quarry's improvisation and trying to box him in. Fitzy sailed off the grassy reservation, squeaking past the electrical junction boxes and swerving back onto Garfield. The closest patrol car growled and hit them in the rear, angling them toward the concrete wall of the overpass and aggressively trying to keep them pinned there. I-90's rushing stream of cars flashed past below them, the windshields and waxed bodies throwing up an endless dazzle of a hundred reflected suns.

Roach leaned out of the passenger's side and joined Grace in a desperate salvo of lead, punching hole after hole into the hood and tyres of the cop car. With a deep *crunk* Fitzy fought free of the cruiser's wall grind, leaving the car leaking oil on the bridge.

"Lose these assholes, Fitz. We got less than three miles." The chase was getting a bit too close to the knuckle for Roach's liking.

"Ah, shit, why didn't ya say so?" Fitzy snapped. In his wing mirrors he saw the remaining two cars racing up to flank him. He knew what came next. The inevitable Pursuit Intervention Technique.

The right-hand car was moving in, nosing toward his right rear tyre. Fitzy braked sharply, dropping back, then accelerated, throwing the needle into the red, and performing his own surprise Pursuit Intervention Technique, causing the right-hand car to fishtail across the Mazda's path and straight into that of the second vehicle on his left flank. The pair of cruisers skidded uncontrollably as if the pavement had become black ice, slamming to a harsh stop opposite the Citgo gas station.

Grace applauded wildly, looking back at the two heaped cruisers shrinking in the distance. "That was tight. Shit, that was tight. Don't do it again, though." Her mask hid her smile.

Roach slapped Fitzy on the shoulder in congratulation, then returned his steely attention to the cloudy sky.

"We're good," Fitzy reassured, letting out a tight breath. He hung a left onto West 57th Street and disappeared into the towers of crushed and rusted-out cars of their scrapyard rendezvous.

"Very nice." Strauss's German accent could draw people in with its polite charm. "Magnificent." He held up to the light of the sky a select few pieces from the hefty bundles of cut gems and gold, a few drifts of exhaust particulate and loose dirt tarnishing the beautiful view. "Our buyer will be ecstatic with these items."

The badly beaten Mazda was already cubed and shelved somewhere amongst the countless columns of automotive death strewn all around in semi-ordered destructive art. Roach continued to watch Strauss ogle the goods, and if he didn't know better he might have been expecting a double cross. In beige chinos and a maroon turtleneck, with a cashmere scarf over one shoulder, Strauss was dressed for an expensive nightclub, not a drab scrapyard. The dapper German opened the driver's door of his immaculate E-Type Jaguar and laid the take on the empty passenger seat.

"Very well, lady and gentlemen. I'll have these properly appraised and will be in touch with Ludlow later on today with an exact figure. You will each be getting a tidy sum."

"Ballpark?" Roach asked.

"Well, I see you got all the specified pieces here, along with some extras…" Strauss bit down on his lip to estimate. "Approximately $290,000. The jeweller will have a more trained eye for these specifics."

Roach extended his large mitt. "Thank you, Mr. Strauss."

"Pleasure is all mine." Strauss challenged the sun's glare with a hard squint and returned his stylish sunglasses to the bridge of his hooked nose. His hand dived into his trouser pocket like a gannet spearing a fish and pulled out another set of keys. He tossed them over to Fitzy and Grace, who were idling in chit-chat. Fitzy snatched the keys out of the air and flicked his cigarette away into the nearest heap of hardy weeds, bolts and rust.

"Don't drive like a madman," Strauss called over with a wry smile.

"It's never me, Mr. Strauss."

"Always the cops, yes?"

"Exactly," Fitzy joked, hitting the fob and unlocking the waiting blue Subaru with a double beep. "Those guys are dangerous."

Strauss left Roach's two stooges to return to their conversation whilst he focused on the main man. "How's the bar?"

Roach calmly stuffed his hands in his pockets, a small, prideful smile doing wonders to hide his tough features. "Pretty good. You should stop by and have a drink sometime."

Strauss rested one arm on the Jag convertible's roof. "I might have to take you up on that generous offer one day. It's not my nature to bury my nose into a man's affairs, but you must be doing well by now—financially, I mean. Have you ever thought about opening a franchise? I could be your silent partner."

Roach thoughtfully inspected the surprise offer for any pitfalls or dubious small print. The truth was, though, he enjoyed running the bar solo far too much to saddle himself with another business partner, silent or otherwise.

"Youth is a commodity in your current occupation," Strauss went on. "You don't want to be strong-arming people and waving guns around when your joints are popping, your reflexes are slow, and your whole damn body is fighting you."

Roach threw a few jovial boxing combinations to deflect the joint business venture in a pleasant manner which wouldn't hurt the feelings of a long-serving associate of Ludlow's, particularly one with such a surprising mean streak. "I got a few years left in me. What you trying to say, I'm not beautiful anymore?"

Strauss eyed him critically and gave him a cynical smile, which, with the help of his dark lenses and combed-back gray hair, made him look like a sinister snake oil salesman, alert for fresh targets amongst the gullible. "Take care of yourself, Mr. Roach."

"Always do." Roach winked and patted the hood of the German's slick transport. Strauss had told him that its color was turquoise green sand. Roach thought it looked like phlegm but kept it to himself.

"Wunderbar." Strauss got behind the wheel and slowly wound out of the spoiled grounds of flaking scrap.

Roach slid the beanie-terror mask off his head and unknotted his ponytail, letting the waves of deep brown hair cascade down his broad back.

Fitzy was in the middle of telling some story to Grace—one of his blue tales involving one of his stripper girlfriends, no doubt— and cracking the girl up. Roach always found Grace's laughter to be infectious. The black south-side kid was hard as nails but there was an innocence to her laughter. Roach left them to run at the mouth for another few minutes whilst he hit a speed dial number. The call was answered after a disconcertingly long time, running close to the automated message service before a deep, raspy voice answered to a background soundtrack of smooth jazz.

"The good news is I'm not calling you from prison, hospital or the airport. The better news is we hit the fucking jackpot with this one. A very happy German will be in contact with you later." Roach relayed the estimated value of the hit.

"That's great, Curtis." Ludlow sounded preoccupied, and it wasn't due to the perpetual jazz which followed him like it was his own externalised soundtrack. Over the course of their long relationship, Roach had been relentlessly abused by Ludlow's education on the city's proud musical heritage. Ludlow only quit in disgust when it became apparent that the art was an irrevocably foreign language to his student. "Have you been to see him?"

Roach was about to ask for clarification but quickly caught himself. There was only one "him". Of course there was only one. He had tried to avoid thinking about Isaac's pending release date for the past several months, for the sake of his own mood, but found that he couldn't successfully muffle the noise. "No. I haven't." He tried to think of a reason which wouldn't make him sound like a heartless coward. "I thought about it. But nothing's changed. Isaac wanted a clean slate." Their time apart had helped him to disguise the resentment in his voice. "I told him I would never turn my back on him. That my door would always be open, but I had to respect his wishes." A pause. "I'm not risking dragging him back into this life after all that. He's a family man."

Nothing in reply but jazz. Roach thought Ludlow had put the phone down and walked away. Finally the reply came.

"I have a bit of bad news. I got a call from Jones at the station. Isaac was attacked last night. He's unharmed, but Maggie and Will are dead. Isaac said it was Wyndorf." Ludlow sounded one part melancholy, two parts whisky. Not a good start to the afternoon. "He doesn't have anyone now. That new leaf he turned over just withered and died on the branch."

Roach couldn't articulate. He kicked up a small hillock of mishmash plastic and loose grit. "Wyndorf? That piece of shit. He actually popped back up?"

Silence on the line. Except for jazz.

"Jesus, Luds. I don't even know what to say."

Silence. The clink of ice against glass.

"Isaac—you know where he is? Where he's staying?"

Ludlow sounded battle-worn. "The detective who interviewed him mentioned that he was going to find a hotel. The police aren't going to give a shit about what happens to him. He's not a suspect. No motive, and Jones said there was forced entry to the home. Not to mention the neighbors seeing a guy haul ass out of there shortly after the shots were fired." A swallow of alcohol. "I'll have a few guys check around. And keep an eye on the obits. If we can't find him before, you could catch up to him after the funeral."

"What would I even say to him?"

"It doesn't matter what you say, the two of you were like brothers. A decade doesn't change that. Just let him know we're here for him. For support. It's not an invitation to backslide."

"What about you? Why aren't you reaching out personally?"

"I don't think I could look him in the eye. I'm afraid he'll blame me. Pathetic old fool, I know."

Roach combed his moustache with a thumb and forefinger, mortified at the idea of a reunion. It was ridiculous how he felt this way. So much blood, pain and death had separated them, like a botched amputation, and now more senseless misery had been inflicted on Isaac and his innocent family.

The bond they used to have would have transcended such trivial matters like time apart. So why was it so awkward to consider a face-to-face?

"I'll keep an eye out for him."

Head Full of Bad Ideas

It was a good job Isaac had squirrelled away a small sum before the iron bars slammed shut on him. It was time to collect.

King Pawn seemed to loiter in the Park West neighborhood like it was casing the place for a hit. It looked like any other pawnshop, an overstuffed box of unloved and neglected possessions, brimming with all manner of assorted goods which were either junk or treasure, depending on the beholder. The old dump had been given a makeover during Isaac's incarceration but it still failed to dazzle, like an old hag who had been slapped with rouge by a beautician. But red trim paint and a fresh neon window sign were probably afterthoughts, or so Isaac assumed, because what was most notable was the enhanced security. The windows had new robust iron bars behind the glass, and the doorway, with its scuffed checkerboard floor, was under constant scrutiny from a small concealed camera wired into the ceiling.

Had somebody got wise to King Pawn's activities?

Isaac pushed through the door, also new and more formidable than its predecessor, and heard the familiar two-tone beep, a call for Roger Coughlin, or whoever he had manning the treasury, to greet the street people with a benign but weary welcome. Isaac was sure he remembered a lot of these abandoned wares from a decade ago: old guitars in need of new pickups or strings, random drum toms and cymbals leaning crookedly around an old bass drum, a few dusty keyboards and TVs, some golf and fishing gear, knives and scratched furniture (not related). The man behind the heavy plastic partition at the back of the store was slumped over a glass case full of watches and jewellery, a newspaper splayed out before him. At the door's chime, he glanced over his reading glasses and did a double take.

"Isaac?" Roger Coughlin didn't look pleased to see him, but he did his best. "I didn't know you were out."

Isaac hadn't slept. He had continued to wander Chicago meaninglessly with a head full of bad ideas until this particular one snagged, sluggishly forming in his fervid mind. "Got out yesterday."

"Hey, congratulations. I still got that old disco ball and DJ light system for sale if you're looking to party? Throw in the dry ice machine too."

Isaac wasn't in the mood to humor him. "I'm a bit cash poor right now. It's why I'm here."

Stress seemed to push down on Coughlin's spindly shoulders. He brushed a hand through his stiff copper hair. Isaac remembered him as being rather placid at the worst of times, so didn't immediately pick up on the bad news circling him like so much cheap second-hand crap.

Roger pulled his glasses off and left them to dangle from their gold chain. "Isaac, you won't want to hear this … I had a bit of a problem. About two years ago now." Isaac waited him out, and noticed that as Roger took a step toward the rear of the shop he was leaning on a cane. That's new. The man was only in his forties. "Somebody got wise to us and hit the place. They went through the holdings like a damn hurricane. Nothin' specific, just a whole lotta everything. My clients couldn't find the crew stupid enough to even think about doing this."

King Pawn's book of clients included numerous mobsters and other questionable businessmen, so Isaac could only guess how much blood ran under the streets in their failed quest to retrieve their loot.

"We think it was a bunch of dirty cops."

Isaac didn't need nor want to ask, but he did anyway. "My nut for the winter?"

"From what I pooled back together…" Roger's jaw clenched, a terminal prognosis. "A deuce or so."

Isaac was speechless for a full five count. "Two gee from ten?"

"I don't know what else to tell you. I had to break this same shit news to the Italians, the Koreans, the Russians; let me tell you, if one of them filthy rat bastard cops hadn't already put a bullet in me, I think I could have expected one or two from either of the outfits."

It was another blow, but right now a thousand dollars would be more than enough for what he needed. Isaac slowly scrubbed both hands up over his face to his hairline then let his arms go limp. "Get it. I'll need a burner and a strap too. Nothing flashy."

Roger slipped his glasses on. "Consider them free of charge. Compensation."

"Thanks."

There was a palpable bad aura around Isaac which Roger didn't seem to dig. He punched in the security code and limped into the back storeroom, returning a minute later with Isaac's plundered capital, a disposable phone and a clean 9mm semi-automatic. Isaac looked at the clip of fifty-dollar bills in Roger's hand. To think he had originally planned to jettison this money to honor his clean slate. Give it to charity, or just try to forget it ever existed, leaving it to rot in Roger's vault until another dirty cop stick-up or a legal police raid scooped it up. He stuffed the clip in his jeans with his phone and stuck the gun in his waistband.

"See you in another ten years?" Roger asked.

Isaac silently left King Pawn and marched off down the street, feeling like a piece of trash buffeted by a cold wind.

GROUNDS FOR DIVORCE

Roach hated using Skype. It felt like such an awkward way to talk to somebody. Impersonal, despite the visual presence. But his kids had been down in Ann Arbor with their mother and her sister for a while, going on forever. He hated using it even more when his conversation broke down into heated arguments with Diane, once she'd bundled little Peter and Vicky away into the next room so the grown-ups could talk.

"Divorce! Can we be civil here? We have an arrangement, right?" Roach's jaw hung open between rapid bursts of shock. "What, the separation isn't enough anymore?" On screen Diane waited him out, fully expecting this response. "They're my kids too, Diane. Please, let me come down there to see them. It will save you the trip. You wouldn't even have to do anything." Roach hated the sound of him begging, but this was the type of highly sensitive issue where being a big-swinging-dick tough guy did very little to help.

Diane shook her head, the determined movement like a sharp spasm. To Roach it looked like this was a decision which had kept her up more than a few nights. Her eyes were firmly pushing back tears. "Yes, they're your kids, and that's what worries me, Curt. I thought you might be willing to talk like adults but I'm wasting my breath. I finally see that, and I'm not happy about it. You think I want to do this?" Frustration carved weary lines into her brow, and she ran a soft hand through her short blonde bob.

"Then don't, please."

"You're incapable of change. All these years I've held on, hoping that this might be the day you grow up. Focus on your bar, or anything, I don't really care as long as it's legal."

"Funny how that never used to bother you, huh? I remember you had no problem spending my money at one point. You were just peachy at looking the other way back then."

"Right! Back then! I was stupid. This mess is as much my fault as it is yours, Curt. But we put these walls up between us a long time ago. And I can't tell you how much time I've spent begging, wishing that you'll learn what it takes to break through them."

Roach sat there at his glass table on the balcony of his plush Gold Coast apartment at the Bernardin. He shot a thoughtful look at the magnificent view of the affluent district's high-rise apartments and splendid architecture. He looked back at her. She had peach lip gloss on her full lips. Who's that for? Herself? Him? Some other guy?

"Everybody's luck runs out sooner or later. I thought you might have learned that from Isaac. I can't have our children around a criminal. How long until you get arrested, or hurt, or killed? It's not fair on them, and I can't let that happen to them. And you shouldn't want it to, either."

"It won't." That was weak, and he knew it.

"I'll be arranging to talk to an attorney, Curt. You should too. I'm sorry." She ended her call, her pained face disappearing.

Roach was left staring at his frown in the laptop's screen. He went back inside and paced the apartment, very much wanting to smash something. There wasn't much to smash. Feng shui took a day off when he moved into his one-bedroom luxury apartment. It was purely minimal. Lots of bright airy spaces, glass and marble, some generic and meaningless hanging art, but little in the way of home comforts apart from a nice TV and a much-used pool table. He homed in on his futuristic slab of a refrigerator and scanned the shelf of non-alcoholic beers. An apple-flavored Holsten. The German brewery had eight different flavors, all of which Roach stocked: strawberry, cranberry, black grape, lemon, pomegranate, mojito, classic and the aforementioned apple. It seemed like an apple kind of mood. He popped the cap and walked around restlessly, feeling like a guest in his own home. The conversation with Diane waltzed around his mind. He sought solace at the balcony, looking for a distraction somewhere in that beautifully designed rat maze of skyscrapers, but he couldn't stand still. He went back inside again and idled by the photographs over the mantel. A few had him looking like the biggest kid in the trio, with Vicky and Pete cracking up about something or other, Diane wrapped around them, putting on a positive front for the camera. The more modern pictures contained only the twins, both parents having amicably removed themselves from the time capsule.

He missed them.

And he missed Isaac. He had learned to deal with his friend's absence over the years, respecting his wishes and wanting only the best for him. He couldn't imagine the pain he must be in right now. Diane was right, Roach knew that. But he wasn't capable of breaking away from Ludlow and his other life as easily as Isaac had done. Could his luck run a little bit longer? With Wyndorf stirring again, he couldn't stick his head in the sand right now. And Isaac would need help with this.

Roach took his bottle back out onto the balcony and pulled his laptop closer. He took a long, unsatisfying slug of neutered beer and hit up the Chicago Tribune, moving to the Beacon-News site and searching the obituaries.

A Suit Good Enough to Die In

Isaac had gone through the slightly unreal process of hiring his funeral suit for tomorrow. It was as black as his mood, with nice shoes and cufflinks. He would have to show his best self even if only from a distance, watching the coffins slowly sink into the earth like some ghoulish voyeur. If he went anywhere near the service, Hank and every extended family member and friend would be throwing him into his own plot.

Dazed, he had considered the likelihood that Maggie had kept some of his old suits back at the house, boxed up for an occasion when they could both dress up again and have a nice night on the town. Making new memories. The thought of going anywhere near North Hermitage caused acid and bile to rage through his stomach, peeling away the layers. The snappy and handsome tailor in the suit store on North Clybourne Avenue had politely gone on about recommending this fabric or that, asking how he found the fit of the jacket. Was the crease okay? Were the shoes comfortable? How about that tie? Isaac had nodded like a bewildered man grabbed off the street for an unexpected makeover, offering the occasional mumble to prove he wasn't a store mannequin.

Leaving the store, he wasn't ready to head back to the hotel yet, so he took his time, bags in hand, strolling north-east to Fullerton and boarding the red line three stops south, south-east down the Magnificent Mile, dimly aware of passing a myriad of restaurants, Washington Square Park, the elegance of the Waldorf Astoria high-rise and the Talbott hotel, before departing at the corner of North State St and East Chicago Ave and walking east to the Water Tower

Place. If an inmate had told him that two days after his release from Menard he would be impervious to the cultural splendor of the city, the exciting hum of activity, he would have told him where to shove his prediction. Yet here he was, borderline nihilistic about the passing spectacles: the historic gothic limestone landmark, the Chicago Water Tower; the functional yet classically proportioned aluminium and limestone façade of the Museum of Contemporary Art; even the simple luxury of the Ritz-Carlton. It all washed over him like empty stimuli.

The gun, though—that was a comfortable weight in the small of his back.

He found himself working his way up the levels of the crowded Water Tower Place, streaming along like a lost tourist without an agenda. Then he stopped when his eyes lit up with silver light. He had sleepwalked his way up the vertical shopping mall, guided by the ghosts of memories toward the Swarovski outlet.

As he stood there, perusing the goods through the glass, that old vice hungered beneath his placid surface, its impatient appetite dangling a poisonous carrot before him. The assortment of high-quality Austrian watches and crystal dazzled his senses, awakening a phantom sensation on his wrist. His own high-end watch had been smashed to bits during the Jensen job. That calamity which sent him down this winding road of misery. He roughly workshopped the store's likely security systems, and estimated the net worth of a quick smash and grab. But it wasn't really about the money. He was thinking about how the rush might distract him from the pain, and how much self-loathing he'd feel if he gave in to his street-honed instincts so damn easily.

Maggie had bought him that watch, right from this very store. Maggie … he'd promised her he'd stay within the lines of the law. He wanted to. He truly did; even in death, he still couldn't stomach the idea of breaking his oath to her memory. The gun grew heavier at his spine, a lump of icy metal. Its comfort now felt like a cheat. Ideas rose and sank in his head: returning it to Roger, lashing it down a storm drain.

But what about Wyndorf? He knew one way or another that their mutual burn for vengeance was going to end in the spilling of each other's blood, with either one or the pair of them dead. Was he meant to give up his life to that animal to honor his word? Would Maggie want that, or Will? His thoughts buzzed like a swarm of angry bees.

No, Isaac decided. They wouldn't want that. He was willing to die, but he was taking Wyndorf down with him, and he'd accept the verdict from whatever judicial system awaited him beyond the mortal threshold.

He took the ghost's hand, and allowed it to guide him along happier memories of days he had spent here with Maggie: a bit of cash-burning retail therapy, sharing some laughs and something to eat at Mity Nice, the both of them planning what else they were going to do with the rest of their day. All the basic pleasantries of a life he used to take for granted.

Isaac wanted to sharpen these moments, improve the clarity of their cut. For he would need them tomorrow, and he would hold them tight.

RITES OF PASSAGE

There was a chill in the heart of Graceland Cemetery.

In accordance with Hank Kurtz's wishes, Isaac watched from the shelter of a distant willow as the priest performed his family's funeral rites. Even from his far remove he could still hear the faint wails on the cold air. He waited patiently, hollowed out and wind-sheared, until the ritual was completed and the gathered Kurtz clan slowly vanished behind gravestone or tree, formal wraiths escaping back to the land of the living. He scanned around the grounds again, expecting to find Wyndorf half-hidden behind a grave marker, waiting for an opportunity.

Nothing.

Isaac approached the precisely tended grass and hard-packed fresh soil of Margaret and William Reid's graves, a conjoined tomb of his very world. It was resplendent in tokens and letters, brightly scented wreaths, candles and photos. To Isaac, the bouquet he had picked up had a noxious quality, making him fearful of placing it amongst the heartfelt offerings.

Isaac felt as though he was interred under the dirt with them, murk spilling through his chest like some depressing fungus, sinking deeper and deeper with each passing hour. Head bowed beneath the duo of aggrieved stone angels, a beautiful guardian for each of his loves, he slowly tortured himself with vignette fantasies of a life he could now never build. The tentative November frost reminded him that it would have been Will's tenth birthday in three months, the first he would have spent with his boy outside the hard, cruel walls of the Menard Correctional Center. Before that, of course, there would have been their first Christmas together, prior to Will reaching the milestone of double digits. Opening presents under the tree with him, a ritual Isaac's own father had never shared with him, usually too drunk or distant to care, but one which Isaac would have cherished with his own flesh and blood. A glass of wine with Maggie before the fire. Laughter, fun and festivities. It made a tight and gruesome smile on Isaac's face, the bitter tears threatening to wash it all away. There would have been a lot of lost time to make up for, possibly too much. How many more years would Will's childish optimism and naivety have shielded him from the hard truth that his old man had done very bad things? A life full of wrongdoings and deceit. Will could well have shunned him like a dirty secret when he was mature enough to learn all the facts. Assuming Hank hadn't already aired the dirty laundry.

Isaac stroked the short, frigid brush of grass as if it was Will's hair, or Maggie's, soothing their sleeping minds from a bad dream. Maggie, God bless her, had proven to have had the patience of a saint in putting up with him for so long. The fights after she learned that he wasn't spending his nights pulling pints and mixing cocktails at jazz bars had been brutal, but he couldn't continue to lie to her face when everything was getting so serious between them. And he loved her, the way she loved him.

Isaac's armor was in tatters. He knew this was inevitable. There was no escaping it. No hiding from it. Here, at their final resting place, he would be flogged by his bad choices. The human condition was nothing if not masochistic when it came to brooding over one's faults. He relived it all again. The moment he could have got out of the life, should have got out, but was too stubborn and foolish to change. Viewing everything in this messed-up life as one big gray-toned landscape devoid of good and bad deeds, only haves and have-nots. The fierce arguments between himself and Maggie played in his head, mixed together, a jumble of guilt. Her suspicions about some of his friends from work. Her finding a small black velvet bag of diamonds hidden behind their dresser. His bullshit rationale to ease her worries, and keep her entwined in his life.

Just one last score, baby. I promise. Nobody gets hurt.

The empty justification of a selfish professional thief. He stuck to big heists only, the type with plenty of insurance and staff who were trained to roll over and let the wealthy banks take the hit.

Or at least that was the case until it wasn't.

Nobody gets hurt.

How many times had he told her that, as salty trails ran down her beautiful face? The last time he did, she had her hands resting protectively over her slowly swelling belly. The poor thing had fallen in love with an absolute loser.

Isaac's breath caught in his throat, his nose sniffling as he fought back the deluge of sorrow straining to burst forth. "I'm so sorry." The first tear slipped free and rolled off his chin, thawing a blade of grass. It must have been his thousandth apology but all the apologies in this world and beyond couldn't change the histories of his squandered choices and stupid decisions.

A soft breeze rustled low across the earth, stirring some of the wreaths heaped before the angels. Isaac wasn't the spiritual sort but he liked to think it was Mags and Will silently exonerating him. A man's shadow fell across them. Isaac's prison-honed caution had crumbled under the weight of his grief. Maybe the shadow belonged to the Reaper, his hand of bone gripping his Wyndorf mask, the agent who slayed with a song in his heart and a whistle on his lips. Or maybe a wolf. Isaac stared through his tears at the epitaphs and waited for the cold tip of serrated steel or speeding hot lead to finish the job and put down the ghost wearing his body like a cheap suit. Still crouching, he swiftly drew his gun and spun on his heel.

"Hey, easy, brother." The man's hands went up in half-surrender.

Isaac knew the voice. The sun burned through the cloud over the silent stranger's shoulder, and slowly revealed enough detail for Isaac to make out his features, a quiet sadness on his face. Without a word Isaac got to his feet, staring hard. It was shocking how different and yet how similar the man before him looked after their lost years.

The man was a few inches taller than Isaac, with a wider frame propping up a long, dark winter coat. He was still handsome in his rakish way but underneath his dark beanie, strands of his shoulder-length dark hair were glowing silver. His neat moustache was a new touch, or at least it was to Isaac.

"Roach." Unexpected relief slowly pooled inside him.

Roach looked awkward, his mouth trying to find something to say but only managing to twitch and stumble quietly, the bouquet clutched delicately in both of his hands like it was a sleeping infant. Isaac became unglued. He disappeared the gat and pulled him into a fierce bear hug, mindful of the flowers.

Roach found his voice, muttering over Isaac's shoulder something Isaac himself had been saying a lot. "I'm sorry."

Breaking apart, Isaac kept hold of Roach's shoulders, continuing to look at him like he was a rare exotic species.

Roach had fallen silent again, searching for something to say. "I know you wanted me to stay away, clean break and all that. But I figured, after everything, there would be exceptions to the rule. That okay?"

Gratitude broke through Isaac's painful smile. "It is. Of course it is. Thanks for coming down."

Roach looked at him like he was nuts for showing gratitude. "Fuck, man, don't thank me. Our shared mileage, you can't write that off completely. No matter what. You ever need anything, *anything*, you know you can still call me anytime."

Isaac patted him on the arm. "Thank you for watching over them whilst I was inside."

Roach shrugged like it was nothing. "Ludlow is cut up about this. He sends his best. He misses you, you know."

They both stood quietly for a moment, then Isaac gestured to the forgotten bouquet of roses in Roach's hand. He wiped a tear away with the back of his hand. "They're not for me, are they?"

A wonderful pressure release of laughter eased the tension, helping to guide them out of this heavy morbid spell and fleetingly toward the healing light of day. Roach handed them over, watching as Isaac softly laid them down amongst the others.

"Wyndorf did this?" Roach seemed to hate himself for asking.

Too tired to react, Isaac remained on one knee for a time, feeling the chill radiate through the knee of his trousers. As he rose back up, his face was tight and blank, and Roach could only imagine the cold anger which coursed through his oldest friend at that moment.

Isaac squinted at the sky, dropped his head and nodded softly. "He must have been hiding in one hole or another, keeping his ear to the ground." He almost broke down into a sob but he choked the life out of it like it was Wyndorf's throat. "There was someone else there that night, too. Not inside the house, in the backyard. A guy in a wolf mask."

Letting that sit for a moment, Roach appeared to consider the most diplomatic way to broach the next subject. "You might have severed your ties to us at your sentencing, but I need to know: what're you going to do now?"

Isaac knew exactly what Roach meant. He wasn't wondering about Isaac's career aspirations. There was no room for subtext here.

"I mean, you're not carrying that heater for fashion." Roach's thumb and index finger became a gun.

Isaac felt like he was cheating on Maggie and Will, standing here, breathing, and talking about his future, one of pending illegality no less. He tilted his chin toward the winding paths of the sprawling acreage encompassing them. "Let's take a walk."

They wandered the long, looping pathways of memorial markers and shady trees with no real destination in mind, the crisp air biting skin and scrambling the raked leaves.

"I've been thinking on it. I don't want to go back to that life," Isaac stated. "It's what caused all this senseless violence. But let's call this a hiatus, because right now I don't see any other option than to find and kill this fucker before he comes at me again. Or maybe he'll take a crack at you next. Maybe even Ludlow."

"That dirty fuck messed up real bad by coming out of hiding. Luds already has guys searching for him. He's got a lot of his own pain to pour into that shitbag."

Isaac knew full well about that. He and Roach. But instead of feeling comfort or solidarity in their shared hunt, Isaac felt alarm. His own agonies were fresh, unlike Ludlow's. Was he prepared to share the kill? His rage had a selfish appetite. The distant Red Line L train rattled along the eastern edge of the cemetery.

"Truthfully, do you blame Luds for all this? Adding Wyn to our crew that night?"

Isaac's attention stayed on the middle distance, gears churning out an honest response. "No, I don't. He was hurting bad. Desperation can do awful things to people. And we went right along with it. Shit, we forced ourselves onto the Jensen thing. That's what you do for family, though, right? And Luds and Janine were the parents we never had. So no, I don't blame him. I played my part."

Roach's cheeks were flushed with the cold, his brown eyes glancing over to the large colonnades of the Potter Palmer mausoleum across the pond.

"And I'll fix this."

"We'll fix this," Roach corrected. "Together. I played my part too. For Maggie, for Will, for Janine."

"For the Jensen family."

Roach looked ambivalent for a moment. "For his wife and daughter, sure." That was awkward. "Look, where are you staying? Come back with me, you can crash in –"

Isaac dismissed the inquiry immediately. "No. Thanks, Curt. I got a room at the Versey." He caught the surprise on Roach's face. "I had an old nest egg in Roger's place." The answer seemed to satisfy Roach. "Dirty money, but that's all I have right now."

"All money's dirty. It's a dirty world. Please, let me put you up somewhere. For my own peace of mind. At least until we deal with Wyndorf."

"I still need some space. Time to adjust."

Roach's expression grew serious, his brows knitting together in concern. "Okay, but don't fight me on this." He started skimming through a substantial wad of bills.

Isaac seized his wrist. Laundered money had never looked so filthy, and he was already carrying more illicit funding than he cared to. "Trust me, brother. I'm okay."

Roach looked annoyed, but finally relented in his offer of charity. "But we're in this together, yeah? You'll come in, see Ludlow?"

Isaac didn't like lying to him. "Yeah, together."

They exchanged numbers.

"Hey, I think I need a bit more time with Mags and Will."

Roach held his hand up in understanding. "Say no more. It was fuckin' good to see you, man. Been too long."

"Ten years," Isaac added. The sum total of days burned down to absolutely nothing was too hard to fathom. They hugged briefly, patting backs or shoulders, still feeling the gulf of years between them.

Roach looked wary of leaving his friend again. "Be in touch."

Isaac nodded. "You be careful."

Watching Roach walk away, Isaac slowly retraced his steps to the stone angels watching over his late wife and child.

A Man Walks Into a Bar …

Conway was wiping the bar down with a rag the health inspectors would probably balk at when he noticed the legs of a man through the grimy window, trotting down the steps to his door. Milky, overcast light followed the stranger inside, spilling into the gloomy dive and causing the suspicious scoundrel-types to react like vampires, furtive eyes latching on to the incongruous man who looked very much like he had taken a wrong turn. Some rooms positively crackle with tension and an anticipation of trouble, and Conway's most certainly fell onto such a list. There was a reason the eponymous proprietor didn't go in for any flashy neon signs advertising his basement saloon up on street level. This had been a neutral zone for an outlaw clientele going back to the days of speakeasies and vice right here in Printer's Row of the South Loop.

The guy didn't look like much. Some yuppie type, maybe, and a low-salary bottom-feeder one at that. Could be he was an intern, judging from his bargain-basement black trousers, short-sleeve white shirt and red tie. Conway thought everything about him looked cheap. Even his thick-framed glasses seemed a little off, a trickster's artifice. Underneath the appearance there was something else, and Conway caught a whiff of danger about the man, mania even, like a spring-loaded trap. But Conway was unsure if the man was a threat to himself or externally.

The newcomer walked over to the bar, dishing out a few unreciprocated smiles and nods to some of the patrons. If he had picked up on the simmering mistrust and hostility with his coke-bottle lenses he didn't care to show it.

"You lookin' for somethin'?" Conway grumbled, folding arms which were somewhere between flab and muscle over his generous belly, tautly stretching an old Motörhead t-shirt which was so threadbare a gang of cats might have been rutting and feeding on it.

Mr. Discount fidgeted with his thick frames in such a fastidious manner that Conway inaudibly sighed at this dumb stiff's wrong turn.

However, unperturbed, the visitor pulled up a stool and cleared his throat. "Um, hi there." His voice was quite reedy, hardly unexpected. "I'm looking for an old friend of mine who I was told frequents this bar."

"I doubt it," replied Conway tersely, leaning his arms across the bar and staring at him from beneath bushy, graying brows. "But you piqued my curiosity."

"Yes, well, um, his name is Isaac Reid."

Conway's face was a brick wall. He stared impassively at the gangly, slick-haired trespasser for several seconds.

Cheap Specs held his stare with a cordial patience that somehow seemed insectile. As if concerned that the chunky, graying walrus had suffered some inconvenient stroke, he rotated his neck left then right, first catching the eyes of a few greasy biker types in a corner booth, and then a few flint-hard stares from a couple of pool players.

The fat statue returned to life. "He hasn't been in here in a long time. Surely a friend of his would know that." Conway glanced at the glossy, slicked-back hair of this alleged friend and wondered if he owned shares in a pomade brand.

"I've been on the road for a while. I travel a lot on business, y'see. But I always make sure to catch up with him when I'm in town."

Conway folded his arms back across his barrel chest, shutting down this line of dubious inquiry. "That so, huh? Well, I don't know what to tell you, slick. I haven't seen him in—" His eyes rolled up to tally the annual chicken scratches on his mental wall of time. "Shit. Ten years. And I think it'd be best for you to reverse on out of here. This isn't your scene."

Slick looked impatiently reflective, drumming two fingers on the bar. "I don't want to keep you. I know you're busy." His magnified eyes swept across the small clusters of bad intent locked in their secretive conversations in the four corners. "What about Curtis Roach? He still drink in here?"

Conway didn't appreciate the inquisitiveness of the outcast. "You don't look like a pig, but you smell similar. Who the fuck are you? A fed?" His hand reached under the bar with practised ease, leaving no ambiguity as to what he was taking a hold of.

Specs could feel the hungry eyes of the phantom 12-gauge staring at his stomach. "Honestly, I'm just a friend. Truth is, I heard Isaac's had a rough go of it. Something about prison, and something on the news about—" He rubbed his brow line in discomfort and lowered his tone for decency, "his family being murdered. Just awful. I don't like talking about this stuff." He wilted. "I don't have the nerve for it. I was just hoping I could find a way to contact him to pass on my regards. I know he and his boys used to be fond of this place."

"I think it's time you walk out, while your legs still work."

A small, nervous smile displayed caps of white. "Please, sir, is there call to be so aggressive?"

Conway was about done with his miserly civility and was a cunt hair from introducing this suspicious little prick to both barrels hinged below the register. "Last chance, dick weed."

Slick shrugged in compromise. But his smile of feigned awkwardness slipped into one of cocky amusement. "Christ, man. Can I at least get a beer?"

Conway wasn't in the mood to hire out some bozos to refurb his wet bar, so he brought the shotgun out to play. "If this thing could talk, it could tell some stories."

Slick held his hands up and slowly climbed off his stool in surrender. "Neat-o. Hey, I got a story for ya." Quick as a magician, Slick pulled a concealed ballistic knife from his trouser pocket and fired the projectile blade into Conway's ample stomach.

After several seconds of confusion, Conway shrieked and fell against the beer coolers behind him, knocking over bottles whilst blood poured through his fingers. Slick didn't move, not even as a number of the shocked patrons began to reach for guns or knives of their own. The bar door swung open, ushering in a swollen body-builder type in a black duster coat, urban camo trousers and army boots. The newcomer had sideburns and a stylish Elvis hairdo completely at odds with the rest of his militant fetishism. Pulling an AR-15 out from his coat, the muscle-bound thug put down each and every barfly with remarkable precision and speed, the type that only first-rate soldiers or overzealous gun range aficionados can muster. When the thunder of each fatal strike stopped shaking the dark wooden walls, he checked on Slick, who remained in his spot by the bar, watching Conway yelp in pain and struggle to remove the sharp-pointed steel embedded in his fat padding.

Slick tilted his head a little, listening to Conway blubber and beg. "I guess it was more of a short story. But some of those have pretty gnarly endings."

The rockabilly-coiffed gun enthusiast quickly confirmed his multiple kills and plodded over to his stone-faced partner.

"You were right, Garland," Slick said. "That knife does not disappoint."

"Nope."

"Did you really put the blade through a fence post once?"

"Yep." Garland raised his rifle to one hillside of a shoulder, not caring about small talk under the pressing circumstances.

Slick removed a tiny, camouflaged earbud, then loosened his tie and collar button to pull away the small adhesive throat mic, bundling and dropping the comm-link system into his pocket. Mimicking Conway's blustery lean-over-the-bar routine, Slick sounded genuinely needy. "You really don't know where I can find Isaac? It would be just swell if you could help me out on this."

Conway tried to get words out between mewling. "L-last I huh-heard, he was goin' legit. Roach…" he was practically talking through clenched teeth now, "he's still active. But he hasn't drank here in years. He's got his own place. A sports bar, puh-Pitchers, on North Wells Street, Uh-Old Town. "S'all I know, I swear. C'mon man, help me. I can be useful. I deal in information."

Slick clucked a few times and looked around the bar at nothing in particular. "You do? Because you haven't been overly helpful. And what good will you be when your fat ass is laid up in a hospital bed?"

"Let's move out," Garland prompted. "Cops'll be on their way."

Slick didn't look at his heavily armed advisor. "Get in the truck. I'll be there in a minute."

Garland paused. "You don't give the orders here—this is baby-sitting duty. If Thurman—"

Slick lashed out like an orchestral conductor with a spasm, a silencing finger in the air. He neatly folded his drama back into his carry-on case. "Give me a minute. He could still be a tattletale."

Garland strode over to the doorway and waited like an indignant minder. "I'll be wanting that blade back."

Slick sighed and hopped over the bar, squatting next to Conway. He gave the base of the embedded blade a little wriggle, prompting a horrendous cry from the tavern owner. "You gave me an address so I'm feeling a bit generous. Don't make me regret being a good guy here." Conway looked positively ill in his pain and blood loss, sweat beading his bald, bowling-ball head. "Conway, right?" Slick ignored the pressing matter of responding police sirens and the man's need for medical attention, holding his hand out for a formal, if not redundant introduction.

Conway, delirious from his misfortune and doing whatever it took to kill time until Chicago's finest burst in here, took the psycho's hand in his own.

"I'm Wyndorf," Slick said with a single firm shake, using his free hand and the dirty bar rag to slip the ballistic blade free of its suctioned target. Wyndorf reset the blade within in its handle as Conway's labored lungs struggled to holler further obscenities. With a dripping crimson finger he adjusted his glasses' frame, smudging a few specks of red on the right lens as he watched the shock and blood loss turn Conway chalk white, the way a diligent student hangs on the words of a good teacher.

Wyndorf stared into the wet, glassy eyes of Conway, charming him, luring him to stay with him for a few moments longer. He whispered, "You look good for one more scream." He reached into his trouser pocket, digging out a cylindrical object. It was cherry red, with AN-M14 TH3 stencilled across it in black.

Conway knew a grenade when he saw one. He shook his head at Wyndorf with great futility. Wyndorf nodded, all mellow and serene. He stood up and popped the pin and dropped it in Conway's lap, the barman's mortal wound and rotund torso proving too great an obstacle for his enfeebled dying hands to reach across and clasp. Wyndorf vaulted back over the bar and toward Garland and the exit.

It wasn't a fragmentation grenade. With the hiss of a thousand snakes, the small red cylinder erupted into a huge ball of blinding sparks, hot enough to burn through steel plate. Conway's scream was inhuman for those first few seconds.

"Christ!" Garland watched the incendiary grenade galvanise into an inferno from behind the bar, engulfing hard wood and stained liquor, the screams of Conway rising to subsonic frequencies before becoming smoke. He shoulder-checked Wyndorf on his race toward the conflagration, raising his rifle. The searing heat had already stolen any lingering breath in Conway's lungs, cooking him internally, but Garland believed that a euthanising shot was the very least he could do. His bullet shut off any final dregs of consciousness within the flame-engulfed head.

"What did you do that for?" Wyndorf whined at Garland like the man had spoilt his sport. Standing half in and half out of the thug haven, he watched the wan afternoon light assist the dim bulbs and the spreading tongues of fire in revealing details of the bloodied corpses strewn about the bar and pool table. Sirens swirled in the electric air, growing closer by the second.

"Shut the fuck up." Garland shoved his partner up the stairs to the decaying street, and hopped into the red Ford pickup truck parked at the curb beside several Harleys. Starting the engine, Garland gave Wyndorf a scolding look. "Clean shirt in the back. Lose those stupid glasses, too. And pass me my blade. Handle first."

Wyndorf grumpily eased into his seat, proffering the blade to his walking one-man army, but he made no effort to change into something less conspicuous.

Garland was a survivalist through and through, and driving around the area of a recent shooting with a partner covered in blood just wasn't the done thing. "Uncross your fucking wires, dickhead. We could get pulled over, and you're sitting there in bloody civvies."

"Then we can add a couple of dead badges to the daily total. Bonus points." Wyndorf's smile matched the barren emptiness in his brown eyes. "Now how about less talky, more drivey."

Garland aggressively tore away from the parking space and reined in his anger at Wyndorf's bullshit bravado. Having an animated screaming match in the car could also draw the eye. A few police cruisers could be seen in their rear-view mirror, pulling up outside the smoky basement. Luckily they were a good ways down the street by now and able to blend in with traffic.

"Who the fuck let you into the armory? Huh?" Garland's cowlick curled toward two focused eyes, covering all points of the street. Wyndorf looked bored by the topic. "Answer the fucking question. Who let you in? It's not your personal fucking toy store. Sneaking out an incendiary grenade! Jesus H Christ! In case you're too fucking dumb to remember your arrangement with the major, you supply us with crank, and we cover your ass. But that doesn't make you one of us. You don't help yourself to our supplies."

Despite the blood stains, Wyndorf looked peaceful: he could have been on his way to a spa, or more likely, a hooker's. "After all this time I'm almost hurt, Garland. You might have a problem with how I conduct myself, but I know that a bunch of your boys *and* the major, have accepted me as one of their own. And why not? I keep you assholes flush with cash, don't I? I'm just another crackpot commando."

Garland's powerful grip caused the wheel to squeak. He slowly exhaled and made certain not to let his bad temper cloud his judgement. This part of the mission required finesse.

"Any plans, big boy? I was thinking we go get a bite to eat, then mosey on down to puh-Pitchers. See if Roach has any—what do you guys call it, actionable intel?—on Isaac. Squeak his wheel, then grease him. You know, fun and games."

Wyndorf's mental state was a seesaw in a hurricane, and kept Garland on his toes. "We'll let things quieten down a little. Then you can pay that Roach guy a visit."

"Let's go now, I'm in gear."

"That's the problem. We'll go later. You're not dragging me down into some public fucking meltdown. Remember the law, those guys who want you? I'm the guy keeping you under the radar."

Wyndorf filled the cab with a quiet tension Garland had long grown accustomed to. He remained immobile, staring off vacantly at the streets and passing traffic. "You know, I'm really disappointed in myself about the other night. Slippery little bastard was right there. Why didn't I just gut him first, then do his bitch? Ya live, ya learn, I guess."

Garland didn't engage. He was sorely tempted to slam on the brakes and put the freaky little turd through the windshield.

But the major wouldn't be pleased with that.

Wyndorf didn't like Garland ignoring him. He wanted the big dog to know his place. "If you don't have the stones for this, the major and a few others will." He lazily craned his neck at his disciplined chauffeur. "You can stay at base camp and play army man, and I'll round up the guys who have a pair. And I'll find Isaac without your 'roid-swollen ass. Shit, I'll even pay Ludlow a visit if I have to. That old coot'll know somethin'. He's bound to. Plus I probably owe the old prick an apology."

Garland turned at the intersection, obeying every road sign and signalling like a good and proper driver. He glanced at Wyndorf, wanting him to hurry up and snap out of his little starry-eyed deathgasm and change his fucking clothing already. "Sounds like a stupid risk. Storming the fort to hit an A-lister over a ten-year grudge."

Wyndorf was on him in a blur, practically climbing into his lap and stamping his ill-fitting black shoe onto Garland's brake foot.

The Ford screeched to a fishtail halt in the middle of the road, creating an unwelcome riot of angry honks and a backup of skidding motorists. Garland felt the point of a concealed knife probing his jugular. Calmly, he looked around as if doing so would make Wyndorf get his act together and allow them to quickly move on before they made a scene.

Wyndorf didn't even take notice. He growled through gritted teeth, his breath hot and unpleasant, smelling like the BBQ beef military rations he had scoffed down before leaving the compound this morning. "Do not pretend to understand the shit that faggot's sensitive nature has caused me. Isaac's a career criminal. They all are. But he got a bit jumpy when the job got rough and tried to kill me? ME!" Those intense eyes and snapping teeth inched so close to Garland's earlobe they almost chewed them off. Instead, all the big soldier got was a tickle of hot breath. "Then he feeds me to the law. Forces me to a life of looking over my shoulder? FBI's Ten Most Wanted. $100,000 bounty on my head. My cuz C.B. keeps me at arm's length, knocks me down to some shit-heel small-time distributer. This is much more than some pissy li'l grudge."

Garland was nobody's pushover, and his professionalism wouldn't allow him to sit here as the horn honks grew more aggressive and the pedestrian mobs gathered to gawp. His voice was cool, composed, disciplined. "We're business partners, you know we'll back you up—it's why you pay us. But do you want to stay on the run or get a fitted onesie and a cellmate? Because we're getting popular by sitting here."

After a few seconds the pressure eased off Garland's toecap, and his throat, and Wyndorf flopped back into his seat. Garland got them out of there quickly but without too much of a fuss.

"You're right…you're right. It's been a productive afternoon. We'll let things settle down a bit. We can check out Roach's pad tomorrow. What's one more day after ten years?" Wyndorf started to unbutton his shirt, swapping it for a fresh one. "I almost forgot, my bad, we'll need to go see Rico later anyway. C.B.'s got a new shipment coming through."

Garland bobbed his head curtly. It was a miracle that this brainless maggot hadn't got them all killed or busted ten times over already. Not wanting to talk for a while, he turned the radio on and busied himself with their commute west toward the Van Buren Street Bridge over the river.

Wyndorf grew into a solemn silence, stroking his clean-shaven chin. "Man, I miss my beard."

Up In Smoke

Isaac pulled his white t-shirt over his shower-damp hair, and let it slide down his body, covering the healed pinkish-white stab wound just left of his abdominals, stitched together by thread and the slow salve of time. After leaving Graceland he had returned to his fourth-floor room at the Hotel Versey, and managed to grab a few restless hours of sleep before a nightmare about dying families awoke him. He tied his bootlaces and grabbed the 9mm from the dresser, slipping it back in his waistband, and crossed to the window to watch the meek sun begin to fade on Chicago. Taking stock of his life for a moment, coming up short on optimism.

The room was a bit bigger than the jail cell he had become accustomed to, but the busy wall collage behind the bed made his eyes ache, the imagery of the Navy Pier Ferris Wheel and Wrigley Field cramped together with part of a Les Paul guitar, signposts and various snapshots of the Windy City. On a positive note, he wasn't sharing it with some snoring, farting gangbanger with a penchant for volatile outbursts.

He shrugged into his flannel shirt and headed for the door and his second chance at life. The hallway carpet resembled choppy aquatic wavelets, the soft gray walls emblazoned with large white text, rainbow-colored graffiti and artwork. He took the stairs to the equally hideously decorated lobby. Maybe hideous was a bit harsh. At another time Isaac might have looked upon the kitschy décor with a wry appreciation, but those days seemed a distant memory. Right now most things were on the wrong side of negative for him. At the moment he thought it was like a group of garish and fiercely proud Chicagoan bachelors had gone apeshit and taken full advantage of their ability to design the place unimpeded by good taste: predominately grays and whites, with mustard yellow seat cushions and baby blue wall panels housing bric-a-brac celebrating the colorful history of the longstanding iconic building. The former home to jazz legend Bix Biederbecke turned decades-spanning rock star hot spot.

One of the two blue-blazered receptionists caught his eye from across the room and attempted a polite smile. Isaac wasn't sure if he managed to return one or not. He might have grimaced instead for all he could tell. The receptionist quickly and professionally diverted his attention to his colleague, the both of them all smiles and easy-going banter. He walked past a group of elderly touristy types lounging about on colorful modern-art-y chairs, and left the building.

He stopped and waited on the corner of Clark, Broadway and Diversey, blowing into his hands. Lights changed, cars rambled to and fro. He flagged a taxi.

The ride down was mercifully quiet, leaving Isaac to think things through. Isaac never waded through the currents of the narcotic world. Even when he was regularly moving amongst thieves, he knew names but never had any cause to associate with that crowd. During his stretch in Menard, he'd heard names, too: old-school players still going strong, up-and-comers making big plays and causing friction. One of the old guard was C.B. The man who was at the forefront of crystal meth's rise in Chicago. It used to be that it just passed through to the south, from Indiana to central Illinois to Iowa, chewing up countless lives in its path, remaining too much of a lightweight narcotic to challenge the heavyweights like heroin and crack. But after making room for itself in the city's northern gay club scene, it started to infect more and more of Chicago, becoming almost systemic in certain neighborhoods. Its spread was made all the worse by the toxic vascular system that was C.B.'s meth network. From what little Isaac knew, the man never even came near Chicago. He was content to pull strings from up and down the east coast, NY, NJ and Miami. Isaac had no way of knowing if Wyndorf was still pushing for him or not. He needed some names from C.B.'s workforce. Anyone he could use as a jumping-off point.

That was why Isaac had the cab drop him off on South Wells Street, near the tail end of the South Loop. He knew a place with useful contacts, where info could be bought or learned. A place he had history with. A place where—Isaac came to dead stop. A blockade of flashing police cars, fire engines and ambulances had blocked off a large section of street from both sides. He could smell smoke scenting the air from where he stood. Conway's had become Lucifer's basement, fiery whips reaching out of the heat-shattered window to snag an ankle, dragging any poor souls inside to burn with them. The firefighters were making some progress, though, the water jets mixing and concocting a huge cloud of smoke and steam. If Conway had survived he'd be here somewhere, snarling and phoning somebody. Isaac searched for him amongst the various uniforms and blank-faced observers. But he knew in his gut Conway and his unlucky patrons were still in there. Dead by now.

Something crept along his spine and he quickly glanced around him, feeling the security of the 9mm at his back. He hard-eyed the growing crowd, looking for Wyndorf, or a wolf maybe. Finding nothing. Off balance, he stormed off in search of a quiet place to think of an alternative plan.

Okay, so that was a pretty significant brick wall blocking his investigation. Having found a new café called Mateo's just minutes down the street from the flashing mayhem, Isaac sipped a coffee he didn't really want, as the baristas darted back and forth about the shop in their green caps and aprons like decaf wasn't an option. He reassessed his options, which were currently one above nil. He could still dig for answers about C.B.'s crew, but he'd be digging up a whole mess of worms in the process. But that was fine. It might be nice to feel something other than this suffocating despair for a few minutes. He peered out the window of the café at the world he didn't recognise.

His phone danced about in his pocket, and he had a stab of panic. Was Roach in the shit now, too? He didn't recognise the number, so that ruled Roach out. He stared at the screen like it was a threat, finally deciding to accept the unknown.

"Who's this?"

A throat was cleared; then an unmistakable voice, soft, musical and deep, greeted him. It was like an analgesic, pleasant and welcome, and Isaac couldn't deny the surprising comfort he found in it.

"Luds?"

"Hey, son. Is it okay that I called? Roach gave me your number."

Such unease for a man of his standing. Isaac rubbed his brow, nodding. "Course it is."

"Christ, kid. I can't begin to tell you how sorry I am about Maggie and your boy."

It was as if Isaac's lungs had packed in, breathing in soil, choking him. He locked the pain away and swallowed the key. "I'm sorry about Janine. I heard it was a nice service. Sorry I couldn't be there."

"I didn't expect anyone in a hospital bed with a gut shank to have been there, so don't be sweatin' it. It was, though—a nice service. A good woman like her, she left a mark on a lot of people." It sounded like Ludlow had written a script for how this conversation would go but had forgotten his lines. "Anyway, that was years ago now, and I don't want to turn this into some soppy goddamn mushfest so I'll get right down to it. Wyndorf needs a bad exit and a dirt nap. It's long overdue. He's been on my shit list so long the ink has faded. I thought he'd gone native in some jungle or died in a desert somewhere. But that stupid little fuck obviously likes tempting fate. He won't be pulling a vanishing act this time around. So I heard you're maybe looking to fix him? I'm not pushing, I don't know how irregular your moral compass is right now with the grief and whatnot…but if you are looking for him, I sure would like it if you would come back into the fold. For my own peace of mind.

Dangerous work like this, and hearing that he might not be alone? Partnered with an asshole in a wolf mask or something? I don't want to be worrying about you out there all alone. It'll be safer with me watching your back. Hell, we'll be watching each other's."

Isaac saw the lifeline dangling before his eyes, but his hands didn't reach, they withdrew. Ludlow's position meant he would be negotiating with the other power players whose street soldiers might have seen or heard something of Wyndorf. And if Isaac did ally himself with Ludlow, he could get the old jazz man's cops to kick the names of C.B.'s local street-to-mid-level guys up to him. But then that would also mean following Ludlow's lead, and Ludlow would be patient and smart in his business. He had a reputation, and whilst the man never handled narcotics, he would be careful not to instigate a war with C.B. or any of his friends without a damn good reason.

"C.B. sticking to his old story?"

Ludlow sighed, seemingly expecting this. "He's proving difficult to get hold of, but I'm trying."

A black Audi A8 cruised to a smooth stop opposite the café. A suited man watched Isaac from the driver's seat of the polished and pristine ride, his attention on him like a fly on sugar. Isaac watched back. The man was black with a closely shaved head, but any other features were difficult to ascertain from this distance. Another suit, a stocky white guy with mirrored sunglasses, was in the passenger seat, his attention on the cops still maintaining crowd control nearby.

"Maybe someone needs to grab his attention."

"You don't start a war with a guy like C.B. on a hunch. And I see no reason why he would take Wyndorf back into his business since booting him out in the first place."

"He's family."

"He's a reluctant cousin and a liability. Murdering a highly respected cardiac surgeon—" There was no mistaking the effort it took Ludlow to give the late Dr. Jensen acclaim. "And his darling family brings all kinds of extra heat that C.B. doesn't need.

His empire is booming, flowing from the east coast to the Midwest. He's smart enough to know that throwing a bone to that wild animal would only invite disaster." Ludlow verbally took a step back, not wanting to descend into butting heads with Isaac. "I'll get a line to him, and I'll find out what he knows of Wyndorf's current situation."

The Audi driver pressed his phone to his ear, and the conversation must have lasted less than ten seconds. He then pushed a button and raised his window, a dark mirror of street lights and shop fronts. Isaac caught a lonely glimpse of his self, sitting by the window, engaged in his own phone conversation. He had failed to glimpse the Audi's plates as several emergency vehicles bussed past.

"So what is it, son. Can we meet up? I need to know there are no hard feelings between us. To this day I still blame myself about what happened to you. I should have done more to keep you from that job. Emotions should never enter the equation. You were a thief, not a kidnapper."

The Audi continued doing laps around Isaac's thoughts. Was it just a few pricks having a bad day, or could they be trouble?

"Bury it, old man. We're good. Always have been. The shit with Jensen is on my hands as much as yours. But like you say, I was a thief, not a kidnapper. And I'm not sure if I'm a cold-blooded killer, either. I'll let you know if I'm on board with the payback."

Isaac felt a pang of guilt about this, but unlike Ludlow's, his pain was still fresh and bloody, and he didn't have the patience to see this through diplomatically. He thought of Conway's furnace, and who might have caused it. Isaac was prepared to set fire to the underworld to smoke Wyndorf out, and screw anybody who didn't like his methods.

"I need to sort a few things first."

Food Chain

Isaac kept hearing that infuriating little voice in the back of his head telling him he needed to slow down and think this through. It was doubting his every move. This wasn't a great strategy, but Isaac knew if he knocked on a few doors he'd find something in the end. And if it was a bullet? Well, he was past caring.

Isaac had the cabbie drop him off at 4400 West Monroe. A notoriously dangerous hood on the Westside in Garfield Park. It was a utilitarian development of two-storey brick homes. Urban forts against the rampant gangs shooting it out for drug turf. For the poor, law-abiding folks trapped here, an honest living was an urban hell.

This was as good a place as any for Isaac to start.

He loitered on a small dirt lot on the corner of South Kostner Avenue and West Monroe. The rows of houses and street lights were starting to light up, artificial stars in the purple twilight. He knew there would be eyes on him. Not because he posed a threat. Not because he didn't belong. But because the watchful gangsters were scoping him out for a possible sale. White boys liked crystal meth. Isaac just needed to find a pusher. Wouldn't be too hard. He had seen enough wasters inside prison and out to bullshit his way into some pretty convincing acting. Looking antsy and with a hint of pathetic desperation, he tried to blend into the environment, keeping a practised eye on a group of black thugs looking mean on a stoop down the street. He could hear the ominous bass intimidation thumping away under the sounds of the group's talk.

Isaac slunk down the street like he was up to no good. A cold and edgy survivor looking for an opportunity. He spotted his mark further down the way on Kostner, carefully dropping a small stash on the pavement, letting a skeleton with yellowish skin and moth-bitten clothes scoop it up before staggering off to some dank corner. Isaac slowly moved across the street like a whipped dog, past a fudge-brown deli and toward the dealer, hanging by an alley opposite a lot full of U-Haul trailers. The dealer was an observant type, keeping his eyes peeled from behind his shades, sizing Isaac up. Isaac slowed down, making himself look as non-threatening as possible, a little peppy even, a new user still on top of the world and yet to fall.

"Choo want, man?" the man grumbled like a tremor. He was a black kid in his twenties, dark clothing and leather jacket, Bulls ball cap to go with his shades. The only thing that wasn't dark on him was the white square of bandage on what must have been a broken nose.

Isaac gave himself a case of the shakes, becoming a furtive weasel in need of a pick-me-up. "Ice, man. You got any ice?" His voice was needy, a little unfocused. He didn't want to spook the pusher or his spotters dug in nearby.

The hustler stood tall, showing who was in charge here. He played God whilst junkies grovelled. He read Isaac, checking to see if he was legit. After a quick look to his hidden homies, he settled a bit and became the salesman. "Shit yeah, I got that Tina for ya. I got all kinds."

Isaac saw his sunken eyes and sketchy portrayal in the corner pharmacist's shades. He didn't want 'all kinds', didn't want 'Tina'. He didn't hesitate. The gun was in his hand smooth as liquid. Isaac used some of his new prison muscle to shove Nose Bandage into the alley and against the brick, his speed catching him off guard. Any thought of mouthing off or fighting quickly leaves the dealer's mind when the barrel presses up under his chin. Isaac felt the clock ticking again now, knowing it was only a short matter of time before the Nose's pals swarmed in to stamp him into the pavement.

"Who supplies your ice?"

Tick-tock.

"Fuck you niggah, you're a dead man."

Isaac dropped the barrel and shot the thug in his left size 12 Reebok. The backup would be sprinting over now, steel in palm, gold chains swinging. But from where? The squad on the stoop? A lookout watching from the three-storey brick block across the way? From down the alley? Isaac was rarely this sloppy, but that was back when he still had something to live for. If he died here and now, without killing Wyndorf, at least he could still find peace with Maggie and Will. The street soldier in black was pogoing against the wall, flailing in pain and using Isaac's pinning arm for balance.

"That's crutches." Isaac aimed at his rabbit-hopping right foot. "Want the wheelchair?" The gun was nudging under the dealer's smooth chin once more. "Where's your supplier?" He heard a car slam on the brakes on the street somewhere, angry voices, pounding footsteps getting closer, louder, descending on the alley. "I can die here. Can you?"

The corner dealer must have pictured himself in the grand scheme of things, his lowly position as the lowest link on the food chain. He didn't like the empty look in Isaac's eyes or the chill in his voice. "Fuck! Rico, Rico Perez. Hangs out in Pockets, the pool hall on West Grand, man. Fulton. You're one dumb-ass dead cracker if you roll up on 'em. You think he's gonna sweat a punk like you?"

"Describe him."

"Big Mexican dude with glasses and goatee. Busted nose."

Isaac cold-cocked him with the butt of his gun and let him drop, taking off down the alley just as the gangsters rounded the corner. They were all curses and snarls, liberal with their loud and angry gunshots. Their firing was chaotic, made worse by their running. Isaac sprinted past the rear of a hardware store, several bullets scraping brick and lancing through parked cars. He fired over his shoulder, aiming to give them pause rather than drop bodies. He cut across a small parking lot and pushed hard out onto West Madison Street, sprinting diagonally across four lanes of angry traffic. Sucking air through his teeth, arms pumping, he spotted his cab waiting on the corner of the next block, by the gas station on

North Kilbourne Avenue. The driver had honored his word. He'd earned his tip.

Isaac checked over his shoulder. The gang had just spilled out of the car park onto the pavement at Madison, separated from their quarry by a river of head- and tail-lights. Isaac slowed down, sprint to jog to brisk walk, warm gun tucked away. He nodded to the driver, who still looked bored but now mildly curious about the gunshots a few moments ago. Isaac slid into the back seat, breathing hard but composed, hands shaking from adrenaline.

He had a name: Rico Perez. He had an address: Pockets on West Grand Avenue, Fulton River District.

With C.B. practically dominating this corner of the drugs market, it was likely that Rico was part of his infrastructure. But could he point a finger toward Wyndorf?

I'll know soon enough.

LUDLOW'S SOLO

The notes rang out sweet and clear from the broken-in strings of the 1957 Gibson Les Paul Goldtop. The weathered hands ran fluently over the neck, effortlessly turning out a succession of recycled jazz standards—Stella By Starlight, Autumn Leaves, Blue Bossa—before chopping and changing various blues-style licks of the all-time great Wes Montgomery, and then transitioning into some of the bebop-infused scales and arpeggio chords Joe Pass was known for. For Robert 'Laylow' Ludlow, this was a practice he had enjoyed since he was a young man hijacking trucks during the tail end of the 1970s. Not only that, it was a form of therapy for him, easing his mind during a concerto of soul and technically schooled fingers, deciphering the language of the fretboard. With his line of work, it was little wonder he was so skilful, its many difficulties and hard days and nights shaping his stress and anguish into a wail across six strings.

To his local community and the jazz enthusiasts who frequented his string of lauded jazz clubs, Ludlow was a big, robust beer keg of a man, good-hearted and comical with a twinkle in his eye and a warm smile, always greeting and chin-wagging with his regulars like the roguish sot that he was, and always easy with opening his wallet to buy drinks for the hired musicians who graced his stages, which he might on occasion share with them.

None of these acquaintances were aware of his dual life as a career criminal mastermind.

Back in the 1970s, away from the thrill of jacking trucks full of cigarettes, booze, electrical goods and anything else which could turn a buck, his life had been very much about rock'n'roll, gnarly free-spirited girls and, of course, dabbling in all things conducive to a mellow and righteous good time.

But those glory days of reckless youth couldn't last forever, and he'd known he had to let his brain get a bigger vote than his balls. It was his era of new age thinking which got the fiery Ludlow his ironic moniker Laylow. His old crew found it funny that the crazy bastard who would roll the dice and pull any robbery, on any person or outfit, was now planning for the future.

Opening his first jazz club, 9 Lives, had been an inspired choice. Helping to keep his musicality sharp whilst aiding in the washing of some of his surfeit cash. The obvious business venture first came to him when he was in between jobs, enjoying his downtime and locked in an after-hours jam with a bunch of incredibly talented musicians at the historic Green Mill jazz club on North Broadway. He was sweating under those lights, lost in the beautiful maze of improvisation in front of a thrilled and rapturous clientele, and thought about how perfect the moment was, how everything else fell away: money worries, legal worries, girl worries, worrying about getting an extra hole blasted into his head by a rival. None of it mattered when he played. The music became distilled, boiled down to its purest form of virtuosity guided by the emotive soul.

Times were different now. Shifting colloquialisms, incomprehensible gizmos, and, in his opinion, modern music deep in the toilet. That's what the taxmen of age and patience will do to you. Take what they can, sully what they can't. Thankfully, neither age nor patience had taken music from him yet, and it would have to be a whopping case of arthritis for him to surrender his last expression of his heart and soul. The exciting days of hijacking were far behind him. But the music remained.

The rock-hard tips of his middle and ring fingers trilled some vibrato on the D string's second octave. He slowly paced around the practice room of his private one-acre estate in Hinsdale, Illinois, the single lamp casting soft, homey light on the oak-panelled walls and brown leather suite. Through the picture windows he could see several of his men, Docherty and Woodman, loitering near the potted plants in the falling night, discussing one matter or another as they watched over the huge property's lush garden and Olympic swimming pool. He stopped the guitar neck from swinging with one hand and reached for his tumbler of whisky, downing several fingers. Several remained. He knew he'd need them tonight.

Isaac Reid. That stubborn hard-faced kid who had found a soft spot in Ludlow's old heart early on. Who had demonstrated tremendous loyalty with a silent decade cooped up in the gray bar hotel. Separated from his beautiful and pregnant wife. That knowledge had caused considerable stress for Ludlow, almost bad enough to give him palpitations. The guilt was unfathomable. And now she and her boy were senselessly dead. May they both Rest in Peace.

Ludlow and his late love Janine had been incapable of having their own children on account of her infertility. Barren, the uncouth used to call it, a term which not only incited tears and woe in his love's heart but made him forget his decency and manners toward any careless-tongued individual who uttered it. Still, by the time the millennium rolled around, he and Janine no longer viewed the young Isaac and his thick-as-thieves confidant Roach as employees but rather as surrogate sons. Good young men, smart and dependable.

Ludlow closed his eyes and continued to let the music guide him in small circles about the room, playing for the spirit of poor Isaac and his lost family. He reflected on the number of times he had urgently spoken to Isaac prior to his trial, telling him of his intent to confess to his role of masterminding the mangled abduction of Alfred Jensen's wife and daughter, and to condemn himself right alongside Isaac. Of course, Isaac had told him in no uncertain terms to keep his damn mouth shut, for he needed Ludlow and Roach on the outside, vigilant and protective toward Maggie and his newborn should Wyndorf come knocking for some retaliation. Ludlow respected the hell out of his tight-lipped disposition, but still found himself trying to negotiate with Isaac even after the sentencing, even after Janine's heart finally gave in, telling him with tears in his eyes that with her gone he had nothing left to hold on to, he was a broken-down old man who just wanted to try to take some of the heat off a son he had been too hurt and confused to help. Who he had failed. Stony-faced, behaving like he held the monopoly on martyrdom, Isaac had told him that he would turn his back on him should Ludlow turn himself over to the authorities, thereby forsaking his personal guarantee to watch over Isaac's loved ones. Ludlow acutely remembered that long, quiet drive back home, five hollow hours north from Randolph County.

Without conscious thought, Ludlow had slipped into a minor key, the maudlin notes like whimpers in the oak-rich room.

Such a blood-drenched mess, and it all came down to one bad decision. Hiring an unknown quantity in Michael Wyndorf.

The thought of the man produced a few bum notes and a fumble in rhythm and melody. Ludlow stopped plucking. He ran a workman's hand over his crinkled and sagging face as he turned back to the large windows.

Right in time to see Docherty and Woodman drop like sacks of bricks to the spot-lit flagstones, the spray of pulverised bone and mushed brain barely noticeable from his higher vantage point. Ludlow hadn't heard a single shot. Two pig-masked assailants materialised from the garden's shady hedges like the gloom had bled them out. Their accuracy was chilling. The pair of them ran across the lawn with stretched shadows, the crimson dusk and patio lighting playing sinister tricks with their proportions. Ludlow's heart leapt like a jazz drummer in a crazy time signature. Were there more, swarming his safe home right this second from every side?

Ripping the jack out of the guitar with an angry buzz, he laid the guitar on the broken-in couch and raced for the .38 special he kept in his desk drawer. His brow and armpits were already clammy from the fear sweat. He stepped quietly to the door and eased it open, thankful for the well-oiled hinges. A shattering vase broke the quiet tension that was suffocating him like a plastic bag over the head, the noise coming from some indiscernible corner of the large house. The absence of protective gunfire was nerve-rattling.

Ludlow placed all his hope in the pound of steel in his warm grip and slowly poked his head around the corner, anticipating a quick white flash and permanent black oblivion.

No shots.

Quietly, he crept toward the ornate oak banister to peek at the wide hallway below. All he saw was the buffed limestone tile and polished table near the entrance's double doors. Not a soul in sight. Quiet as death, two shoes slowly walked into his line of sight through the living room's archway, the sight making his blood run cold. Wanting to keep the advantage in angle and height, Ludlow waited for more of the intruder to step into view. Maybe if his shakes allowed it he could place a round squarely into the top of this bastard's head. He raised the five-shot revolver with both hands, steady and experienced despite the surge of adrenaline. The legs continued toward the hall, toward him, shins quickly becoming thighs, becoming torso, becoming gun-wielding hands, becoming…Smith. Ludlow sighed with relief. Smith was young and hard-looking with neatly combed brown hair, and, most importantly, was not wearing a marauder's mask.

"Smith," Ludlow whispered. "What's going on?"

Smith kept his gun up, scanning the hallway and putting a pin in his boss's pertinent question. With rapid, catlike steps, he came around to the wide staircase and effortlessly took the steps two at a time. "Sir, I need to get you to the garage right away. We have an unknown number of armed intruders on the premises and the safest precaution is to get the hell out of here."

"I know," Ludlow quietly snapped, indicating his gun. The pleasant numbing effects of his afternoon's liquid diet had turned to corrosive unease in his gut and veins. "Where is everyone?"

"Dead." Smith was a seasoned pro but Ludlow saw the professional demeanor quiver at the unwelcome odds facing them. "They didn't crash the gate. They must have scaled the walls and taken out Slavin and Nowak in the guard hut. The alarms have been disabled."

"I saw Docherty and Woodman go down in the garden," Ludlow said sadly.

"Let's go." Smith took charge.

"I'm regretting not installing that panic room." Ludlow quick-stepped after his guard in his slippers and sweatpants, his white t-shirt feeling sticky along the base of his back.

Even on the thick beige carpet their steps sounded deafening in the quiet house. Moving off the long landing, they tiptoed down the rear staircase, the wrought iron spiralling them down toward the large kitchen. Ludlow bit his lip as he set his foot down on each step, expecting the muted clangs to bring the whole mob toward them from all corners of the house. Those pig masks didn't sit well with him. Not at all. Were they a coincidence? Or had Wyndorf grown a set in his time away? A set big enough to attempt such an invasion as this?

As he descended toward the harshly illuminated kitchen, all he could envision was the pigs waiting near the bottom of the steps, just out of sight, with very large butcher knives. However, he and Smith touched down without event. They hadn't entered a shooting gallery or butcher shop. Neither of them basked in relief. It was far too bright in here; the light fixtures lit them both up like sitting ducks for any killers lurking outside in the garden, hidden by the windows-turned-mirrors.

Ludlow quickly slapped the light switch at the base of the stairs, wrapping them in a protective cloak of gloom. The last image he saw before the bulbs went out was the outstretched leg poking out from behind the kitchen island, forcing a knot into his dry throat. The polished black wingtip pointed up toward the recessed lights of the ceiling, a spreading pool of black blood soaking the back of the trouser leg. Steam rose from the mug of coffee on the island. Judging from the issue of Field & Stream on the table it was Davies. Ludlow had never had any interest in fishing, but he had bought the now deceased Davies a St. Croix Legend Tournament Musky Casting Rod and fishing tackle box for the anniversary of his five years on the payroll.

Smith caught his attention and tilted his head back toward the door leading into the garage. Ludlow kept his iron sight on their rear as they backed away from the kitchen. Smith nodded to him, you ready? Ludlow might have nodded yes but everything existed in a bubble of fast-moving uncertainty. Smith bolted through the door into the four-car garage, his gun eager for a target. Breathing deeply through his nose, he waved Ludlow into the poorly lit room, smelling of earth and a pervasive hint of engine oil. Smith bundled Ludlow into the passenger seat of a 4x4 and jumped behind the wheel, punching the button on the garage door remote.

He had just fired up the engine into a throaty grumble when two neat and silent shots did unpleasant things to his face. Ludlow gasped in horror. Smith's blood was running down his cheek, onto his undershirt, momentarily suspending rational thought. The gun and its five lead slugs lay uselessly in his hand.

Standing in a ring across the gravel driveway were a wolf and four pigs in funeral suits, each holding a suppressed pistol. Each of them had him dead to rights.

Hanging in the Pocket

The crack of pool balls sounded like bones colliding to Isaac. He'd had another night of poor sleep. After ruining that punk's dancing days back in West Garfield, he had gone straight to Pockets and proceeded to stay until closing time. Rico was a no show.

The next morning, Isaac showered, had a tasteless breakfast and went right back. He had nothing to fear. The crippled dealer and his boys would have been in Rico's ear immediately after Isaac's questioning, but all the interested party would know was a white guy was looking for him. And Isaac was just another pale face in Pockets.

Isaac felt like a small fish inside the hall, its interior lit up like a cold aquarium, columns of sapphire LED bulbs and tables of pale, mint green felt. He was growing impatient. He couldn't foresee himself spending an entire day drinking water, potting shots, and expecting Rico to pop in. He retired his cue, letting a group of guys take over his spot, and was walking back to the bar when his phone went. Ignoring it, Isaac took a pastel blue bar stool, sponging up the groups of faces in the hall, double- and triple-checking that he hadn't somehow missed Rico. He wasn't in the mood to listen to Ludlow or Roach fret about bringing him close, but with nothing other than time on his hands he punched the button and got Roach.

"Somebody hit Ludlow's house last night." Roach came right out of the gate, knocking Isaac back momentarily.

"Hit? He dead?"

"We don't know. Only found the bodies of his men. The job looked professional. Surgical."

Ludlow…dead? Wounded? The news hit him, just another punch to his gut. Ludlow, the man who had taken a petty, hard-faced criminal straight out of juvie, a kid whose only discernible talent was a rudimental knack for thievery, and taught him how to be smart, how to stay clean. How to survive in the only world he was meant for. Better than a self-medicating, vanishing mother or scrounging, fuck-up father.

"You done a job on the wrong person lately? Somebody with the teeth to bite back?"

There was confusion in Roach's voice. "We smash and grab jewellery stores and banks. Places with insurance. We don't fuck with people who'll hit back outside of legal channels."

"No suspects?"

"I'm asking around. Got a few more names to cross off. That greasy little prick Payton, a few other guys who duked it out with Luds over the years. I don't know, though, it feels like I'm reaching here. This seems like retaliation, but I can't think of anyone who'd be pissed enough to pull something like this."

"I'd have said Wyndorf, but surgical isn't that sloppy fuck's style. And it was me who really fucked him, not Ludlow."

"And Wyndorf already fucked Luds plenty by killing the surgeon. And why wait all this time to do it? I mean, a decade?" Roach took a slow breath, contemplating something. "Unless he's been busy making friends. Maybe he wanted to wait until you got out so they could scoop us all up."

"I don't think Wyndorf has the brains or the patience for a move like that."

"That's great, then we got Wyndorf and someone even worse up in our shit."

"I was talking to Ludlow last night," said Isaac. "He said he'd been trying to get C.B.'s ear about Wyndorf's return. Said he couldn't get a hold of him."

"You thinking C.B.'s behind this? I don't know, brother, I can't see the motive. He and Luds have no history. You think he's defending the honor of his shit-heel cuz ten years after the fact?"

"Maybe not. But maybe some of his local guys are tight with Wyndorf." Isaac impatiently eyeballed the pool players and the few slow drinkers at the bar.

"Where are you now?"

A bulky shadow entered the hall, looming in Isaac's peripheral vision. Glasses, goatee, tight haircut, thick sleeves of gangster ink, and a brown pugilist's face which looked like life had gone a few hard rounds with it. "I'm still at the hotel. Hey, I'll get back at you soon, stop by your place for a beer. Talk this through." He disconnected the call, keeping watch on the big Mex in the mirrors behind the bar.

Rico was alone, orbiting the pool hall's entrance and engaged in his own phone business. He looked agitated. Besides the Hispanic gang ink coating his arms, he went in for the respectable look in his fashion: a dark blue polo, beige chinos and brown leather shoes. Rico angrily ended his call and headed right back out of the bar, no time for leisure. Isaac carefully glanced around the place, checking for signals to see if something was about to pop off. His stomach felt twitchy, the way it used to before a big job, and he was anxious to get out on the street before he lost Rico. Forcing a mellow gait, he ambled out of the hall, keeping Rico in view. Knowing his target was wobbling on foot east down Grand, Isaac checked the avenue both ways. The roads were fairly busy, but Isaac didn't spot any likely cars angling in to pick up Rico. He kept a wise distance in his casual pursuit, feigning interest in an ongoing text conversation.

After a couple of blocks Isaac started to weigh up the likelihood of Rico having a lab set up nearby. The likelihood grew in plausibility when Rico left the sidewalk and headed toward a five-storey self-storage building. Maybe Rico or his powers above owned the property, if not for cooking then maybe just for some legit income. Isaac felt his options thinning out quickly. Was Rico about to enter a huge brick box full of hired guns? Should he run up on him now, twenty yards from the street, and cause a scene?

Rico went past the entrance's glass doors and toward the south of the building. Isaac stayed on him, tracking him into the large chain-link parking lot at the east side of the storage block. The lot was almost at capacity, and Isaac felt more exposed than ever. The storage building had almost as many windows as it did bricks.

Isaac now had his gun against his leg, carefully tailing the husky guy to a blue Toyota Tacoma pickup truck. He still felt a little twisted up about blasting that kid in the foot. For him, the gun was always a motivator, not an executor. His first major mistake as a professional criminal had cemented this opinion for him. The memory of that security guard lying in the street, bleeding out, still messed with him, proving his appetite for violence was strictly limited. And he wanted to reserve every last drop of it for Wyndorf.

"Rico Perez?"

Rico kept his back to him, inked arms dangling at his sides like big decorative hams. Isaac heard car doors opening behind him and realised his desperation had got the best of him. But he didn't feel afraid. He felt free from his suffering. Two of Rico's guys, one sporty, one smart casual, emerged from a silver Mercedes S63 AMG. They were smart enough to eschew the obvious low-rider gangster mobiles, opting for more sophisticated and professional vehicles. Rico ran a business, not a crew of wild banditos. Evidently the pair had been waiting for this. They both circled slowly around into Isaac's view, their guns giving their own angry stares.

"You're the pendejo who popped Leroy in his foot. What's the matter with you, blanco? You looking to die?" Rico slowly turned, hands in pockets. A man with time on his hands.

"I just want to talk."

"You start all your conversations with a pistola?"

"Wyndorf. You know where he is?"

"I'm going to need that gun of yours, cowboy."

"That's not happening."

"You need to reassess the balance of power here, holmes. You say you need info, but if I'm dead you ain't got shit. If you die, I go and get some ribs. Comprende?"

Sporty racked his slide.

"I don't like having conversations with guns being waved in my face." Rico knew he held all the cards here.

Isaac gave it a few seconds, jaw clenched, and dropped the 9mm, kicking it over to the shaven-headed soldado in the tracksuit.

Sun glared off Rico's glasses, hiding his thoughts. Isaac stood quietly for a moment, gauging which one of them was to talk first. Rico folded his arms across his chest and started to inquire about Isaac's business with Wyndorf, when he shut off, his head tipping to the right to see something over Isaac's shoulder. Before Isaac could turn around, he watched thin jets of crimson splatter out of Sporty and Smarty. A second later, another soft pulsing caused Rico's left lens to crack into red shards, and the distributor fell against his pickup.

Isaac turned around, wondering where his bullet was. The wolf stood in the center of the lot's entrance aisle, returning his suppressed pistol to his shoulder holster. Two Audis with tinted windows had quietly crept in like panthers, one blocking the shared entrance and exit, the second slowly moving deeper into the lot. So the wolf had an Audi. Isaac wished he had trusted his instincts after seeing those men outside Mateo's yesterday.

"Who are you?" Isaac asked the stationary wolf. The Audi hovered confidently close in the distance, hemming him into this chain-link cage.

The wolf stayed silent.

"You know where Ludlow is?"

The wolf nodded curtly.

"You working with Wyndorf?"

The wolf slowly shook his head. One leather-gloved hand reached inside his suit jacket, slowly pulling out a cattle prod. Isaac heard the crackle and hum, followed by the pop of the moving Audi's boot.

Isaac rushed for his gun on the pavement next to where Sporty was leaking his brains. His hand was chased away from the grip by several neat warning shots. The passenger window of the approaching Audi was down, and a gloved hand gripping steel was warning

Isaac to leave his piece on the concrete. Isaac spun and sprinted toward the fence at the rear, hearing the slap of the wolf's black wingtips reverberating off the concrete right behind him. The throaty grumble of the lead car declared its supremacy, coming to aid the wolf in his hunt. Isaac didn't dare glance over his shoulder, knowing the car would be on him in a second. He just poured more coal onto the fire in his muscles. Isaac had a mental image of the sleek and powerful car slamming him down, not fatally, but just enough to slow him. To allow the wolf to shock him and toss him into the boot.

Isaac slipped right out of the aisle and dodged and weaved through the ranks of parked cars. Bumping, sliding and half-climbing through the narrow gaps between cars, he caught a sidelong glimpse of the wolf, still hot on his tail, clearly in great shape and unfettered by breathing through a rubber mask, shock stick still clutched tight.

The chain-link fence was just up ahead. Luckily it had no barbed wire across the top. He could practically feel the wolf's breath on the nape of his neck. Isaac scaled the fence faster than he thought possible, dropping into a crouch back on the paving of West Grand Avenue. He stared at the wolf through the links, watching him step aside. An engine revved with fury. Isaac sprinted, knowing what was coming. The Audi crashed through the fence at his back, hand braking into traffic, tyres squealing and the clatter of the broken fencing harsh on the ear.

Isaac raced until his legs and lungs burned, scurrying catlike across the four lanes of traffic, using the cars to impede the Audi roaring at his back, shifting its way through the blockages. He made it several blocks to North Halsted, his momentum failing as he recklessly threw himself across the intersection of Grand, Halsted and North Milwaukee, his salvation pinned on the Grand Station subway. Both Audis swung around the corner into the erratic mess of junction traffic Isaac had created. The lead Audi nipped at Isaac's legs as he barely made the pavement, bolting down the grimy steps toward the blue line.

He vaulted the turnstile, shoulder-checking the security guard aside. The angry commands at his back shut off like a switch. Isaac had a good idea why but chose not to look back for confirmation. He all but flew down the staircase, slipped and dodged his way along the platform and skidded through the subway car's doors a half-second before they closed. A single frustrated blow slammed the door at his back. Isaac turned. The wolf stared back. Mask to glass, huffing and puffing.

The subway pulled away, the wolf marching alongside for several angry strides before jogging back to the stairs and climbing topside.

Isaac stared at the concerned faces watching him and his drama. They all lost interest soon enough. He walked in short circles with his hands laced on top of his head, breathing deep. Okay, he thought. Maybe it's time I call Roach.

Q & A

"You got that look in your eyes, Roachie. You ain't goin' to go all Hulk-smashey-smashey-Nick Cage in here, are ya?" Fitzy was leaning into the lift, looking casual but also trying to keep a safe distance.

Roach, bolt upright in the center of the lift like a treacherous peak, glanced at Fitzy and tried to dismiss his concern with a calming, controlled expression. Unaware that Fitzy and Grace saw a jovial-looking time bomb.

Grace, hands in pockets of her denim jacket, appeared to have accepted the likelihood of Roach getting rough in here. "I'm with Fitzy on this one. I know you're pissed an' all, but starting a gang war over a hunch is like…fucking bananas. Use your words, boss man."

Roach fixed her with the same cheap plastic mask of imposed peace. "Simply a Q&A session. Cool it, both of you."

Grace and Fitzy exchanged a troubled glance.

The doors opened onto a large, sleek reception area. They were on the tenth floor of a high-rise office block on East Jackson Boulevard. A nice commercial space with the ubiquitous floor-to-ceiling windows and glass-housed conference rooms. Roach clomped through the veneer of glass, steel and professional courtesy, seeing through all the bullshit for what it was. This was a back-alley enterprise as old as the wheel but with a paint job and some nice potted plants.

Roach stopped primly before the mid-range reception desk, glanced into the black crow's eye of the security camera then turned his charm onto the high-range cosmetically daubed bimbo occupying the hot seat. "Curtis Roach. I have an appointment with Mr. Payton." If Roach had to guess, the tight little brunette spent as much time on her knees beneath Payton's desk as she did typing emails and answering calls.

However, she could at least read, which caught him by surprise, and promptly threw up the inevitable bureaucratic roadblock. "I'm sorry, you're not on the list. But if you leave your contact details I'll have him call you back at the earliest possible convenience."

"This"—Roach pointed at the ground, at the very moment—"this is the earliest convenience."

Her smoky-shadowed eyes looked distrustfully at his large black peacoat, then to his two associates standing a few feet behind him.

"Don't worry yourself over it, sweetheart. I'll see myself in."

Her lipstick-coated mouth made to protest but Roach was already cruising past her desk toward the closed office door at the far end of the hallway.

Grace and Fitzy exchanged an exasperated look. Fitzy made himself comfortable in the nearby waiting area, taking a seat in one of the plastic chairs. He was delighted to find the latest issue of Automobile amongst the scattering of periodicals, all of which catered to the typical interests of gruff men, such as the leg-breakers, arm-benders and wise guys who made up this pleasant little enterprise. Using the magazine to hide his gun, he carefully divided his attention between the articles and the lift doors.

Grace parked her rear against the secretary's desk, gently took the phone out of her manicured hand, and offered a peaceful open-hand gesture, calming her back into her seat. "This'll go much silkier if you don't get the goomba brigade involved."

The secretary read Grace's big brown eyes, drawing on her experience of dangerous people of both genders to judge that there was no inherent threat in the cool young lady, and kept her dainty hand away from the silent alarm button under the desk. Grace nodded cooperatively, and enjoyed the decent view of the Loop's skyline, her smooth reflexes primed and ready to draw her gats should any of Payton's employees stumble out of their corrupt little offices.

Roach burst through Payton's door with just the right amount of energy to make the eel-slick loan shark spring to attention, his neat handwriting taking a sloppy arc inside the notebook columns of client names and their outstanding crushing debts.

"Roach? The fuck you think you're doin'? You back on the sauce?" Payton looked like the dictionary definition of a sleazeball. A sly, aging imp with calculating eyes and a taste for expensive and gaudy jewellery. He also continued to dress like an 80s Wall Street criminal, with red braces over a pinstriped shirt.

"Leave the gun in the desk or I'll break your hand." Roach spoke like a prophet. "I only need to ask a few questions."

Payton's hand hovered near the drawer for a moment, then thought better of it. "I know how you ask questions. They normally come attached to expensive hospital bills."

"Not like you can't afford it, Jack. Still adding the customary ten points to your generous handouts?"

"You come up here to discuss business practices? Or you looking for work?"

"I'm looking for Ludlow. Where is he?"

Payton looked blankly at Roach for a few seconds. "No clue. I heard about what happened, but my knowledge extends no further than Chinese whispers. His security detail was hit, he was taken. That's all."

"Detective Wu tell you that?"

"Like I said, Chinese whispers."

Roach loomed large, hands down on the bureau, one palm over a suspiciously dark-stained gouge in the wood, a constant reminder of a poor beggar who'd had his hand pinned down with a stiletto blade. In a more scrupulous office, such sordid events would be covered up. As it was, this office, the whole blood-spattered credit company, looked like it had been thrown together in five minutes and could be disassembled in the same time. Some ugly metal filing cabinets in a vile shade of olive green, a few shelves, a cheap desk lamp and some random geometric paintings passing themselves off as sophisticated art.

"You and Ludlow have a rough-and-tumble history, and I know you're pissed that he recently bought up that piece of real estate you had your eyes on. A nice little earner like that, a respectable front, must stick in the teeth of you and your Italian pals."

Payton looked incredulous. Placing his fountain pen to one side and closing his debt collector's diary, he laced his fingers over his flat stomach and sat back. "First of all, you know full well that I'm only a peripheral associate of the Trentinos. They have their own interests, and let me assure you, I doubt purchasing some modest restaurant was even a blip on their radar. And secondly, whilst Ludlow and I have a spotty history, I'm not going to go to war with him over some steaks. It's a big city, Roach. There's enough to go around for both of us."

"You're known for your generosity," Roach squinted at him, still having a difficult time swallowing Payton's line. "You still got a side line distributing C.B.'s speed?"

"Maybe I do. So what?"

"You heard from Wyndorf?"

"You crazy? Course not! Why the fuck would I have heard from him?"

"I'm just trying to deduce a few things." Roach clucked his tongue in thought. "Hey, remember that avalanche of heavy shit that rained down between you and Ludlow, you know, after you had the bright idea of vouching for Wyndorf. Telling Luds he was reliable muscle."

Payton rubbed his eyes in exasperation, his gold-ringed claws looking as though they might burrow into his brain to end this repeat. "You're fucking kidding me. This? Again? Were you a history professor in a past life or something, because you sure love the subject. I held my hand up to that. Wyndorf was my contact in moving his cousin's stuff. He'd been nothing but reliable for me. I knew he was a bit fucking crazy, but up until his…wingnut episode with that doctor and his family, it was a manageable kind of crazy. Shit happens, Roach. Ludlow got heated over that mistake and things got a little bloody between us. We thinned out each other's payroll a bit, but we formed a truce, didn't we. You survived it." He spread his hand out to Roach. "Its business, you know that. Now can you get to some kind of point, because as you can see I have quite a bit of homework to be getting on with," he gestured to his black book of future casualties and corpses.

"I'd say collectively, your past friction has cost you enough bank to make the restaurant spat seem like a good reason to pull a stunt like this. The proverbial straw busting the camel's hump. Why not get Ludlow out of your oily comb-over once and for all? You're a greedy little shit, Payton. Always have been. Always will be."

Payton developed a dew of nervous sweat. The look in Roach's eyes wasn't just anger, it was worry and pain. It was the look of a man who wasn't intending on leaving quietly.

Roach reared back up to his full height, spine rigid, chest out. "Where's Ludlow?"

If Payton could resolve this peacefully, he would. "Roach, ask yourself something: if I had any hand in what went down last night, don't you think I'd have made damn sure that you and your two jokers outside would have been dealt with, too?"

Roach slowly took a warning step around the desk.

Payton clearly knew Roach was only moments away from swinging his big mallets. He didn't go for the gun drawer, he went for the secret dial-a-goon button under his desk. A lock clicked open behind Roach, a secret door opening into a small security cubicle.

"Fucking weasel," Roach spat.

Payton's two largest and most loyal henchmen spilled out in silk shirts and slacks, street dirt done up in elegance. These two dumbbells clearly spent a great deal of time in the gym, but Roach had never needed to pump himself up with weights; his right hand made him a born finisher.

"There's a lot of cornfields in Illinois, Roach. If you don't want to become fertiliser you better control yourself right fucking now," Payton threatened.

Roach didn't waste a breath. He stepped in and popped one neckless thug with a stiff jab, launched a freight train right cross into the jaw of the other, collapsing him as if his stylish clothes were suddenly void of a body, then returned to the first, blocking his punch and smashing his teeth together with a counter upper-cut. Just for the hell of it, Roach thought he'd help him on his way down to the floor with a completely unnecessary overhand right to the temple, but his steaming anger got the best of him, throwing his timing off slightly and causing him to punch the rock-hard forehead instead. Roach heard something pop and felt a white jolt of lightning turn his hand into a limp dead fish. Shaking it off, he rushed Payton who had his hand in the drawer, scrabbling for his only available equaliser. Roach slammed the drawer shut on his wrist, ripping a sharp hiss from Payton. Then he dragged him out of his seat and threw him into the wall, cascading books from the shelves. He knew one way to confirm Payton's honesty. Roach picked his chair up, and with a snarl of effort raised it over his head.

"DON'T!" Payton cried out.

The wooden base of the chair shattered the floor-to-ceiling pane, leading the glass shards in a rapid descent to the pavement below. Luckily nobody had been walking directly underneath the landing zone at the time. Nevertheless, a sizable commotion was soon stirred up by a gathering of pedestrians looking upwards in anticipation of more falling office furniture.

"You stupid fuck," Payton spat, hunched down like a cornered animal. "You stupid little—"

Roach ripped him up by the scruff of his neck and easily dragged him toward the edge, the wind chill and bladder-clench-ing terror turning Payton's insides to ice water. Roach hooked him by his suspenders, letting him dangle outside the window at a forty-five-degree angle.

"Hey, Payton. You don't happen to know where Ludlow is, do you?" Roach quickly checked the pair of brutes across the room. They were still out of the fight.

"NO!"

Peyton stared at the sickening drop, then looked back at Roach. "I HAVE NO FUCKING IDEA WHERE HE IS! HEAR ME NOW, ASSHOLE, YOU DROP ME, YOU'RE A FUCKING DEAD MAN!"

Roach allowed the elasticity of the suspenders to bob Payton back and forth, testing to see if the material might rip. He didn't think the Trentinos would be best pleased if it did, but it was a risk he was prepared to take. "You better not be lying to me, Jack." He squeezed out every last drop of false bravado and honesty from the scumbag. After a few more paralysing seconds, he ended the interrogation and dragged the parasite away from a much-deserved death.

Payton wheezed and gasped, his face caught in a frozen snarl of rage and trepidation. He fell against the wall and clutched his damaged wrist, the wispy hair of his balding pate resembling a wild black tumbleweed, and stared with unmitigated wrath at Roach.

Grace and Fitzy burst in behind them, pointing guns and trying to keep a fragile peace despite the crescendo of angry hoodlum threats in the hallway. They looked from the dazed and bloodied lumps at their feet to Roach and Payton near the broken window.

Roach turned back to the slime-bag gangster. "Just business, remember. I had to be sure. I'm not exactly tripping over leads here." He kindly adjusted Payton's skewed tie, receiving an unappreciative shove in return. Roach slapped a wad of bills in Payton's hand to cover the damage to the window, then joined his team at the door.

"I'm willing to let this one time slide, Roach, on account of you being clearly upset." Payton was still talking through his teeth, body quivering with rage. "You do anything as stupid as this again, well, use your imagination."

Roach flapped his coat, buttoning it against the unhospitable cold wind which was fluttering the vertical blinds and notebook pages on the desk. He nodded once in understanding and left the office into the mob-populated corridor.

The three of them made it to the lift without further violence, but a few of Payton's roughs appeared eager to act independently, like riled guard dogs.

Roach carried his quiet intensity into the lift. Grace and Fitzy were quietly shaking their heads and goading one another into breaking the silence.

Fitzy relented first. "What now?"

"We hit up the remaining spots and ask around. Someone must know something." Roach discreetly rubbed his swollen knuckles. "This whole thing feels off. Isaac gets targeted by Wyndorf—who might have some fruit-basket backup in a wolf mask. A professional job getting pulled on Luds in his own damn house. I hate stumbling around blind like this." He stopped short of punching the lift wall. His knuckles didn't need it, even if his disposition did. He checked his phone instead, noticing the missed call from Isaac. "On second thoughts, you two snoop around. I owe Isaac a few beers."

KILLING TIME

Wyndorf lay on his aluminium fold-out camp bed, its blanket half on the floor. It was the only unmade rack in the huge basement-turned-barracks. He was trying to focus on the badly dog-eared survival handbook in his hands, one of the many pieces of prepper literature which was on the bug-out brigade's suggested reading list. For the past five minutes he had been attempting to read one damn paragraph, only to be repeatedly distracted by the grunting of Higgins doing press-ups in the space between their cheap beds. Even without Higgins' sharp exhalations, Wyndorf found the prepper material hard to take seriously. He had been trying to read through a short instructional essay on water purification tablets when he got bored, thumbed through a large number of pages and stopped randomly, squinting at an introduction to the joys of black powder DIY. Now this could be interesting.

Higgins' almost sexual gasping made Wyndorf slap the book shut. Leaning up, he tossed it onto the floor beside the trim and firm posture of the regimental crew-cut busy descending and ascending, descending and ascending. Higgins huffed and shot Wyndorf a red-faced warning. Even the bulging veins in his forehead looked critical of him. Wyndorf didn't catch it, he just grabbed an equally dog-eared—if not more so—copy of Penthouse from his bedside drawer. Whacky old Major Thurman's utilitarian compound had an internet connection and a few well-maintained laptops, but Garland had made it clear during Wyndorf's induction that they were strictly reserved for coded forum discussions between other cells of the Midnight Frontiers, and not for sexually explicit entertainment.

One of Wyndorf's few pleasures during these claustrophobic years had been testing the boundaries of Garland's harsh disciplinarian role, but the sense of technological paranoia that pervaded the compound was palpable, so much so that the computers were practically kept under armed guard. So Wyndorf continued to stare tiredly at the corrupted beauties on the pages, finding lust and its promise of quick relief too evasive for his restless mind.

He was bored of waiting. Bored of constantly being watched, sat on, and treated like a golden goose. All because Major Thurman had a giant meth-flavored monkey on his back. Wyndorf blamed himself for that though. Now, following last night's collection from Rico, Wyndorf had once again been relegated to bench-warmer duty, superfluous and muzzled, whilst these idiots were charged with running manoeuvres all around Chicago's doper hotspots, turning profit for the cause.

He had behaved.

Now it was time to go see if that cock Roach was hiding Isaac in his bar. Maybe flush them out of there with another fiery piece of stolen ordnance from lock-up, but only if it was one of the more amenable shitheads on duty. The Penthouse joined the prep manual on the floor next to his current babysitter, emphasis on 'baby'. The kid must have been about twenty, for shit's sake. Higgins let his slender but steely arms drop, and sat up. He was fighting for breath after that last set, but still managed to drill Wyndorf with those same old tired rules and regulations about keeping oneself and one's environment neat and tidy. Blah-blah-fucking-blah.

Wyndorf ignored the young trooper of the coming apocalypse and stared at this rectangle of cinder-block walls. His prison away from prison. His gaze found Higgins' perfectly made bed—like the dozen plus others down here—and scrolled across to the neatly organised stack of books at his bedside, his lockbox full of various prepper items underneath his bed, then finally landed on his own skin mag and survival guide, heaped on the floor like sagging paper tents. Wyndorf scooped them up just to stop Higgins from whining any further and dropped them on their shared bedside unit.

Wyndorf stared at the kid—back at his press-ups—and thought about how good it would feel to go Rambo on these losers. They spent their whole lives dreaming of war, so why not give them one? He'd most definitely get shot to shit within a matter of minutes against these boys and their toys, but it could liven things up at least momentarily. Anything beat all this waiting. Cabin fever, that's what this was. All these bullshit rules and pissy little rants about discipline. Why did any of them still bother preaching to him? He wasn't a member of their little loony army and never would be. So why couldn't they leave him to be him, and they could all do press-ups and polish their power fantasies until they gleamed so bright that they went blind?

Family wasn't worth shit, Wyndorf censured. One mistake. That was all it took. Just one go-a-bit-crazy-and-kill-a-respected-quack-and-his-family-and-land-on-a-federal-watch-list mistake and suddenly C.B., the meth king of four states, gets all holier than thou. Now here he was, on the margins of his cousin's business. Forced to fend for himself and reduced to hiring out these borderline goose-steppers to protect him.

Wyndorf had first latched onto Thurman and a few other Midnight Frontiers cell leaders six years ago at a New York gun and knife convention. They spent time bouncing between camps in the Midwest, doing this and that, for the cause, but mainly for food and water. Then, a little over a year ago, he was bounced back here with Thurman. Thurman and his ultimate authority. Thurman with his ultimate weakness. A boon for Wyndorf. Easy to exploit.

All things considered, his situation could be a lot worse, Wyndorf supposed. At least C.B. had finally opened his door a crack, permitting this arrangement, allowing Wyndorf to act as liaison between Major Thurman and Rico, thus enabling them to distribute product to Chicago's networks of psychologically damaged war vets.

Wyndorf started whistling tunelessly, the ghost song of frigid gusts slicing through a window crack. All this thinking wasn't good for him. He felt the restless rat clawing at the insides of his skull, determined to get at the cheese. Isaac wasn't going to kill himself.

He plonked his cheap dress shoes down on the bare concrete, fixed the blue tie knotted over his fresh white shirt and sprang off the bed, leaving Higgins to his vigorous extracurricular exercise.

Marching out of the basement's sleeping quarters, he trotted up the steps to the staff-only area of the large gun emporium and firing range, and walked out the back door, feeling the camera watching him. The large rear of Down Range was off limits to customers and the public, but its location in Lyons, Illinois, adjacent to the I-55 and thirty-five minutes out from Chicago, put it at little risk from random nosey punters. The area was laid out like a budget military base: several fair-sized cinder-block buildings used for dining, personal storage, and one for the optimistically titled Command Center; an area of greenhouses and pens for chicken and rabbit livestock; several guard towers; and a modest fleet of vehicles, all surrounded by a twelve-foot-high brick wall with electronic iron gate manned by a guard hut. Wyndorf sneered at a bunch of Frontiers doing laps around the compound in full combat gear: night vision goggles strapped on their heads, rucksacks full of supplies, the works. If The Man ever did track this place down, it would be smashed through like a tank-tread over a child's crib. But Wyndorf had to hand it to some of these fringe asshats, they would probably fare pretty well operating in a mobile guerrilla fashion, hanging out in the woods and sewers.

He swung open the door to the mess hall in search of Garland, expecting to find the big old 'roid machine struggling to assuage his ridiculous appetite. Instead, all he found was a cluster of the badly wired militia, hunched around the benches discussing various globe-destroying theories over bowls of greenhouse vegetable and rabbit stew, and drinking from canteens of purified rainwater. Wyndorf backed out of the building, leaving the Omega Man candidates to feed and discuss their backward politics and insane hypotheticals about brewing race wars and mortal combat between the wealthy and the poor.

He entered the Command Center next door, feeling the room grow suddenly quiet. Like most times when he entered rooms occupied by Garland and Schecter, all conversation was quickly stifled. But it wasn't just Garland and Schecter in here: three former troopers turned strung-out mules were standing before Garland, awaiting their orders. The five of them glanced at Wyndorf, Garland and Schecter viewing him like a foraging rodent, the other three with an almost reverential light. Wyndorf waved his hand as if to say please, carry on and propped one sole against the wall, waiting quietly, looking like a Jehovah's Witness on break.

Schecter, at his desk by the window, returned to his inventory lists. Garland dropped the rucksacks on the scarred and beaten briefing table with a clear measure of disdain. His powerful presence owned the large, sparsely furnished nerve center of the DIY militia. The day's three scheduled dealers flicked their hungry, reptilian eyes from their superior to the three bags of product and back again. As with any army worth their salt, everything was organised and scheduled, even dealing ice. Garland glowered and folded his arms across his chest, watching each of the three sheep-in-military-surplus-clothing grab a bag loaded with a healthy portion of their latest methamphetamine shipment. Off to the side of the table was a corkboard with a well-used map of Chicago pinned up like a geographical battle plan: red pins indicated the military vet centers, white pins the drug treatment clinics, and blue pins to indicate any other miscellaneous non-profit charity centers and counselling groups established to aid the broken and chewed-up soldiers abandoned by spoilt brat-brained government officials.

Bruhl, a skinny white-trash poster boy with a mullet, glanced at the board and then to the stoic right hand man of the major. He was awaiting their official orders but none seemed to be coming. Bruhl, like most of the cell's manpower, had become accustomed to the growing preoccupation in Garland's stony gaze.

"Sir? Who's going where?" Bruhl asked the mute muscle.

Wyndorf could see the itch take hold of Bruhl. The boy was trying to contain himself. To keep his nails from scratching at the blood ants running riot beneath his pale skin, not wanting to wave his craving in front of Garland, the large reticent slab of killer.

Wyndorf liked watching Garland continue to struggle with Thurman's amended mandate. He knew how much the mountainous ex-marine wanted to grab those bags and burn them out back. He knew how the big motherfucker ticked, with his current dosage of anadrol pumping through his system, an ireful rhino frustrated with his own weak obedience, overseeing the transfer of Wyndorf's toxic salvation into the veins and lungs of Chicago and Illinois' downtrodden ex-soldiers. That's why Wyndorf didn't have big ideas about loyalty. Sooner or later some asshole's ideas will clash with one's own, and something will have to give. Fuck loyalty. But watching from the outside? Seeing someone else's internal dilemma? He enjoyed that. For Wyndorf, half the fun was guessing if Garland would snap and decide to buck Thurman's new regime.

"Sir?" Bruhl tried again, squirming.

Garland turned from them to the map and the pins, an enraged god preparing to obliterate a city from on high.

Bruhl looked crabby now, wanting a simple command to get the ball rolling. The longer it took to get out there and earn a crust, the longer it'd take to get back to a pipe and an episode of bliss. He glanced at his two perplexed mules, then looked doubtfully at Schecter, the quiet burned man, in the corner of the room, too busy appraising the army's checklist of food stores and munitions to pay them any mind.

Bruhl silently promoted himself in the moment and took point with his nasal tough-guy voice. "I'll take the rehab clinics. Wohler, you fly by the vet shelters. Hunt, you get the rest."

With one final baffled look at the statue of Garland, Bruhl grabbed his bag. Hunt and Wohler did the same and followed him out of the Command Center, nodding at Wyndorf.

Captain Crank.

Wyndorf rolled his eyes—finally—and stepped away from the wall. "You ladies got a minute?"

Schecter pretended the peddler wasn't in the room, consulted his list and reported to Garland. "Apart from a few crates of beans which are nearing their expiration date, we're loaded for winter.

Plenty of canned goods, water and grains. Kershaw's happy with the supplies of antibiotics and first aid equipment. Gas for the generators is good. We're ready to dig in at a moment's notice."

Wyndorf glanced at him, taking in the horribly burned skin snagging on the neckline of his NRA t-shirt, and facetiously crossed his fingers, "I'm still just praying for the day you get to live your Mad Max fantasy."

Wyndorf got a nice tingle from the combative challenge cooking away in Schecter's hot charcoal stare.

"It doesn't matter to me if your face looks like burned oatmeal. You still have really beautiful eyes." Wyndorf spurred the man's hate, curious to see whether he had the balls to finally make a move.

Schecter continued to prove that he had more self-control than Wyndorf gave him credit for.

"Man, I guess your sense of humor got scorched away with your face back in that lab explosion, huh?" Wyndorf dared, begged for Schecter to take a run at him, even with that big fucking greaser troll standing by.

Schecter stared quietly. Under the singed and soft white putty of his scorched eyebrows, he was most likely frowning, but it was hard to tell. Yet his gaze alone was a withering storm of ash. Wyndorf continued to stare right back, having a grotesque fascination with the waxy and distorted mouth of the burned militant, and the wispy clumps of dark hair smeared into the cooked terrain of his scalp.

"Personally, I'd be blaming the S.W.A.T. team, but if you're still that sore about how it went down, come on over here and we'll get to the heart of the matter."

Schecter had his fully loaded Sig Sauer on his person, but he was gripping the pen in his hand the way a starving, crazed woodland cannibal might hold a grisly bone knife.

Garland put an end to the building maelstrom, telling Schecter, "Give me a minute."

With a shrieking scrape from his chair legs, Schecter pushed himself away from the table, dropped his pen and left the makeshift briefing room, vanishing into the back room. The sound of an outer door slamming rang off the cinderblocks.

Garland stood proudly, monolithic, his torso-clinging gray vest and urban warfare trousers helping sell the image of a brutal gung-ho warlord. "We need to re-establish your position here at the compound. Your disruptive influence is blunting the troops. Despite your financial value, some of us here are still taking serious issue with how you're warping the perspectives of our ideology, how it's altering our long-term mission parameters. Some are even starting to believe that the meth distribution should become our primary objective instead of gearing up for the inevitable societal collapse. They're content to act like ass-wipe gangsters, profiteering from destroying patriots, the troubled men and women who should be joining us instead of killing themselves in flophouses and gutters."

Wyndorf played the innocent stooge. "I ain't the boss around here. What your men do, say and think is down to you. Isn't that the whole army mandate, to erase any sense of individuality? Sounds like you might have to put these troublemakers in their place, boss."

Garland's expression was stone. His biceps swelled to the size of grapefruits, his large jaw clenching hard enough to bite through steel. "Make no mistake, if they don't re-evaluate why they joined up for this in the first place, they will be discharged."

"You mean like you were?" Wyndorf gave a snide quarter-smile.

"I was dishonorably discharged from the weak, foolish and blind imperialistic regime of the United States Army. A discharge from our ranks is something more permanent."

"I'm glad you take all this so super-duper seriously. But you see, here's the problem. You of all people know most of these "survivors" are gun aficionados or deer hunters. Not real, genuine soldiers. But you're getting your panties in a bunch because they've realised they enjoy making money more than doing jumping jacks. And don't forget, it's my connections to our glorious tax-free revenue which has allowed this piss-weak militia to get balls deep in army surplus gear. Thurman makes out okay with the gun store, I get that, and some of you idiots teach that bi-seasonal prepper workshop survivalist bullshit for asswipes who play too much Call of Duty, but I turned the safety-catch off of you guys. Now I'm beginning to feel a little unwelcome around here, so just say the word, and I'll make the call, turn off the meth tap, and I'll find some others willing to offer me protection."

Garland thumped over to him, his boots rattling the tables and chairs.

"You try to project this air of control," he said, "but I see right through it. You hired us because everyone else either wants you dead or nothing to do with you, and let me tell you, I get that. I really do. Even C.B. and his scumbag partners wouldn't give a wet shit if you turned up dead. Having spent one very long year with you under my roof, I understand how skilled you are at burning bridges. You're a goddamn arsonist to camaraderie. But I know behind this cheap front of yours is a man who doesn't want to be out in the cold, where the law might find you. Some of my troops have already raised the issue of hog-tying you and turning you over to the L.E.O.s for an easy payout. Just to get rid. But I'll admit, your revenue is useful … for now."

Wyndorf shivered in mockery. "You just best remember that if you want me to keep milking my cash cow for your little revolution, you'll protect me like your fucking life depends on it. I'm your mission. I'm your objective. I'm your whole fucking campaign. Don't forget that."

"Only until this system fails. After that, the global infrastructure, the economy—it'll be nothing more than a chapter in the new history of humanity. Once that happens, your money won't be worth the paper it's printed on, and it'll be hunting season." The sincerity in Garland's eyes spoke volumes about his fanaticism.

Throughout Wyndorf's prolonged stay at this ranch of mishmashed patriotism and paranoia, he had yet to truly discern exactly which catastrophic end they were all eagerly anticipating, but what they lacked in a clear, comprehensible ideology they made up for in disturbing combat efficiency. They clung to the Bulletin of Atomic Scientists' Doomsday Clock model of impending global demise as if it was their own personal compass, guiding them through the wilderness.

Wyndorf moved a few inches closer to the taller, wider man, his dark eyes burrowing into those of the warlord of weekend warriors. "You of all people should know that man is the most dangerous game." He began clapping his hands, as if he was trying to motivate a lethargic cow. "Now, how about we get out from under this day care center for fuckwits and go check out Pitchers, you know, since I'm such a good earner and all."

Garland loomed over him like a big white bear for a few more seconds. "Fine." Wyndorf didn't even see him slip the Ka-Bar knife up under his throat. "But you make another scene like yesterday, or you pull a knife on me, or anything else which I consider a hostile act, I'll sever your carotid and leave you to die where you fall, tell the major you were K.I.A."

Wyndorf felt the cold tip pressing into his neck and gave the trained killer a vacant smile. "Sounds like a good time." He pointed toward the back-room armory. "Shall we?"

Garland marched into the armory and grabbed a suppressed semi-automatic pistol and holster from the rack. "We're not going to play this like we did at Conway's. This is purely recon. If your man Roach is there, we'll handle this quietly and wait until he leaves, grab him when he's alone." As an afterthought he grabbed Shauna, his favorite assault rifle, from the neatly ordered stockpiles of firearms and explosives. "Shauna is just tagging along in case this gets FUBAR." He shrugged into his large duster, to help conceal the feminine wiles of his assault rifle. "You understand what I just said?"

Wyndorf gave him a half-assed salute. He could tell Garland was waiting for him to leave first, to make sure his sticky fingers didn't attach themselves to any more incendiary grenades or the like.

Wyndorf led the way to the compound's small fleet of motors. Garland pushed past Wyndorf and the red Ford, selecting a silver Range Rover instead. Swapping out vehicles was always good practice. One never knew when the CIA, FBI or even the DHS were snooping around.

PITCHERS

Roach had got the both of them a quiet booth at the rear of the bar to discuss matters. It wasn't that hard, really, considering it was his bar. Pitchers was just starting to liven up with the late-afternoon rush: the white-collars finishing up long, alcoholic business meetings, college kids getting an early start on a night of socialising, and the regular bar hogs watering down another uneventful day. Isaac was on his second beer.

"That's not your style, Isaac. I might even go so far as to say it was fucking stupid," Roach chastised him, not impressed with Isaac's recount of playing the defective detective.

Isaac considered Roach's opinion on prudence, then glanced at the ice pack resting on his swollen knuckles, courtesy of his enthusiastically quizzical nature. "No argument here."

Roach noticed him twiddle his wedding band a few times.

"I don't know what happened." Isaac looked blank for a moment, trying to recall some missing memory, a name or song lyrics, perhaps. "I didn't think it through." He gave his head a shake. "I thought if I could just get a hold of Wyndorf, I could end this quickly. My way."

Roach sipped his orange juice, the ice clinking against the glass. "And what happened to going straight?" He seemed to be appraising Isaac, curious as to what the lost years had done to his friend.

"I am going straight. I mean—I want to. This isn't taking down scores. Something real bad is hovering around us. And either we take care of them or they take care of us."

"So, to recap. The wolf—possibly a bald black guy, or a nondescript white guy—has an unknown number of friends, with a couple of black Audis…and they're not working with Wyndorf."

"I think we just blew this thing wide open." Isaac sucked his beer.

Roach chewed a sliver of ice. "Even so, if I'd known that a bit earlier I probably wouldn't have gone through Payton's place like a bull in a china shop."

Roach glanced around at his bar in thought, watching a minute of the Black Hawks game on the large screen over the bar. Isaac sipped his beer in the quiet moment and admired the hip spot, the roomy brick and neon interior. Of course, with Roach being the proprietor, only the hottest barmaids would suffice. It was a simple business strategy: hire flirtatious good-lookers and watch the suckers roll in.

"You know, when I heard you owned a bar, I feared for the worst. Figured you might have drunk the place into a pit of debt."

Roach smirked and tipped his OJ toward him. "Actually, you're not too far from the truth. I…" He sighed. "I had some pretty hairy troubles there for a while. I'm five years sober now, though."

"No shit?"

"I go to meetings every Tuesday."

Isaac tried to look supportive, but part of him still felt out of touch. This was a friend who had been a huge chunk of his problematic life, and yet he had been willing to let that relationship starve and die because it had been slowly poisoning his aspirations of a noble life. Was he really proud of Roach? He felt like a hypocrite. "That's great, man. About time. I lost track of the number of times I had to carry your stupid ass home."

Roach flashed that youthful smile again. It seemed incongruous with his thick and refined moustache.

"Remember that time you threw up on the bartender in that rock bar—what was it called? Out by Wrigley Field…Trace. I had to pay him off before he kicked the shit out of your drunken ass!" Isaac laughed and felt some of the day's dread ease off as he relaxed into the red leather of the booth.

"Not really, no. But I remember you droning on about it at great length. What were we … Jesus, twenty-two, twenty-three?"

"Those were the days, huh. We'd pull off a small-time score and you'd spray most of your earnings everywhere in piss and vomit."

"Don't forget charm." Roach chuckled. "Drunk me could be pretty charming when he had to."

Isaac snickered, thinking of the number of disastrous relationships Roach would begin with his inebriated, debonair charisma, only to subsequently destroy with passive-aggressive sobriety. "I don't know why, but I always found myself waiting for you to ease off the juice after we graduated to Ludlow's bigger marks."

Roach shrugged. "More money, more bottles. That's what forced Diane to finally tire of my shit."

Isaac fidgeted with the glass. "I'm sorry to hear that."

"I'm not." Roach looked wistful. "She was right. Amazing she put up with my boozing as long as she did."

"When was the separation?"

Roach sifted through the debris of past events. "Seven years ago. It wasn't on good terms. It finally dawned on her that I was too in love with "the lifestyle". She moved to Ann Arbor to be with her sister."

"You seeing anybody new?"

"I've realised I'm not cut out for relationships."

Isaac sipped his beer, trying to come up with some redundant comment which would fork the conversation away from past mistakes, of which they both had many. "You've pulled it together now, from the looks of it."

Roach glanced around his kingdom of sports-themed drinking, appreciating it as if he hadn't laid eyes on it in a long time. "It's okay."

The quiet spaces between words was beginning to feel less and less awkward, but Isaac knew reminiscing about the glory days of their sketchy youth wouldn't solve their problems of today. "So what are we going to do?"

Roach leaned into the table conspiratorially, his game face slipping back into place. "We wait for my guys Grace and Fitzy to get here. See if they've learned any names or leads as to who these guys are. If not, then we can shake more trees with four pairs of hands than three."

"We're 0-for-2 in our disastrous attempts at playing the big dick hero."

"Well, what are you thinking? Find a basement somewhere remote and hope they don't find us?"

Isaac fidgeted with the rim of his glass. "Aren't there any other guys who can weigh in and help us out?"

Roach's expression took on a downbeat cast. "I don't have too many favors I can call in at the minute. Particularly when it comes to backing us up against an unknown crew capable of snatching a name like Ludlow from his own home."

"That's not exactly a no." Isaac pushed the issue with a raised eyebrow.

Roach shut him down with a non-verbal response, choosing instead to use his fingernail to squiggle moisture trails on his cool glass. "You know, it's funny. Yesterday Diane warned me about my luck running out. And remember Strauss? He implied the exact same damn thing. Told me that I should think about getting out of the rough stuff. Focus more on this place. Talk about bad omens."

Isaac tilted his head. "Or a professional warning."

Roach waved the suggestion away. "No, it's not like that. He and Ludlow have, like, stacks of volumes of history, man. You know that. If there was even a hint of something rotten between them, Ludlow would have told me. He's still our go-to guy when it comes to shifting the hot stuff. Nothing to gain for him by randomly turning on trusted long-time associates."

After being off the board for so long, Isaac no longer knew up from down, but he still trusted Roach's shrewdness when it came to reading people. He glanced at his pal's ice-rimed knuckles again. Admittedly, Roach's methods of reading occasionally lacked subtlety. Despite his soulful eyes, he'd always had a penchant for violence which far exceeded Isaac's own.

"If we get through this, maybe you should think about cashing out. Open up another bar on a beach somewhere."

Roach solemnly held his gaze for a long pause, and Isaac knew the spinning wheels in Roach's head were grinding down any notion of retirement into broken junk. Before he got his inevitable answer, Isaac heard the thick glass doors of the bar swing open, ushering in frigid air and street noise, and found himself bracing for the worst. Had the gun-toting wolf sniffed them out again so soon?

From Roach's calm reaction, Isaac knew it wasn't the wolf. He turned slightly in the booth, seeing a chubby guy in jeans and a Celtics jersey with a spring in his step, with close-cropped rusty hair and a trimmed beard of fiery gold. An attractive dark-haired barmaid popped the top off a bottle of San Miguel for him with such practised ease and timing it must have been a daily routine. Behind the big guy wandered in a younger, attractive black twenty-something woman in jeans and a denim jacket, her tribal braids hanging off her shoulder. The woman paused for a brief moment, leaned over the bar and kissed the barmaid. They were clearly more than just friends. The pair of them joined the booth, pulling up free stools from the adjoining table, closing the circle.

Roach quickly made the introductions for Isaac, aiming a pistol-like index finger at the pudgy pale guy and then the dark lean youth. "Fitzy and Grace."

Fitzy gulped his first mouthful of beer and exhaled with pleasure. "You're Isaac, right?" He extended his non-beer hand, giving Isaac a hearty shake.

"Yo, Roach told us some of the stories about you two back in the day. One of the old school," Grace said. She didn't offer to shake, just smiled all cool and nodded.

"Christ, kid, I'm only thirty-nine."

"S'old to me, pops. I'm twenty-three."

Isaac conceded the point. "I feel fifty."

Fitzy harnessed his tough Boston accent into a meeker, star-struck speech. "My condolences. I heard about what that sick fuck did to your family. Some shit ought to be off limits."

"Straight up," Grace agreed.

Isaac didn't want to get into the matter with people he had only just met, but he nodded his appreciation for the man's sympathy.

Fitzy placed his bottle on a damp coaster and flipped back to business mode, telling Roach, "Got some news. Conway's, it's—"

"Torched. Isaac told me. You checked the news?"

"You were there?" Fitzy asked Isaac.

"After the fact."

Grace passed her phone, an article from the Chicago Sun-Times website already open, to Roach. "Not just torched. Some dude with an automatic weapon dropped everyone in there. Including Conway."

Roach skimmed the article and passed the phone back.

Isaac looked from the two replacements to the leader of his old gang. "The old employment office."

"Place is an institution…was," Roach corrected. "We stopped going there a while back. Back when most of our older eyes and ears got out of the life, got dead or got out of town. The newer locals coming in were mainly wrapped up in different lines of work, but now and then you could still count on the place for some useful sources."

Isaac was glad Maggie couldn't see him now. Sitting here with hoodlums, on the precipice of death and criminality. But what choice did he have? 'Who's keeping their ear to the ground now?"

Fitzy answered. "MacKinnon was an old pal of yours, right?"

Isaac hadn't thought about Lou MacKinnon in a long time. "Purely in a professional sense. We performed a few jobs back when she"—he pointed at Grace—"was in diapers."

Fitzy nodded. "Uh-huh. Well, we know he's fallen off the face of the earth. No one's seen him in over a week. And that guy likes a routine."

Isaac and Roach exchanged a glance at this detail. Did Isaac catch the ghost of a memory in Roach's eyes?

Fitzy continued listing their lack of available insight. "Man, we spoke to everybody who's anybody: Alonso, Bowen, Loco Molinero,

Green—they're all clueless on the subject. Nobody knows dick about Ludlow and some wolf."

Isaac was no longer paying any mind to Grace and Fitzy's list of dead ends. He was busy trying to figure out where MacKinnon's piece fit into the puzzle. Assuming he too had fallen foul of the wolf's pack, what would they want with him? What had Ludlow done that warranted such extreme action, which also somehow connected to him and MacKinnon? Isaac unspooled the connective thread, surprised and horrified at how quickly the yarn ended. If he was right, it put Roach in the crosshairs too, and explained why the wolf and Wyndorf were not partners. Wyndorf was a target, too.

Isaac found his voice. "Did Jensen have any other family? A close friend? Someone who, for whatever reason, has decided to make a move on us now?"

Grace and Fitzy looked at him for an explanation, with only Roach grasping what Isaac had said.

"Who's Jensen?" Fitzy asked.

"Alfred Jensen," Isaac repeated, testing how it sounded. "He was a surgeon. He and his family were killed by the same man who murdered mine. Maybe the reason nobody knows anything about Ludlow is because this isn't some business dispute. It's personal."

Roach didn't want to hear this and stared at Isaac, scepticism and belief duking it out behind his eyes. "You think some white-collar friends and family of Jensen are behind this? Like who? A bunch of tough-guy doctors from the country club?"

"Think about it. MacKinnon had been reliable enough to us and Ludlow back in the day, to the point where he knew about the Jensen cluster fuck. So these guys ask around a little, maybe grease a few palms to find somebody who might be clued up on me and that job. They find MacKinnon, and that guy was reputed for two things: being a so-so thief, but also, for being a useful contact." Isaac thought about MacKinnon's final moments and imagined them being deeply uncomfortable and verbose. "They make him give up the full crew involved in that job. Ludlow's done. But they're still gunning for us."

Roach shifted uncomfortably. "We didn't harm a hair on their heads. That was all Wyndorf."

"You think they'd give a shit? Would you give a shit? We were all complicit that night. It makes sense. It's no secret I was involved. These people could have been biding their time until I got released. Look at the time frame: MacKinnon goes missing, a few days later I step off the bus—my family is killed by Wyndorf but the wolf was there, beaten to the punch. A day later Ludlow gets taken, and now they're circling me again." Isaac wasn't aware how agitated his tone had become, his raised voice catching a few curious looks from some of the drinkers at the bar.

Grace and Fitzy were mute.

Roach rubbed the bridge of his nose, looking like he wanted to grab Isaac's and Fitzy's beers and drink away the conversation. To hell with sobriety.

He held Isaac's stare. "I don't give a shit who these guys are. We can find out when they're dead. You said the wolf came at you with a cattle prod, but they all had guns, so we know they want you alive."

Isaac felt his back being pressed to the wall and was ready to fight if the situation called for it. "We can draw them out. Let them come for me."

"And bleed the answers out of those motherfuckers." Roach was getting a fire in his belly. "First we're going to need a secure place to get our bearings. You mentioned calling in a favor. Well, I do have one. Monahan owes me. He'll give us shelter, help us until we figure out the best way to handle this thing."

Isaac had a flashback of Monahan—patron saint of the desperate and endangered criminal—singing his praises after he secured him a staggeringly attractive jewel in another distant life.

"Even if you're bait, you're going to need a new piece."

Isaac looked ambivalent. Yes, he wanted to deal with these killers. Yes, he would happily intimidate them and take great satisfaction in inflicting harm on them if forced. But could he terminate another life, other than Wyndorf's?

"We need to get this right, Curt. I've only got one more kill in me, and we both know who I'm saving that for."

"Then we better find Wyndorf before the wolf does. Don't sweat that for now, though. We need to get going." Roach adroitly tied his hair into a ponytail and stood up. "I don't want my bar getting shot up. It just passed the health inspection. Fitzy, Grace, start the car."

The pair hopped to his command. Grace kissed her girl goodbye then followed Fitzy out to his black Mercedes-Benz C220. It was starting to get dark out, neon signs, street lights and headlights warming up for the cold closing fist of night.

The four of them sped away in the high-end car, unaware that by the time they'd reached the end of the road, an Audi had caught their scent. Further back, behind the wolf, a silver Range Rover fell into line.

Safe House

"It's just fucking awesome to be riding with you. I could blush, I swear. I've been a wheelman for enough names in my time—Roach, obviously—but now to be driving the both of you? It's like driving Jagger and Richards, or something. The Parkway Bank & Trust job you pulled. $70 mill. Your Marshall Pierce jewellery heist. $53 mill. Those two are my personal favorites, but you guys are a living highlight reel showcase."

Isaac begged to differ, but allowed Fitzy to run at the mouth if it meant he kept his focus on the road. Now he knew why Grace had graciously given him the shotgun seat with a mischievous smile. Punk, Isaac thought, knowing she was sitting peacefully in the backseat with Roach, who was haggling over the phone with Monahan for the nearest haven off the streets.

"The way you carried those jobs out. The precision, the control. Like a damn military unit. I wish I could have drove for you back then. I'm a damn good driver."

"If you can drive like you talk, I don't doubt it," Isaac answered, silently begging for him to let the radio, or even sweet silence, dominate the journey.

Fitzy chuckled, patting the wheel with his ham-like fists as if trying to coax some laughter from the leather. "I hear ya. I know I talk a lot, it's what I do when I'm excited, but I'm quiet when I need to be, ya hear? You like this sweet ride?" Isaac grumbled assent. "I borrowed it from an old friend back in Charlestown," Fitzy went on.

To his credit, Fitzy was very efficient at yammering away whilst smoothly slipping and dodging in and out of lanes. "Must be a kind friend," Isaac said.

Fitzy's grin was more like a gurn. "I say friend—he's really just some guy I grew up with in Southie. Mitch "Dopey" Roscommon. He used to be small time, working for the O'Connell family, and I was more, ya know, freelance. We'd keep runnin' into each other. He'd ask for tax from a sideline I had going, I'd give him a drunken slap in Whitey's; he'd shoot my car up, I'd fuck his sister. Just small tit-for-tat stuff, ya know? I actually quite like the guy. Wouldn't dream of wasting a bullet on him. Not even the skin off my knuckles. Anyway, he's a mid-level guy now with a nice new home in the South End and a Benzo, and last time I checked our scoreboard I owed him one, so I drove back to Boston and boosted this. Stupid design flaw in the vehicle, if you ask me. Would have been a little harder to steal if I'd had to hotwire it from his driveway. But keys and locks are just too old-fashioned now, I guess."

"Dino-tech," Grace added from the back seat.

"All I had to do was some grade-school-level iPad tinkering to amplify the key's fob signal from inside Mitch's home, and boo-yah! I was away." He chuckled with a machine-gun cadence.

Isaac humored the loquacious racer, growing impatient with Roach's prattling to Monahan. "Does Mitch know you took it?"

"Not directly, but I'd like to think he knows in here." He patted his Celtic-clad chest. "I might even swap the plates back and return it to him after this. I'm sure he'll laugh about it."

Isaac was slowly starting to realise that Fitzy was not playing with a full deck, and wondered if Roach was slipping in his vetting process. The last thing he needed right now was allies who were too flaky and goofy to make a stand against their shadowy enemy.

Finally, Roach ended his conversation. "He's got a free place in Chatham, South Saint Lawrence Avenue. We're to go there and wait. His guys will watch over us until he arrives."

Fitzy's jaw-wagging energy was redirected to his quick hands and reflexes as he moved them with a bit more purpose, silently cutting left at the intersection and gliding through the chains of traffic with crisp, judicious ease, heading back toward I-90 East.

Four cars back, the wily Audi proved just as competent in its maneuvers. Three cars behind it, so too did the Range Rover.

They arrived thirty minutes later, finding a reserved parking spot waiting for them outside the safe house. Isaac had pulled only the one job for the wealthy racketeer, so he was unfamiliar with Monahan's level of protection. From outside, the three-storey graystone looked unexceptional in terms of security measures. However, closer inspection would reveal the front door to be composed of bullet-resistant fibreglass with a wood veneer finish, and the iron-barred windows couldn't help but offset the normalcy.

They took the porch's wide stone steps and Roach rapped on the raid-proof door. The heavy curtain to their right twitched and Isaac was sure an eager, suspicious eye was glaring at them through the peephole. The door opened soundlessly and Roach led them in, Grace and Fitzy bringing up the rear. Neither the doorman nor the gunman at the bottom of the staircase to their right offered to take their coats or indulge in any such pleasantries. In fact, their hard stares were distinctly unwelcoming. Wearing a shoulder rig and a loosened tie, the goon by the stairs blew at the steam of his coffee and trudged back up to his post.

The room off to their left was a large open-plan living room and dining room separated by a wide archway. Isaac noted four more guys occupying a card table in the latter. They wore black trousers, dress shirts in various colors and ties. Isaac gave them all a quick study and considered that if working conditions were as bad as their faces suggested, then they should probably start a union. He also took note of the several electronic eyes installed throughout the spacious, cold lobby, and deduced that the man upstairs was probably watching and recording them right now.

The doorman was as large as the front door and looked just as physically dense, his bald pate gleaming in the light from the wall sconces. He quickly patted Isaac and Roach down, not being shy about it, as a second dour-faced triggerman left his seat at the communal poker table to perform the same action on Grace and Fitzy.

"How long will Monahan be?" Roach asked, mid-pat down.

Grace and Fitzy were compliant as their inspector, wearing an ugly, almost reflective purplish-blue shirt, removed their handguns, his burning cigarette glued to his bottom lip.

"He's on his way," the bald wall rumbled unhelpfully.

Having passed the security test, Baldy and Smokey returned to their card game at the green felt table in the dining room, leaving their unwelcome guests free to sit or roam about the open lobby and parlor. It looked like Monahan was aiming for some sort of faux-cabaret aesthetic with the bare limestone walls, soft light and black cherry-colored divan couches and beanbag box seats. Isaac flopped down onto a box and stared at the floor between his shoes, something he'd had a lot of experience of doing in Menard—if not the floor, then the walls and what might lie beyond.

"This place looks like it can't decide if it's a whorehouse or a safe house," Grace said to Fitzy. The pair of them took up positions near the thick vermilion curtains to keep an eye on the street outside. Neither the upstairs guard watching the house's perimeters through a bank of screens nor the card table of complacent killers filled the young enforcer and driver with a whole heap of confidence.

Roach took the box seat opposite Isaac, hearing one of their babysitters curse and fold his hand.

"What's room service like in these places?" Isaac asked, looking at how his friend's face had aged and wondering what stories each deepening wrinkle and gray hair could tell him. He assumed Roach had at some point pondered similar queries about him.

"I've not been in this particular resort before, but I'll be sure to leave a review on TripAdvisor."

"You done a lot of work for Monahan?"

"Bits and pieces. After Janine passed on, Ludlow pulled back from the life for a good while there. Between her death and your sentence, the guy was verging on becoming a recluse. I had to keep busy, though. I missed her too. And I missed you, brother. I was hurting. Had to stay busy or go stir crazy."

"I shouldn't have been so harsh, distancing myself the way I did. It's just, for the first time, with Maggie and Will, I saw a future I never thought possible for me." Isaac thought he saw a flash of burning indignation in Roach's eyes, but if it was there then it was extinguished quickly.

Roach nodded solemnly. "You're a better man than me. Maybe I can't change. Diane was always there, and I always went the opposite way. I needed the work to keep my mind off the fact that my only real family was either dead, or not answering my calls, or locked away. That's when the bottle really became a problem for me. But I was still functional to an extent, getting some more hands-on, rough work from our new host. Eventually, Ludlow picked up his phone again and it was business as usual. Sobriety and armed robbery. Yeah, I'm a selfish prick, but at least I own it. That's got to mean something, right?"

Grace dropped onto the divan along the back wall, with something on her mind. "We're getting our gats back, right? Last time one of Monahan's monkeys patted me down, the motherfucker kept it."

"You were itching for a fight."

"He was running his mouth, and he scuffed Fitzy's ride. Guy was a prick."

Roach softly patted the air to calm her. "You'll get it back when the boss gets here."

"For when the big bad wolf comes scratchin' at the door?" Grace was trying for amicability but Isaac's wordless glare took the mirth out of the cocky jibe.

Isaac focused on Roach. "What I said before: when it comes down to it, if I can wound this guy and we get some answers out of him, someone else will have to finish him off."

Grace looked confused. "You don't wanna blast the wolf back into the woods?"

Isaac paused, already sensing further hassle. "I'm a thief, not a killer."

Amazement remoulded Grace's perplexed brow. "You mean you, big-time bagman, have never popped your cherry?"

"Once." Isaac took a breath. He would have preferred to reminisce about one of his and Roach's big scores, but what the hell, he had no place else to go. "An armored car guard. It was one of my first jobs for Ludlow. I got sloppy, and he tried to take advantage of my mistake. He reached for his gun. I didn't have a choice. And I shot him." His eyebrows knitted in a despondent frown. "Before we left, I saw he had a picture of his daughter on the sun visor. She was only a kid. Sweet-looking thing."

Grace wasn't particularly sympathetic. "Sounds to me like it was his own stupid-ass fault. It wasn't his money, why take the risk?"

"The why isn't the point. I took that girl's dad away from her." Isaac's posture had become tense at the talk of the murder, the corded vascular muscles in his forearms bunching up like ropes. "I'm not going to destroy any more families."

"Such nobility." Grace smirked.

"Look darlin', have you got a problem?"

The card players heard the word 'problem' and forgot about the pot of cash mounting on the table, their cutting stares boring holes into their bellicose wards. Fitzy watched the guards at the table and understood why the five of them had disarmed their house guests. Frayed nerves and the spectre of death had a way of coloring the moods of hunted men and women.

"Shit, I'm only playin'," Grace grinned. "No need to get tense, I run my mouth. I read up about it, it's a coping mechanism. There you go, now you know you can kick my ass in poker."

Isaac smiled thinly, which Grace almost celebrated. "That's better. We're on the same team, let's all chill."

The guards continued their game.

"How did you start working for Roach?" Isaac asked her.

Grace's dangly earring flashed gold as she raised her head up like she was preparing to dive into the story. "I'm from K-Town. I don't think I need to ask if you've heard of the Vice Lords?" Grace didn't. People on both sides of the law knew of the Almighty Vice Lord Nation, one of the biggest, oldest and most ruthless gangs in the city. "Or the Mickey Cobras?" Isaac listened intently, interested in where Grace was going with this. "Right, well, I wasn't in either of those. Instead I grew up getting my ass beat and trying not to get blasted any time I left the house. I spent so much time avoiding people for fear of getting shot that most of my friends were dogs. Paws can't pull triggers," she snickered.

"Except you," Isaac added.

"Right, "cept me. But I did know a few kids, all scared and abused losers just like me, tired of living with nothing, no future for any of us. Time was running out. If we didn't join a crew, we'd wind up dead. Some guys from the A.V.L.N. and Black Disciples were starting to pressure us hard. We wanted the paper, nobody else would pay us more, but if we did join we'd wind up dead too. So the nine of us had the brilliant idea to form our own gang, some weak-ass outfit that didn't even have a name." She attempted to smirk at the memory like it was some coming-of-age misadventure, but an earnest shadow drained it of its humor. "Shit seems funny now, but I was only sixteen, and Wrecks, the brains of the crew, was only nineteen. Wrecks, he got this wise idea to sneak in and bust a Mickey Cobra dope stash we knew about, sell it off quickly and jet out of K-Town, out of Chicago, go anywhere else. Stupid kid fantasy. We had a few gats, ones we found from some fools who got themselves dead. At first we all thought the plan was suicide. Fucking bonkers. But Wrecks wouldn't let it go, made it sound like a good idea. We knew the guys who guarded it, big mouths with little brains, always high in those dust clouds. In the end we all started to believe our own hype. And we did it, thought we were fucking ninjas. Made off with bricks of herb, it was beautiful. Those bricks were freedom to us right then, they unlocked the chains pulling us toward prison or six-deep plots. We didn't get around to selling it. Wrecks and the crew all started turning up dead. Quickly. And the Mickeys had their stash back. It was a dumb fantasy but now I had to make that shit a reality. I needed to get out of K-Town and fast. I needed money, and I knew about Conway's place. Word on the street. I talked myself into goin' there, so sweatin', freakin', expectin' to get cut down any minute. I ran from my block, tellin' myself that I had to be prepared to do any stupid shit which would pay me quickly. I had to look legit when I got there, but dumb-ass me was too panicked to realise I had zero rep and was lacking a dick. Anyway, I get in there, and I see this wasted dude about to get into it with a few jacked-up dudes, and for some reason I jump in. This white guy might have deserved gettin' his ass beat, I don't know, but I thought if anybody in there was going to take me seriously they would need to see something good. So both of us fought our way outta there before we got swarmed. I was swinging bottles, stools, ashtrays, kickin' guys in the nuts, whatever I had to do."

"I think I can guess who the lightweight was." Isaac flicked a glance at Roach who held his hand up, owning his reputation as the drunken asshole.

"Man, he was so grateful I stopped him from getting fucked up, he offered me a job."

"So you took it," Isaac wryly surmised.

"I took his damn hand off and got my ass away from K-Town." Grace hacked up a pretty laugh. "Never looked back."

"Like a fairy tale." Isaac smirked. "This would be about the time you stopped going to Conway's?"

Roach gave a soft chuckle. "I'd say that's accurate."

"Hey, this him?" Fitzy asked the room.

The confirmation came from the top of the stairs in the foyer. "Boss' here." The guard with the brown leather shoulder holster had the door open before Monahan had come up the porch steps.

Mr. Monahan walked into the parlor, a large man with dark, neatly combed hair and a ruddy face, a gray overcoat draped over his shoulders. He primly greeted Roach, nodding at his party, and lastly, allowed his eyes to settle on the subtle alterations to a familiar face. "Isaac Reid. You made it out of the clink in one piece."

Isaac shook his firm hand, cold as an ice sculpture. There was definitely a bite in the air but Isaac could only assume the old-timer had some circulatory issues. "Good to see you, Mr. Monahan."

"Likewise, my boy." Monahan let his coat sag off one shoulder and made toward the staircase. "Let's have a word in my office. I could use a drink."

Monahan's stately office sat on the top floor. It was warm in temperature but cold in décor: deep royal blue curtains and matching carpet, sapphire-tinted lampshades, and lots of dark wood. It made Isaac think of an ancient seafaring vessel smashing against glaciers.

"I need to warm up." Monahan poured brandy from an elegant decanter into a small glass. "Anybody else care for one?"

They all politely declined and hovered around his desk in wait. Monahan eased into a leather wingback chair, then gestured at the four of them. "Would you all mind sitting down? You're making me nervous."

The desk lamp revealed the weathered and worn features of Monahan. He was a man who looked like he had enjoyed the finer things in life for a long time: tanned skin from holidaying in Italy or the south of France, the beginnings of a turkey neck, bags under his humorous eyes. But his dark, wavy hair was untouched by Father Time, either from regular drownings in dye or by good fortune.

Isaac and Roach took the seats before the desk. Grace and Fitzy made a din of cracking leather as they took to the blue couch along the wall.

Monahan sipped his cognac and regarded Isaac with tired, hooded eyes. "I've been out of town for a few days. Roach filled in a few basics for me on the phone. Some men fear getting out of prison because they've become institutionalised, but you get out to a freak with a mask fetish trying to stuff you over a mantelpiece."

Monahan paused, delicately adding, "And I try to keep up with local news even when I'm away. I'm very sorry for your grievances."

Isaac dismissed the apology, not needing or wanting the sympathy.

"Roach mentioned "Laylow" got hauled off last night. I guess he didn't lay low enough this time. However…" He nursed his brandy and sighed tiredly. "Pissing people off is an occupational hazard. Any idea what level of security you're all going to need? What type of threat do these men pose?"

"I think they're hitmen. Hired by a relative or close friend of Alfred Jensen's. Real Old Testament, eye-for-an-eye deal," Isaac said. "I'm just spitballin', but the few things we've pieced together add plausibility."

Monahan squinted in thought. "The dead heart surgeon? I know the broad strokes, some hearsay, but that's about it. Would you fill in the details for me?" He sipped.

"It was the damn cigarettes. Janine Ludlow smoked like a tire fire her whole life, ended up needing an emergency heart transplant. No surprise, Ludlow became distraught, started running around like a crazy person looking for the best cardiac surgeon he could find. He found Jensen. And this guy ticked all the boxes. A superstar in his field, so naturally, there was a waiting list. Ludlow hounded the guy, bending his ear at every opportunity, calling and calling, talking about Janine's chest pains. Well, Jensen finally gets around to assess her candidacy, and then he gets cold feet. Turns out Janine had been suffering with chronic obstructive pulmonary disease for a time, which, as it turns out, is a risk factor for surgery."

Isaac snapped his fingers. "So just like that, after keeping her waiting and letting their hopes, our hopes"—he gestured between Roach and himself—"build up, he wipes his hands of the whole idea so he can keep his unblemished surgical record." Isaac took a deep breath. "Ludlow didn't take that well, and decided that if he had Jensen's wife and daughter kidnapped, he could leverage him to operate. Lud was hanging on by a thread. Kept saying how he didn't give a shit about going to prison, he just wanted Janine to be okay. So he starts putting a crew together, already has a driver in mind, and Roach and I jump at the chance. Not our usual type of work, but for family you make exceptions. He fought us on that until he turned blue, but we didn't give an inch. We weren't taking no for an answer, and eventually we wore him down."

"That's quite impressive. He was widely regarded as a stubborn prick," Monahan added. "No offence."

"He needed one more guy. Some seasoned extra muscle as insurance. Ludlow and Payton were sharing one of their truces, and Jack told him good things about this new guy, Michael Wyndorf, who'd been dealing for him and doing some rough stuff on the side. We meet him, no alarm bells start ringing, so he gets the green light."

Isaac slumped back in his chair. "We drive to the doc's townhouse, burst in, wave the guns, yell, the whole deal, and Jensen, his wife and daughter are putty in our hands. All going smoothly." He exhaled slowly. "Until the doc tries to be a hero. He grabs a vase and tries to bust it over Wyndorf's head. Wyndorf didn't handle that well. The vase only glanced him, but it was like hitting a switch—he went from cold and professional to complete fucking maniac, whipping out a butcher knife from his coat." Isaac closed his eyes, the imagery haunting his memories.

Roach sat quietly, wearing his own look of disgust at the recollection.

"We tried to stop him but it all happened so quickly. He was stronger than he looked. Roach landed some good shots but got dazed when his head was bounced off a doorframe. I didn't fare any better, fucker stuck me in the stomach; luckily I was angling away, but it was still deep. Then he turned to the wife and girl. They were on the phone to the cops when he got them. He sliced…and hacked…until they looked like they belonged in a butcher shop window. Then he went back to work on Alfred, and he started to fillet the guy's face. The police sirens were on their way when I managed to crawl back to my gun and put a bullet in Wyndorf's leg. I was aiming for his head." Disappointment bloomed on Isaac's face. "My blood was already all over the place, and I wasn't running anywhere, and Wyndorf had already fled, forcing our driver to get the pair of them out of Dodge. Roach was shaking off the cartoon birds when I told him to get back to Ludlow. No sense in us both getting pinched, and with Ludlow climbing the walls and my Maggie being pregnant, I needed him on the outside to watch over them." Isaac cleared his throat, and looked like he had extracted another sliver of the evil which had pierced his frail soul.

Roach's large frame had shrunk a few inches in his chair.

Monahan placed his empty glass on the blotter. "Tragic story." He wasn't speaking facetiously, he was merely too spiritually calloused to be surprised by such a tale of woe.

Becoming introspective, Isaac took a moment to think his answer through. He shrugged lightly. "There's one more thing I can't stop turning over in my head. The wolf mask. Janine was originally scheduled for a pig valve transplant. Wyndorf thought it would be hilarious to get us all pig masks for the job. Having a wolf hunting us feels like a taunt."

"Sending a wolf to eat the piggies who killed the doc and his family. How poetic." Grace broke her silence, and this time there wasn't a hint of mockery in her voice.

"So you're likely dealing with contract killers."

"The manpower you got here will be enough. We're not planning on turning this into a six-month vacation. We only need time to knock a few plans around to draw these guys into an ambush," Roach answered.

"And I'm going to need a gun." Isaac's voice was as low as his mood.

Monahan gave Isaac a crocodile's smile. "I understand that Ludlow's welfare makes this a personal matter for you. A real "Cry Havoc, and let slip the dogs of war" type scenario. But tell me, when you find these individuals, how far are you prepared to go? If I recall correctly, one of your idiosyncrasies was a cast-iron insistence on killing no more than a target's nest egg." The explanation didn't make the act sound any nobler in speech than it was in practice. "Have your recent sorrows made your code a bit more flexible?"

Isaac's countenance became worryingly abstract, leaving Monahan looking baffled.

"I'll kill 'em," Roach intervened.

Monahan hummed softly, scrutinising Isaac a moment longer. "What the hell, for the man who stole me the Cardinal Ruby, I'll give you two guns."

RAID

The 9mm was feeling more and more familiar in Isaac's grip. It was as if one of his muscles, long atrophied, was regaining lost strength. The gun was a Smith & Wesson M&P Shield. Monahan had led him down to a Spartan basement, lined with cheap wood laminate and unfurnished apart from several wall racks weighted heavily with a variety of concealable, and a few not-so-concealable, weapons. The room felt like a discount coffin to Isaac.

Monahan gasped at how Isaac wielded the gun, like it was a shoddy piece of equipment waiting to go off and take his fingers along with it. "For Christ's sake, you didn't use to do stick-ups with a paintball gun, now did you? Stop acting like a debutante. You know where the business end is."

Isaac didn't feel the pistol grip, he felt death's hand holding his. Some extra-sensory phenomenon, a universal snitch, was telling him that his choice to kill or spare a life was inevitable. He was too far down this path, and wicked men were at the toll. Isaac grumbled, and to appease his host and armorer, quickly and efficiently dropped out the eight-shot magazine, checked it was full, slapped it back home and racked the slide. "Happy?"

"Delighted, Isaac." Monahan didn't sell it. "Well, that's me. You and the boys and girl upstairs are welcome to all this stuff whilst you're here."

Isaac revisited the ample supply of hardware and damn well hoped none of them would need half of the collection to get the job done.

Monahan started for the stairs with Isaac at his heels. A sudden thought struck him. "When all this blows over—if you're still alive, that is—I'd love to hear from you. I always have plenty of work."

Isaac chose not to feign any interest. Monahan tipped his hand in a fair-enough gesture.

Wyndorf watched the quiet activity unfolding around the black Audi parked further up the street, his eyes alight with a territorial greed. Several occupants had slipped some lumpy, indiscernible masks over their heads and were using the shadows between the street lights and the parked cars to sneak closer to the house.

"Who the fuck are these guys?"

Garland was slumped down behind the wheel, his instincts screaming at him that this was a bad scene. "We're leaving."

The soft clinking of a pistol against the passenger window froze the pair of them. It was a snarling wolf, beckoning them out slowly and carefully.

"Fuck." Garland didn't fancy his chances of waking Shauna up in time to get a shot at such close proximity. Instead, he slipped his ballistic knife into his hand.

Slowly, they opened their doors.

Roach, Grace and Fitzy were idling in the parlor, while Grace was cockily twirling her gun like a flashy sharpshooter, jubilant that the security had returned their weapons without any bullshit or dick-swinging.

With the gun secured snugly in the back of his waistband, Isaac followed Monahan from the basement into the kitchen. The big, bald behemoth left his seat at the poker table and tailed them both into the living room, ready to lock the door after Monahan's exit.

Monahan stopped in the hallway and looked at Roach. "This is your favor paid back in full. Remember, you can always earn another."

Roach nodded. Monahan wormed about under his overcoat, bracing for the cold night air that would rush in when the henchman unlocked the door.

As if recalling something, Monahan stopped on the threshold and threw a departing glance at Isaac. "Oh, and Isaac, buy yourself some new clothes. You look terrible."

Monahan stepped onto the porch and shuddered twice. The back of his coat billowed outwards in red squirts as two bullets punched through his chest. The ogre of a doorman bellowed out a yell of alarm and reached for his sidearm. Several shots thudded into his massive torso, the coup de grace punching through his rock-shaped head.

Outside, two men in rotting pig masks quickly emerged from the shadows between the parked cars, walking swiftly but softly to minimise the spoil of their aim. Several more suppressed shots cracked against the bulletproof wooden door Roach was attempting to slam, whilst aiding Fitzy in dragging the guard's cumbersome body aside. One of the pigs pulled something from a pocket in his dark suit and tossed it into the closing mouth of the doorway. It bounced and rolled along the hall floor. A brief moment was all it took for them to identify it.

A brief moment too long.

The flash-bang went off like an enraged Odin, calling down thunder and lightning from the firmament. Still standing in the parlor, Isaac managed to dive and pull Grace away from the doorway and the retina-cooking flash of the blast, but their ears bore the brunt, the piercing trill of violently displaced air drilling into their eardrums.

Cards and cash rained down as the players tipped the table over in their haste to jump into action, taking defensive positions. Two moved into the kitchen to check the windows for a rear assault. The back door was bulletproof steel set into a steel frame, but the bars on the windows would only resist so much. The other two joined Isaac and Grace in the living room, keeping their guns trained on the open front door.

Blind and deaf to the world, Roach and Fitzy rolled about in the hallway. The two frontal assault pigs cautiously took the porch steps, spotting a gunman descending the hallway staircase, his gun strafing for a target. He was too slow. The lead pig tightly grouped two shots into his heart and he collapsed down the remainder of the flight, landing several feet from where Roach continued to fight for his equilibrium. He and Fitzy fumbled across the floor toward the living room, the white flare in their eyes beginning to fade back to a blurry semblance of normality.

The masked duo stepped over Monahan's body and were drawing on the two crawling targets when a fusillade of bullets splintered the doorway around them. Before they could take cover, Roach rolled onto his back, his gun up, and squeezed off a couple of shots, hitting the lead attacker in the neck. The pig stumbled backward, hand pressed over the red geyser in his throat, and tripped over Monahan's splayed arm, tumbling back down the porch steps. Fitzy pulled Roach to his feet, the both of them still wobbly and half-blind, and Isaac dragged them into the parlor. Then, providing his own cover fire, he charged for the front door, leaning into it like a shield and working to shove it closed.

The second pig was still on the blood-slick porch, crouching defensively. As Isaac began to shift the door, he leapt forwards, throwing his shoulder against the other side barring Isaac from shutting it.

Out on the street, the surprise peal of automatic gunfire perforated the quiet of the siege. At first Isaac was going to poke his gun around the bullet-beaten barrier and blast the triggerman in the leg, until he realised that the body was now dead weight. The hitman slumped across the threshold with several high-calibre exit wounds in his chest. The din of breaking glass and short controlled burst fire lit up the opposite side of the street. Everything was happening so fast it was difficult to process, but it sounded like somebody else was mixed up in this.

"Now what?" Fitzy shouted over the racket.

One of the housesitters approached the window and peered out, shifting the curtain with his gun. It was exceptionally poor timing. Another pig-faced assassin, pink rubber flesh turning necrotic, was crossing the pavement and placed several shots into his stomach. The latest victim on Monahan's payroll fell backward in a screaming fit, his white shirt pooling into soaking warm crimson. The pig's hand flailed up into view outside the window, a smoke grenade following in the wake of the bullets, passing through the bars and rolling along the floor, hissing like an angry viper.

"Upstairs!" Roach yelled out, the smoke billowing out and rapidly enveloping the ground floor.

A deafening boom rocked the house as the brick wall of the kitchen collapsed, crashing one of the hired help against the refrigerator in a ragdoll tangle. Gagging on acrid smoke and disintegrated brick, the remaining kitchen guard backed up and fired several shots into the dark, craggy mouth of the improvised doorway. He was just into the dining room when he was punched backward by a cluster of silent lead emanating from the smoking hole.

Eyes watering, Grace and Fitzy opened up, their shots lighting up the smoky parlor and searing through the obfuscating air toward the kitchen invaders, hitting nothing but cupboards and a coffeemaker. The final house guard abandoned his gut-shot companion and joined Grace in focusing his fire at the kitchen doorway. Several shapes loomed through the wall of smoke, shapes with big, swollen jaws and floppy ears. The pig-men moved in formation through the kitchen, alternating cover fire to close the distance. The final poker player cashed in his chips when through the roiling smoke he was lanced with two precise shots to the lung and heart. Quiet impacts peppered the stone wall over Fitzy's shoulder. They were boxed in and the box was shrinking fast.

"Upstairs! Now!" Roach repeated. "We can hold them off."

The street outside sounded like a battleground.

"We'll be trapped like choking rats," Isaac yelled, still using the front door as a shield and waiting to pop anyone else who made a run for the porch. "Fitzy, get the car."

With killers swarming in to flank them from the rear, options were limited, but Fitzy still didn't look too keen on the plan. Leading by example and staying low, Isaac was the first out the door and off the porch, gulping heavenly fresh air. What he saw confused the hell out of him. Across the street was a humongous guy in a long coat and boots, the stock of an assault rifle propped against his shoulder, tagging well-placed shots at several Audis blocking the north end of the street. Amongst the carloads of war pigs stood the wolf, commanding them as he gripped and tugged at something stuck in his shoulder. Shimmering street light showed it to be a small blade. Isaac didn't know who the big guy was or what the hell his stake was in all of this, but the figure taking cover near him froze Isaac for a heartbeat. A clean-cut killer, crouching amongst a pile of shattered glass and reloading a suppressed handgun.

Wyndorf.

The pair of them locked stares across the battleground. Roach, Grace and Fitzy ignored the seemingly helpful big guy with the cannon and hopped off the porch steps, blasting at the Audi blockade to the north. Fitzy was about to jump into the Mercedes when he noticed it was squatting lower than normal. The tyres had been slashed.

Wyndorf smiled at Isaac and pointed his quiet iron, firing and laughing joyously like each round was a sharp punchline. Isaac ducked low beside one of the parked cars, sliding his gun hand over the roof and praying that one of his shots would give Wyndorf a sucking chest wound.

Over the sounds of mechanical destruction, Isaac heard Wyndorf curse when his gun dry-fired. Then racing footsteps slapped south along the concrete, away from the deadly mob block-age. Isaac wasn't sure if the wolf had more on the way, maybe planning on blocking the south side too, but he couldn't allow Wyndorf to slip away again. This could be his only chance. He spared a quick look to his right. Roach and Grace were running rapidly through their limited ammunition, giving Fitzy time to attempt hot-wiring another getaway car. Roach caught his glance, deciphering Isaac's psychotic intent in his wild eyes. Roach shook his head at him. Isaac didn't say anything. He broke from his cover and ran.

The two rear assault pigs stepped out from the smoky murk of Monahan's conquered garrison, surveying the scene from the porch. They didn't go for kill shots; rather, they tried to hit Isaac in his sprinting legs. Two shots chipped the pavement before Roach spun back around from the northern beachhead and emptied a clip into their torsos.

Isaac didn't look back, not even when Roach screamed his name over the sky of hot leaden hornets.

Wyndorf was getting away, sprinting down the street and cutting through an alley between two houses. A part of Isaac hated himself for leaving Roach back there. They might all die at the hands of these lunatics. Then, Isaac knew he too might die at the hands of the lunatic he was pursuing into a dark backyard. That was fine. No matter what the night had left in store for him, he would at least cure the world of this frothy-mouthed animal before the wolf chewed his throat out. Wyndorf's life was forfeit.

Up ahead in the murky light, he heard Wyndorf gasp and heave, throwing himself over the rickety wooden fence into the yard. Isaac was possessed, utterly incapable of exercising caution, feeling the spirits of Maggie and Will speeding him on. He clambered over the fence, his hands slick on the damp and flaking wood. Several pulsing shots punctured the boards, wood chips erupting and scraping past Isaac's fingers and left shoulder.

A motion-sensor light unexpectedly flooded the garden, illuminating Wyndorf on the yellowing grass. Isaac swung his leg over to straddle the high gate and fired back from his perch, aiming to sever his spine. Wyndorf feinted left and right to prove a more difficult target, Isaac's shots bleeding soil from the tufts of grass and bark from the rough trees. As he scaled the chain-link fence, Wyndorf looked back to throw Isaac a look of raw hatred.

Isaac noticed the noise of urban warfare seemed to be dying out. And not a moment too soon. A soft thud came out of the darkness at his back. Choking on a lump, Isaac glanced down at the inky movement of a silhouette slinking through shadow below him. A blue spark appeared in the Stygian shroud like a crackling firefly, and the wolf leapt up out of the darkness, swiping at Isaac's dangling leg with the cattle prod.

Whipping his leg out of the way, Isaac compromised his balance and fell off the fence onto the stone flagging of the backyard, the jarring blow to his ribs stealing his breath. On his back, he ripped a few shots through the wooden barrier separating him from his hunter, hoping to hit him in his legs. Isaac glanced over his shoulder and panicked, seeing that Wyndorf was gone, each passing second putting more and more distance between them.

He pushed himself up and pounded across the grass, sucking in air despite his aching ribs, and going so fast he looked as though he might be attempting to shoulder-charge the chain-link fence off its post. Instead he practically hurdled the obstacle, and walked out into the wide, poorly lit division between the backs of the houses. Over his rushing blood he imagined footsteps: the wolf on his tail; Wyndorf preparing to pounce out at him from behind a rubbish bin or a tree. Isaac cleared his head of them and focused on the real sounds, his pupils dilating to drink in the meagre light from distant street lamps or the odd rear window. A bottle smashed off to his right, and Isaac's weapon sprang up, ready to kill. Wyndorf seemed to lunge from out of nowhere, knocking the gun away and tackling him to the gritty path. Strong hands closed on Isaac's throat, thumbs crushing his Adam's apple.

Ambient light played tricks across Wyndorf's spectacles, flashing white lenses mixing with the demented rage lurking within his dead eyes. "I could have killed them sooner, you know," he snickered wetly. "I watched that fine piece of snatch pay you your little visits for months. Dragging along your little brat to the market and the movies, baseball practice and the planetarium. Almost made me want to play big papa to the both of them. Remind her what a man feels like." His breathy voice heaved.

Hearing the enjoyment in his voice did something to Isaac. The war drum of his heart and the surge of hot blood fully unleashed his grief and black rage.

Isaac jammed the knuckles of his two fingers into Wyndorf's metacarpals, grinding them against the bones and ligaments until the strangler gritted his teeth in pain, loosening his choking grip. Isaac coughed and grabbed the back of Wyndorf's head, pulling it down into his rising headbutt. Clutching his nose, Wyndorf attempted to drive a fist into Isaac's face but the shorter man was quick, managing to writhe away. The dropping fist missed Isaac's ear by an inch, smashing into the hard ground instead. Isaac thrust his legs out, kicking Wyndorf in the chin and toppling him into an awkward heap. Surrounding homeowners were cautiously peering out of windows now, and a couple of distant neighbors had poked their heads over their fences, having no doubt called the police during the mass shootout.

Back on his feet, Isaac was wary of the bigger man's longer reach. Wyndorf didn't fight with any particular technique other than an enthusiastic desire to inflict pain and damage. He swung a haymaker, connecting with Isaac's cheek and sending him staggering backward. Through the white concussive haze, Wyndorf became a shimmering penumbra, wrapped up in the gloomy ambience and the heavy blanket of night. Isaac circled about to clear his head, putting steel in his legs to hide the buckle in his knees, and stepped into Wyndorf's next overly ambitious swing, beating him to the punch by slamming him in the jaw with a powerful right cross. The blow stilled Wyndorf's momentum, his brain processing the hit and giving Isaac time to step in and go for another swing.

The hit didn't land for some reason. One second Isaac was midswing and the next he was a quivering mass of jelly, falling to the ground, with Wyndorf mimicking his dance right beside him.

Through squinting eyes Isaac saw the wolf step over him, eyes shining through the mask's eyeholes. Human eyes which lacked humanity. The wolf regarded Isaac for a moment, then looked at Wyndorf with more interest.

"Michael Wyndorf, or is Clark Kent now?" The wolf's voice was deep, like gravel churning in his throat, a charming devil in a smoking jacket. "Alfred Jensen was delighted when I told him you were back in town."

The electrical shocks had stopped but the news hit Isaac just as hard. His muscles were cramped from charged tension, leaving him like a bundle of wet noodles on the dirt. He felt the probe darts of a Taser being yanked out of his back when an Audi slowed to a stop about ten feet away. Hearing police sirens closing in from the distance, Isaac saw several pigs quickly loom into his peripheral vision.

And everything went black.

Déjà Vu in Digital

The scene unfolded the same as the time before, and the time before that, and so on, and so forth for Dr. Alfred Jensen. The details of the scenario couldn't truly replicate the worst moments of his life, but they were accurate enough to dry his throat and squeeze his innards.

To an outside observer, the former surgeon would appear to be exploring a sterile empty room. What Jensen saw, though, with the VR helmet covering his eyes and ears, was the digital mimicry of his psyche's scar tissue. He was now back in the wainscoted hallway of his old home, his once safe and secure abode locked away in the beautiful gated Kane County.

The doorbell rang again, its evening intrusion summoning him from his easy chair. His wife and daughter were ensconced in the living room.

The beeps of Alfred's heart rate monitor gradually accelerated.

The white front door seemed to reel him in, as if his feet were on a conveyor belt, but Alfred knew he was in complete control of this re-creation. If he wanted, he could simply stop right there, turn his back on the door and what waited behind it, and return to his loving wife and promising teenage daughter, keeping that hell barred and bolted away from his family and himself. It wouldn't mean a damn thing, of course, retreating back to an artificial comfort like a coward, an imagined happy ever after. Would it have turned out differently if he had chosen that course of action in reality? Knowing what was politely ringing his bell? He knew it wouldn't have. And hiding behind alternative histories and what-ifs had done very little to help him so far.

The bell rang again.

He pressed on down the hall toward the vestibule, and, remaining faithful to his naïve former self, once again didn't bother with the door's peephole.

The heart rate beeper sped up marginally, while the blood pressure monitor and other machines attached to him like industrial veins pinged and blipped in a smooth, controlled ascent. The controller in Alfred's clammy palm used to make him feel as if it would open a trap door beneath him, dropping him right back into his six-year coma. His holiday in Hades. Now the controller was a supportive confidante, eagerly pushing him through this endurance of the soul. Strength through suffering. He pulled the trigger, opening the front door, and the nightmare which had redefined Alfred Jensen's life for the past decade spilled forth into his home and his mind.

The heart monitor plateaued at seventy-one beats per minute, and for Alfred, each one seemed to have downgraded from chest-bursting jackhammer to the dull silver discomfort of a lump hammer's tapping.

At the end of it all, in the aftermath of all that pixellated blood and the artificial screams of his family's off-screen avatars, the image of the rubbery pig-mask looming over his heaped, helpless body froze mid-frame. The distorted voices of carnage cut off and the virtual reality program paused and faded out.

"Mr. Jensen?" The headset was gently removed, the controller pried from his grip.

The final impression of the three little pig-masked assailants ransacking his home faded, returning Alfred to the empty room. Dr. Marianne Velez, one of the lauded pioneers of medical virtual reality therapy, began to pack up the VR equipment, storing it in the adjoining observation room whilst Jensen's personal physician, Dr. Steinway, unclipped the heart rate monitor secured around his subject's thin chest, the flesh of his torso and protruding ribs as pale as his white undershirt.

"Your tachycardia is lower than the previous session," Dr. Steinway said. "Your blood pressure looks a lot better, too." He smiled warmly beneath his bushy gray brows and glasses. His demeanor projected a deep care and support for his long-time colleague and friend, but Jensen knew that at his core, the personal and explicit nature of the radical treatment still upset him.

Velez returned, pleased with the latest data but disquieted by the more human aspect of her results, for Steinway wasn't the only one who found the re-enactment ghoulish. Even after a year's worth of their patient-doctor relationship, Velez still sounded queasy when referring to Jensen's prescribed computer program.

"Very encouraging, Mr. Jensen. I'd dare say you have officially conquered your swinophobia. That stimulus, played at the highest stress setting to such a moderate physiological response, proves the trauma has significantly depreciated in potency."

Alfred's mouth remained a tight line, just another slash to match the rest of his sliced-up putty face. He nodded distastefully, not particularly proud of the fact that he had finally learned to overcome a counterfeit rendition of his life's most traumatic event. It couldn't undo the physical and familial damage. "I've been getting some extracurricular exposure."

Dr. Velez leaned against the door frame of the chamber, hands in the pockets of her tan corduroys, and regarded the white patchwork of scars holding Jensen's countenance together. "That's good. Now, truthfully, I don't see much use in persisting with this treatment, but I'm willing to continue if that is what you'd prefer; although—professional opinion—I think you're ready to close the book on your trauma."

Jensen began to button up his shirt, a distinct absence of relief on his face. Velez continued to look slightly troubled at this detachment. Having watched Alfred Jensen dedicate himself to overcoming such a debilitating phobia, she didn't like the way he continued to behave like a living phantom, a void with a pulse and purposeless eyes.

"Mr. Jensen, when you first came to my office a year ago, you made me give you the hard sell on virtual reality exposure therapy. And I went on at great length about the tremendous results it has yielded in curing everything from battlefield PTSD to arachnophobia. Now, I can't imagine what it must have been like, having gone through what you did, but you've come out the other side now. Yet despite your commitment and courage, and all the suffering and vast improvements you've made in overcoming your fears…" She gave a dispirited sigh and crossed her scrawny, birdlike arms across her chest, a few loose bracelets jingling. "Your success doesn't seem to have offered you much in the way of comfort."

Alfred remembered swimming up from the eye-crusted, disorientating depths, screaming and panting in delirium, limbs dead, the tendrils of a never-ending nightmare coiled about his blazing neurons, trying to pull him back, deep into the horrors of his coma. He had awoken, a husk in a gloomy hospital bed, dried out, confused and lost to time. He remembered the private doctors scrambling around him, and little by little some of their faces began to conjure up memories from his professional past.

Dr. Terence Steinway had been one of them, a benevolent visitor from some blurry epoch of his life. Steinway had completed his residency at the Medical Center Hospital of Vermont alongside Jensen, and after parting ways during their fellowships they had eventually crossed paths again here in Chicago. It was he who'd had the atrocious task of walking Jensen through his last memories, reconnecting the dots of what had led him to the hospital bed. Steinway had held him, staving off inconsolable tears and screaming rage. He had been forced to tentatively show him his reflection in the bathroom mirror. He had tried in vain to promise him everything would be okay, but there was no sedative or magic pill which could mend a fractured soul.

And it wasn't long before the pig-men started to stand in the corners of his room like sinister statues, waiting for him to fall asleep. Nobody, not even Steinway, had ever been able to see them. It got to the point where he would insist on sleeping with the lights on, a cold sweat soaking him into a paranoid shiver. Even in the bright and safe light of day, the forms would occupy the periphery of his vision, following him, darting from sight and hiding, trying to get behind him to finish the job.

After some dark, ungauged passage of time, Jensen began his physical rehabilitation to strengthen his atrophied muscles, and valiantly he got out of bed every bleak morning on slightly stronger legs. He wanted his awakening to remain out of the gossipy circles of the medical profession, worried that some snooping journalist might think it would make a tragic but inspiring human interest story, so had himself declared dead. His body finally giving up the fight. In actuality, with his body slowly rebuilding itself, it was time to contend with the fever dream stalkers lurking around him. With a little research he learned of Dr. Marianne Velez from MIT and contacted her with shaky resolve, desperate to overcome the demons that hounded him. Underneath it all, he knew the names of two of these devils: Isaac Reid and Michael Wyndorf. He just needed to learn the names of the others involved in dismantling his life.

Jensen snapped out of his trance and skewered the short, pony-tailed doctor with a look. "I paid you and your squeamish team to construct a program that simulated the attack." He gestured at his ravaged face with one dispassionate hand. "But I never said it was purely to remedy my phobia."

Velez raised an eyebrow suspiciously. "Then what was the point?"

Jensen couldn't tell her it was to keep his hate alive and strong. He began to calmly fasten the buttons on his cuffs, parrying the question. "There is no more comfort for me, Marianne. But at least I can come to terms with what happened without falling into a piss-soaked panic attack." He walked Dr. Velez into the adjoining room, where Steinway was finishing his latte.

"I don't believe that, Mr. Jensen. And I don't think you do. Nobody bothers to make such an effort as you did because they're throwing in the towel. I've personally dealt with many extreme cases where patients have been through absolute hell, similar to you. Assaults, acts of terrorism—they all lost people they love. And the majority of them managed to rebuild what they lost. There can be a silver lining; you just need to be open to the possibility of seeing it."

Jensen hung on her words, ever a polite listener, but inside his head he was already shutting down the optimistic sentiment.

Velez checked her slim Rolex, surprised by the hour. "If you do wish to continue the sessions, I'm willing to oblige, but honestly, I think at this stage you would benefit more if you spoke to somebody about your perspective. I can put you in touch with a great psychiatrist who could—"

Jensen softly halted her with a firm handshake, allowing her to escort him and Dr. Steinway out to the building's lobby.

"Don't hold on to the past too tightly, Mr. Jensen," Velez encouraged, but resignation tinted the sentiment. "Allow your progress to push you forward." She left them to lock up her office. As usual, the session had been conducted outside of her normal hours to accommodate Jensen's dislike of attracting morbidly curious stares. The cubic Foundation Counselling building was eerily quiet in the dark evening, with their voices ricocheting off the polished floor and the pristine glass creating mirror worlds of Jensen's awkwardness.

"Mister Jensen." Steinway seemed to tut-tut. "It still doesn't sound right to me. Have you given any more thought to getting in the saddle again, Al? Quite frankly, it's a damn disgrace to allow your talents go to waste. You could be helping people again, saving lives."

Jensen saw his Halloween features reflected in Steinway's spectacle lenses. "How can you ask me that?" he snapped, instantly regretting the harsh tone. "I can't, Terry. There's no going back for me."

Steinway slipped on his duffel coat, knowing the professional impasse signalled the end of the discussion. Whilst Jensen had come on strong in his therapy, he had remained hopelessly rooted to the spot in terms of piecing his life back together.

"Thank you, again, for helping with all this. It means a lot." Jensen wrapped his thick navy scarf around the lower half of his face and tugged on his peaked cap, keeping it low over his eyes.

"It always does, but I hate seeing you stuck in this cycle. Call me if you need to talk, Al."

They pushed through the glass lobby doors of the small private facility into the empty parking lot. Jensen could feel his friend's solicitous stare as Steinway waited for a reply, trying his best not to zoom in on the ugly details of Jensen's passivity.

"I will," Jensen offered, voice muffled and distant behind the concealing fabric. Steinway gave him a doubtful look. "I promise."

Steinway hung there for a moment longer, then nodded and headed off for one of the three parked cars. Jensen watched him walk ahead, becoming a shadow against a backdrop of lamp posts and the cold, humbling beauty of the distant, attractively lit tower blocks. He remained a castaway on an unchartered island.

A hornet buzzed from Jensen's coat pocket. Colquitt had good news.

FALSE FLAG

Kershaw's steady hand sewed the black thread through the raw, but luckily, rather shallow bullet graze in Garland's shoulder. The large man barely winced as the needle slipped back and forth through the red valley of the sliced deltoid, the harsh white glare of the lamp beaming down on the area as bright as the Afghan sun.

At least the bullet hadn't done any real damage. Kershaw had explained how nobody wanted a shattered humerus, acromion or clavicle. Garland had seen some heinous battle damage but to him it was just red meat and gristle, so he took the medic's word at face value. As it was, he would be ready to carry Shauna again unimpeded in no time.

After clearing some distance between himself and the masked hostiles, he had left them to contend with the trio from the raided house and retreated to the Range Rover. It had been a narrow escape. No sooner had he fired up the ignition than he'd heard the wail of approaching police cars converging on another of Chicago's Wild West displays.

Now, hunched in HQ like a large white gorilla, he observed another of his company wander into the makeshift medic bay.

The fresh arrival, Velazquez, appeared to be confused as to what he was meant to be doing, standing there uncertainly with speedball eyes and scratching at his arm. "Garland...um, sir," he mumbled, scratching a little harder, a dozy grin playing about his lips. "Major Thurman wants a word with you."

Garland had a few choice words of his own for the major and his growing squad of piss-poor soldiers. He stared at the tweaking traitor to their credo and wondered if these men's mush-minds still remembered they were commandos preparing for the fall, not two-bit cracker-ass crystal dealers. After five seconds of stony silence, which could have seemed like a full minute to Velazquez, Garland dismissed him with a firm, silent nod. Private Spaceman seemed to comprehend the response and floated back out to relay the message, assuming he remembered it. Kershaw cut off the thread and applied a gauze pad, dropping the wrappers and scissors down by the bottle of surgical spirit and reddish-pink cotton swabs.

Garland confided in the drawn-faced ex-army medic, looking for signs of disloyalty in his darkly humorous eyes, but the man appeared clean: his pupils were no more dilated or edgier than normal. "How many of our unit are using that poison?"

Kershaw looked stern, disapproving even, taking his time to answer. "The number's risen. Up to fifteen now." He unsnapped his latex gloves and tossed them into a plastic bag. "The major still holds much of the influence over our faction, and when the commander is a user, and an outspoken advocate, some of the men seem content to dabble in the product, too."

"Fifteen." Garland rubbed his eyes. "Our whole division is only nineteen strong." He jumped off the metal table, rattling the whole frame, his boots bombing the rough wooden floor.

Kershaw watched him pull his vest back on, looking at the angry red acne pocked across his mountainous back like landmines, visible evidence of steroid abuse. Garland caught the look, reading the criticism but not taking it personally. Actually, he had been reflecting on the myriad forms of addiction, and knew that if he was to continue his vehement rhetoric about leading a pure-blooded army then he too would have to do better. Any dependency was a crutch that couldn't be carried over to the next phase of survival. Walking wordlessly over to the racks of antibiotics and medical supplies, he grabbed the few glass vials of anadrol and smashed them in the stainless steel basin.

"Don't let it be said that I stand for hypocrisy."

"I'm glad you brought that up and not me, but maybe you should have weened yourself off instead." Kershaw threw his hands up. He stroked his handlebar 'tache. "Doesn't matter. I have some anti-depressants lying around if you experience any withdrawal symptoms."

"No, no more drugs. If I can't man-up and deal with it then I don't deserve to be here. Our people need to be hard as stone and as cohesive as water." His thoughts were a tempest. "Our people. Fifteen. I warned the major about this. Time and again. He won't listen."

"He's a troubled man," Kershaw said. Yet it was clear his enthusiasm for defending the major had waned over time.

"Yes he is. And a decorated war hero, and he deserves better than what this country gave him. He should have died over in 'Nam if this was to be his legacy. He went over a living warrior, came back a living ghost." Garland's uncompromising tone softened with sympathy. "Who he is now, what he's become…he's detrimental to his own cause. Our cause." He stabbed his finger downwards like a falling sword. "The Midnight Frontiers. As for the others, they're showing their weakness. It's one thing to fall in line and obey unquestioningly for the mission. It's another entirely to get hooked on some chickenshit narcotic because their superior officer is a bad influence."

Kershaw crossed his arms in thought, his olive green t-shirt and brown trousers pressed to a fine razor thinness. "What are you getting at?"

"I'm going to go talk to him. After that, I think it's time we clean house. He's probably so out of it I can sell Wyndorf's death without too much of a confrontation. And by the time he's a bit more sober, that little prick should hopefully be dead for real."

"And if Thurman pushes for an exfil for that little turd?"

"An extraction?" Garland quietly thought that problem over, not happy with where his contingency plan was taking him. He glanced about slowly, checking for ears in the walls. "Then I might be forced to relieve him of his command."

A breathless cadence welcomed Garland into the major's private quarters—his office at the back of Down Range—the awkward breathing another symptom of his addiction. Physically, Thurman had seen better days, even after shrapnel took his right eye in the muggy, death-littered jungles of Saigon. Age had turned his bristling buzz cut the color of inhospitable winters, but it was synthetic ice which had reduced his remaining eye socket to an exhausted and hollowed-out pit housing a restless, paranoid eyeball. His indiscretion had only been eating away at him for little over ten months, proof of Wyndorf's insidious toxicity to the otherwise regimented pack. He had incurred some pretty horrendous dental attrition, the effects of meth mouth leaving his few remaining teeth like frag-blasted yellow jags of enamel in bloody gums.

The hard-bitten ex-marine rattled about his room of fading maps, his worsening psychosis leading him into a fantasy of grandeur, past glories of leadership, proud conquests. His Purple Heart was pinned to his urban commando attire, a heart-swelling souvenir for his injuries during the hellish fallout of the Tet Offensive.

Garland hated seeing him this way. They were supposed to fight side by side when the world tilted on its axis and civilisation crumbled; brothers-in-arms across this once great nation, finding purpose and getting back to the roots of how man was supposed to abide. Thurman had rescued him, fresh from his discharge. The military court had spared Garland prison, but stuck its hands deep into his shallow pockets. Struggling for work, unable to vote or even register for a gun, Thurman had found himself another disenfranchised bird with a broken wing. He had listened to his troubles, and he supported Garland's views on his own personal episode of manipulated conflict, this one in Afghanistan, agreeing that dying in the desert so some asshole can put gas in his car was a prime example of how fucked civilisation was.

"Wyndorf. You lost him?" Fist hammered table, his respiration sharp and shallow. "We need to pull his ass out of the fire."

Garland expected this response exactly. "Sir, I think we need to take this moment to reassess our mission. Losing Wyndorf is a great"—he couldn't believe his own lie—"setback. But I believe his business venture has distracted us somewhat. Captain Hooper at our Des Moines faction is pushing his men to the limit. He's making some hard-assed bastards and I fear some of our men are getting a little too soft. Their discipline and training has slipped."

Thurman couldn't stop moving, wearing out the boards under his feet, going back and forth. He brazenly poured out some powder onto the barrel of his service pistol and inhaled deeply. At least he wasn't smoking it now; he couldn't afford to ruin that smile of his. Hacking and coughing, he clearly hadn't heard a word his subordinate had said. "Who was it? Who took him? You think those dirty fucks have killed him?" He was arguing with himself, his voice rising in agitation. "We need more of his glass, Garland." His hand shook in the air as he tried to pull a word out of the ether. "It's a powerful tool. Keeps you sharp. The Nazis used meth, you know. Hitler swore by it—not that I approve of that maniac's vision, but goddammit if they didn't come this close to conquering a damn planet. It was a Berlin pharmaceutical company, government sponsored, Temmler. Dr. Hauschild, their chief pharmacist, was trying to emulate an amphetamine called Benzedrine which our own guys used in the 1936 Olympics. Instead he created Pervitin, the blueprint for crystal meth. Factories produced the stuff by the ton, and the Wehrmacht waged a sleepless, tireless war against the Allies whilst up to their eyeballs in the stuff. Think what we could be capable of if we got in deeper with C.B.'s business." The 9mm rattled in his restless hand until he slipped it in his waistband. He leaned across his desk, his eye burning like a chemical spill into Garland's. "I know Hooper and Lisiewicz, all our faction leaders think I'm up the creek, but they just need to be brought around to my way of thinking. We could bring them all in, all the camps, become a relentless united front against the candy-ass pen jockeys who are shitting all over our country. Better killing through chemistry. I haven't slept in days—it's allowed me to accomplish so much."

Garland thought about asking his unhinged despot if he recalled the part where Hitler and his master race lost the war. He scanned the room: indecipherable codes and keys scrawled in red marker on the maps, books on extinction-level events and natural disasters, a prepper handbook explaining how to build a DIY Faraday cage should an EMP be launched at them by the Man in the White House. Garland was no longer certain what the major was cognisant of during his episodes and felt it prudent to put the man back on a firm track before continuing with their supposed discussion.

"You asked me if I think Wyndorf's K.I.A.?" It was a genuinely tough question. "I'm not sure. But I do know that those guys were good. Trained, from the looks of it. I don't like Wyndorf's chances against them."

"We're not leaving a man behind. That's not our way, soldier. You should be fucking ashamed of yourself." The major's mood swung to aggression on a dime, another charming symptom. "He has a tracker in him," he barked, "so go find him."

Garland set his jaw, biting back the retort. This was pointless. Thurman was beyond help, and he was running the whole unit into the damn sewer. A solution was slowly forming in his head. "Major, how about one last mission? I would be honored to take these guys down with you beside me on the field."

Garland suspected the wolf and his spoilt bacon brigade were ex-military due to the way they moved, their formations, skill, weapons handling. If they were not official military then they were at least highly trained by someone who knew what they were doing. A good, strong test for the army of the new world. Great experience for his true, clean warriors. And a great threat to the fouled war hero and his undisciplined acolytes. If the gangrenous limb of this faction should be removed during this healing campaign then, well, friendly fire was a risk of warfare. Garland watched the promise of combat stoke the dead embers of vitality and purpose in the major's watery, unfocused sight.

"Son." His single eye briefly flashed with a keen intelligence before passing behind a glaze of narcotic hunger as the major clamped a steely hand on Garland's shoulder. "The honor would be all mine. Let's go get our piggy bank back."

Garland found Schecter in one of the watch towers, flicking a match head and watching the beautiful power burning away. Warmth and safety. Death and destruction. Scars and nightmares. He tossed the match off the top of the guard tower with the others. One by one they had sailed down to the bare earth like miniature wooden Hindenburgs. He pulled another from the book and glanced at the horizon.

"Keeping busy?"

Schecter craned his neck toward the deep voice but continued to slouch in the deck chair, his boots propped on the wooden guard rail. Ignite and toss. "I heard some whackos in masks crashed Wyndorf's little reunion party. You okay?"

"Just a scratch," Garland answered.

"Please tell me that prick wasn't so lucky?"

"Too early to tell. That's why I'm here."

Schecter sat up, throwing a disparaging look at his superior.

"I'm organising a rescue mission."

Schecter gave a bitter chuckle and lit another matchstick, holding the glow to the ruined half of his face. "This a joke? You think I'm signing up to save his ass?" He extinguished the flame with his thumb and index finger.

"The job isn't to save him. It's to save this camp. The other cells' respect for us is almost tapped out. They view us as a bunch of fuckwits only interested in getting high. We need to detox this whole platoon. I just spoke to Thurman again, stared him dead in the eye…he's too far gone. Hooper told me Thurman returned from the jungle with a smack habit, and he beat it, eventually. A proud moment. Started piecing his life back together. Opened this gun store, found some like-minded people. But some demons never truly leave a person. I think Thurman was like every other junkie, only ever one moment of weakness shy of letting the demons whisper in his ear."

Schecter might have nodded at this but the dim perimeter lights around the gates below made it difficult to ascertain, and the cloud cover dimmed the starlight. "Wyndorf is a demon, all right." Another matchstick blazed. "It takes a demon to laugh whilst a man burns half to death. You know a part of me was actually amazed I could hear anything over my own screams and the crackle of my skin igniting. But I heard him. Laughing as he took off to save his own skin. You saved my ass back in that raid. When the S.W.A.T. boots were stomping down doors and their bullets were tearing the lab apart. You kept me from being charcoal on a slab." He blew out the dancing flame. "You know I'll have your back."

A proud smirk spread widely across Garland's huge jaw. "I know you will. Okay, so the good news is Kershaw has provided me with a list of all the junkies dragging us down. The bad news is, it's everyone 'cept you, me, Kershaw and Higgins." Schecter shook his head sadly. "I propose a false flag operation. We drop in under the pretence of rescuing Wyndorf, and the four of us hold back as his tweaking sympathisers are weeded out by a better, more coherent enemy."

"And Wyndorf?"

"His captors are good. This will be dangerous. But I believe that once the shit hits, they'll be distracted enough for the four of us to sneak through and neutralise Wyndorf."

"And if by some miracle these clowns come out on top?" Schecter stared down at the camp below, wondering how many of them were this instant smoking and snorting by torchlight?

"Then we mop up what's left."

"The major?"

"Him too. His old self would have been the first to lay down his life for his men. It's what he would have wanted before he became this disappointment."

Schecter stared unresponsively out across the dark interstate. His expression was that of a man about to make a very big leap.

Even with his evident troubles, the major had been the figurehead of this outfit since the beginning, starting their whole movement with a handful of fellow 'Nam survivors left insulted and disgusted by the deceitful leaders of their beloved country. "Wyndorf can't go quick. I want him to suffer for what he's done. We need to carve him up like the tumor he is."

"I'll hold him down for you."

Schecter hopped to his feet double-time, the promise of correcting their course adding some much-needed vigor to his morale.

"Thurman is bugging out, desperate to relive his glory days. I'll go pinpoint Wyndorf's GPS tracker and get an idea of the terrain. Move it, we roll out in fifteen," Garland ordered.

Schecter slid down the ladder like his palms were greased. Garland held on a moment longer, thinking about the all the itchy, manic chaff sequestered below, waiting to meet his sickle.

Feeding Time

Alfred stood in a large study that was slowly falling into disrepair. It wasn't a room of quiet respite. It was dedicated to his surmounted terror. He was surrounded by it at every turn.

Sus scrofa domesticus.

Pig.

He inhaled another steadying breath, a man tensing before the plunge into icy water. Pushing himself above his fear. The walls of the gloomy study held paintings of pigs rolling about in each other's company, portraits of their wide, eternally hungry and simple faces. Small ornamental statues and models of the dirty things littered the dusty, empty bookshelves, the tables and windowsills. There was even a large stuffed boar mounted over the rough-hewn stone hearth, the log fire creating a malevolent blaze in its dead eyes.

Jensen puffed out his chest, proud but melancholic, rejoicing in his victory over the pig icons' diminishing power. He walked amongst the artful sty, lit by the blaze's hellish light, toward the windows, and saw the electric eyes of a van's lights sweep around the courtyard of the decrepit private estate. He watched the dark figures pile out of the van below, only to look through them, becoming entranced by his pale deformity in the cool glass. His gaze was only interrupted by a polite and firm knock at the open door. Alfred beckoned Colquitt into the fire-lit study.

Colquitt entered halfway into the den of pig propitiation, his splendidly tailored double-breasted navy suit and coal black tie giving him an air of efficiency, a Swiss watch made flesh. "We have them, sir."

"Isaac Reid and Curtis Roach." Jensen spoke to his reflection, closing his eyes, his voice expressing something like wish fulfilment.

"We found the bonus prize during the collection. I think your stars must have aligned." Colquitt watched as relief deflated the mangled surgeon, a man finally sighting the terminal station of a long and challenging pilgrimage.

Jensen silently turned toward Colquitt, unable to find the words, the crackle of embers and flaming wood filling the quiet. "You ... found Michael Wyndorf?"

"He and Reid were beating the shit out of each other. Got there in the nick of time." Blood trickled down from Colquitt's saturated cuff, pattering on the old wooden floor, the firelight illuminating the perspiration on his face. Briefly he bared his teeth in a throb of pain.

"What happened?" Jensen glanced at the wound.

"Wyndorf had a friend with him, if you can believe that?" Colquitt clenched his jaw in fury at the huge son of a bitch who had managed to stick him and shoot his way out of there. "He won't be a problem, though."

Jensen drifted across the room toward his hired gun. "Any other complications? Police?"

"No police. I lost four men, though."

"Their shares can be divvied up amongst the rest of you." The surgeon paid no mind to Colquitt's loss. They were mercenaries, after all. "Let me check the damage."

Colquitt took half a step back. "That won't be necessary, sir. I can take care of it. I'll have one of my men prepare your other guests. We'll be at the pen when you're ready." Colquitt faded into the shadows of the large landing.

"Thank you, Mr. Colquitt." The doctor's voice was stricken with a surge of emotion as he battled for composure. Dr. Velez had been wrong: he was open to happiness, but their definitions were night and day in comparison. He buttoned up his winter coat and replaced his armor of scarf and hat.

"Wyndorf…' Dark ecstasy leaked through the spongy folds of his brain. "Finally…the beginning of my end."

Isaac felt the damp chill of the earth channelling through his knee-caps, making them ache, as if filthy ice shards were crystallising within the bone. His hands were bound tightly behind his back. The sack was torn from his head. His eyes exchanged one dark world for another. After a few seconds his eyes adjusted. Two other figures, similarly bound, were lined up in his row. Their bags were ripped off, too.

Three pig-masked lackeys stood quietly before them in the dark field, cattle prods at the ready. Behind them was a structure, a huge tunnel, looking like a monstrous worm that had broken halfway through the surface of the soil to sleep under the starless sky. The stench of undisturbed nature and the odiousness of aged, lingering animal shit choked him. From somewhere in that large structure emanated a faint, languid symphony of honks and oinks. The sound made Isaac shrivel inside.

It was the sound of avarice and hunger.

Isaac and Roach exchanged a troubled look, relieved to see each other alive, yet knowing the clock was rapidly running out. A fourth man, wounded but still clearly dangerous, stepped before them. Fortyish, black, bald, clean-shaven with mirthless eyes. Isaac recognised him from the Audi outside Mateo's.

"You the wolf?" Roach asked the stranger.

"He works for Alfred Jensen," Isaac answered.

"Jensen? That faggot still alive?" Wyndorf chuckled with cruel astonishment. His lenses had been lost during his abduction, and strands of his otter-slick hair had come loose, hanging into his eyes. "I'm bettin' he's camera-shy these days. So what's your deal?" Wyndorf thought he was in the market and was ready to haggle. "This personal? Business? What?"

"Bit of both. Business primarily, but I just lost four men back there, so I'm taking that personally," the pack leader answered, his voice deep enough to send tremors down their spines. "And the name's Colquitt. I feel like we can now dispense with the mysteries."

"Where are we?" Roach asked. He could make out a few barns and a creepy old farmhouse.

"Lockport. A former family-owned business Jensen was able to snatch up for a steal. Almost an hour from the city. So don't expect any helpful strangers stumbling by to help."

"Will we be seeing Jensen, or is this a quick and neat shallow-grave type of situation?" Isaac asked.

"He'll be here shortly." Colquitt winced momentarily, a splinter in his professional façade, a steady trickle of dark blood dripping from his temporary patch-up job.

"Look here, Colquitt, whatever burger-face is paying you, I'll raise it. I got a solid connection with the biggest meth distribution network on the entire east coast. If you're smart, you'll take me up on what's a very generous deal, and all I'll ask in return is that you allow me to personally gut this bitch before we split." His malevolent eyes sliced across Isaac.

Isaac wanted to tackle Wyndorf and tear his throat out with his teeth. He might not get another chance. But Colquitt and his two-man deterrent standing by would never stand for it.

Colquitt seemed to find the negotiation amusing. "My men and I are professionals; we do our research. Your cousin Cameron Beech and his associates can't stomach you from what we've been able to piece together. Why else would a family member be working as some disposable low-level mutt instead of having a seat at the grown-ups' table? You think he's loyal enough to buy me and my men just to spare a fuck-up liability like you?"

Wyndorf took it with good grace. "Ah, can't blame a guy for trying. Remember one thing for me, though: I offered you a way out of this. You see, I have new friends now. That guy who ruined your suit? He's one of them."

Colquitt seemed to pay no mind to the knife wound leaking in his shoulder. "A charming man like you? I'm sure you have lots of friends."

"What the fuck were you thinking back there?" Roach said reprovingly, catching Isaac unawares. "Outside Monahan's," he clarified. "Twice in one day you act like an impulsive dog chasing the mailman. It's not you. Not who you were. You got a death wish?"

Isaac craned his neck to the left to look at him, but he couldn't find a worthy answer. His attention kept slipping to Wyndorf, kneeling beside Roach.

"Do you?"

"Doesn't matter. Looks like we would have wound up here one way or another," Isaac answered.

"Death wish?" Wyndorf almost choked on his own words. "In case I was being too subtle back there, asshole, I'd be happy to kill you."

To hell with the guards. Isaac went for it, but with hands bound by flexicuffs, his wrath was checked. He landed a kick on Wyndorf's jaw, then collapsed on top of him. They both writhed and flapped about like gasping fish in six-pack holders, all expended effort and little else, but Isaac managed to land a nasty headbutt, chipping Wyndorf's left incisor before two square-shouldered pigs separated them with their own occasional punch or kick. Roach shouted at them to leave Isaac alone, receiving a stiff jab for his trouble, almost doubling him over backward.

Wyndorf smiled through bloody teeth at Isaac. "I bet your dead wife hits harder than that."

Isaac's facial muscles contorted and he became fluent in a language of violent prehistoric beasts, one step away from foaming at the mouth like a rabid dog.

Colquitt received a text message, neatly slipped his phone back in his pocket. "Okay, get them up."

The armed pigs hauled their three prisoners to their feet, keeping enough distance between them to nix any further bright ideas with a quick cattle prod shock. Isaac trudged behind Colquitt, their death march leading them across the moon-clouded field to the huge pen. The excited scoffs and snorts grew steadily in volume the closer they got.

At the maw of the tunnel, Colquitt flicked a switch on the wall. A series of flickering strip lights revealed a flight of metal steps leading up to an elevated bridge that extended the entire length of the tunnel. The walkway was suspended over a large walled-in enclosure, at the heart of which came the excited noises of hunger. In the light, the dark pig masks became livor mortis red and rotten apple green. Isaac knew very shortly he, like Roach and Wyndorf, would be nothing more than another dead pig.

Colquitt climbed the steps, each clang like a spoon banging against a pan. Isaac was pushed forth. The dark beneath the bridge seemed hungry. Colquitt stopped the procession in the middle of the walkway. Walking toward them from the opposite end was a beaten and dishevelled old man, wearing nothing but his white briefs, another pig-man prodding him on toward the submissive gathering.

Robert Ludlow: bruised but alive.

A few paces behind Ludlow's guard was another figure, taking deep, soothing breaths, moving from electric light to brief shadow, to light to shadow. Isaac knew who he was, but couldn't recognise him at first glance, at least not until the figure removed his flat cap and scarf. Alfred Jensen's visage was enrapturing, so much worse without all the blood to mask the finer details of Wyndorf's handiwork. A bad slasher movie come to life. Isaac side-eyed Roach and noticed a similar look of awe and shame on his face. Wyndorf cackled in disbelief.

Through swollen raccoon eyes Ludlow stared at Roach and Isaac with a combination of paternal support and sorrow. "Curt, Isaac, you boys okay?"

Colquitt kicked Ludlow in the back of his bare knee, dropping him painfully into the bridge's metal grating. Colquitt and his men, and Jensen, their director in all this, made a looming cluster about him.

"Jensen," Ludlow whispered, swollen lips puffed up like a squashed rosebud. "Jensen, you don't need Isaac or Curt. I told you, it was my plan." His venomous gaze tried to strike down the other man, recognising him as Wyndorf. "This cocksucker, though—I know you're going to have plans for this sick sonuvabitch. Me and him," he beseeched, "we're the only two you need. Let the others go."

Jensen stepped closer, the electric light and shadows making interesting and atrocious peaks and troughs in his redesigned face. Ludlow's lamentations carried on for several more moments until Colquitt kicked him in the stomach.

"You have the gall to beg, and make demands of me?" Jensen's voice was empty, his inflections and cadences left far behind in his coma. "The four of you tear my fucking heart out and now expect lenience? Mercy?"

Ludlow got his coughing under control. "I told you, it was me and that cocksucker Wyndorf who're responsible. Isaac and Curt tried to stop him. They tried to stop me, too. Tried to talk me out of ordering it. I didn't listen. I refused to. I couldn't sit there as you left my Jeanie to die."

Jensen nodded. "Of course, these two just wanted to kidnap my wife and daughter. Not that big of a deal, I suppose. And what then? Kill them after I'd served my purpose? Dump them in the lake?"

"No! Never! They would have been safe. I would have released them and turned myself in. I just needed to see that Janine was okay." Tears ran freely down Ludlow's bruised palette of a face.

"You really are just a bunch of misunderstood saints, aren't you?"

"None of this would have happened if you weren't such an egotistical piece of shit," Isaac spoke up. "Your precious surgical record is more important to you dick-measuring assholes than a patient's life. You're just as much of a fucking murderer as this cunt." He tilted his head and spat at Wyndorf, trying to dive at him again, once more blocked by quick, brutish hands.

"You dare compare me to him? I didn't make the system what it is! I only worked within it. There shouldn't be ratings. Patients shouldn't have access to our records. Insurance companies shouldn't be keeping their greedy little eyes on our successes and failures. If you had a problem with that, then you should have taken it to the medical board. Not sent your barbarians to come and pay me and my family a visit one night!" Jensen screamed, some life returning to his dead, slumbering voice.

Ludlow stayed quiet, hunched over in defeat, his old anger spent. He couldn't argue with Jensen. Too many years spent in doubt and contempt for what he'd set into motion. He thought about their shared grief and emptiness, and tried to find the humanity in the face of a man who had had his humanity stripped away from him.

Jensen squatted down before Wyndorf, examining him like he was a bug. "I only have vague flashes of that night. One thing I am keenly aware of is that this"—his fingers caressed his ruined face almost proudly—"was only superficial. Hard to believe, I know. Sutures had to be applied to the incisions in the musculature, iodine spread across the expansive wound edges to prevent infection. A drape had to be taped to my face to keep the skin aligned and sterile." His voice took on the tone of a medical lecturer as he used his hand to mimic the procedure in question. "I declined reconstructive surgery…much to the chagrin of friends and colleagues. It felt wrong somehow, like I was trying to forget what happened. How could I?" His lips peeled back to show white teeth. "You see, the blow to my head was considerably worse than this skin-deep horror. You know, there are reports of some people awakening from comas telling of endless dreams they lived through. It all depends on which region of the brain suffers the trauma. For six years I was chased, and mauled, by stinking, squealing, laughing pigs. Feeling an endless dread as my wife and daughter screamed…cried…died somewhere in that haze. Over…and over…and over again. Always out of my reach. Six years. Six years of porcine dreams."

Wyndorf locked eyes with his long-suffering victim. "Well, you look great."

Isaac expected Jensen or Colquitt to lunge at this jester and inflict some much-deserved pain, but the room was still. Instead, Jensen stared at Wyndorf for what must have been fifteen seconds, until Wyndorf started to get angry at the silent inspection.

Jensen, not remotely intimidated by Wyndorf's unpredictable temperament, grew bored. He paused a moment to search for the fear in Ludlow's blackened eyes. The swine noises had grown deeper in pitch, suggesting animals larger than Isaac had at first assumed. The enclosure beneath their feet seemed to mock and shun the strip lighting, swallowing it, hors d'oeuvres before the main course.

Jensen took a few steps over to a small, wheeled surgical tray positioned next to an opening in the railing. The tray held some type of bulky tool, looking like an alien hairdryer with a lime green handle and dark gray barrel. The trigger cinched it. The trigger, and the cardboard box with STUNNER LOADS and .25 CALIBER printed along the side of it. It was no child's toy or grooming product.

Jensen picked up the penetrating captive bolt gun, emotionless in the face of his big moment, his power fantasy subdued to nothing more than cold, empty method. He stared at Ludlow, watching the former king of thieves sway through exhaustion and head trauma on the edge of the drop-off, Colquitt's hand the only thing steadying him.

Ludlow sighed, his voice filled with weary resignation. "So this is your courtroom? Your method of balancing the scales? I can guarantee you this won't bring the peace you're searching for. It won't make sense of all the agony and the emptiness." Head bowed, his toes over the edge, he stared down at the roiling murk. "This isn't the answer, but I'm ready to prove that point for you. Do what you must to me and Wyndorf, but please let the others go. They can be better men."

"Fuck you!" Wyndorf launched into a short-lived tirade toward Ludlow, bowing at the knees as a pig guard's thick trotter slammed into his right kidney.

Isaac waded about, lost and directionless in the blind, violent rage he harbored for Wyndorf, and realised he was not about to live up to Ludlow's hope that he would be a better man. He stared at the choices scrolling behind Jensen's dark eyes. Ludlow didn't glance at his judge. Instead he looked over his shoulder at Isaac and Roach, his stare full of sorrow and regret, but most of all penitence.

"Drop him," Jensen ordered, passing his wolf the gun.

Colquitt placed the bolt gun just above Ludlow's knee and squeezed the trigger, the gunpowder round blasting the bolt deep into bone and muscle with a splash of dark red like a burst paintball. Isaac and Roach cried out as they watched Ludlow fall fifteen feet, landing badly onto the cold, hard muck. The pig-faces pushed their hostages against the railing, shining torches into the gloomy pit, the beams like cold searchlights pinning Ludlow. He lay there, groaning in agony, hands pressed to his ruined leg, spilling blood like a faucet.

The pit wasn't the open pen Isaac had been expecting: the design was more like that of a man-sized mouse maze. From somewhere in the network of tunnels, blind turns and dead ends, the grunts grew in volume, echoing off the dull corrugated walls until finally, a tremendous bulk of filth-encrusted flesh and hide-hair waddled into the roving searchlights of the torches. The wild boar was easily seven feet long, an absolute monster.

It wasn't alone.

On its tail came another, and another, and one more, all nearly as large and lethal as the lead animal. Isaac wasn't sure who screamed louder, himself, Roach, or Ludlow, their shared outrage and grief forming a wail of discord as the greedy quartet descended on Ludlow, charging their tusks with over 700 pounds of mass and piercing his arms and legs over and over. It was difficult to tell if he was dead before their insatiable appetites reduced him from man to morsel with each scoffing, wet, flesh-tearing, bone-crunching bite.

"This is your big plan? Turn us into pig shit?" Wyndorf grinned facetiously.

Jensen took the gun back and emptied the spent brass cartridge, reloading it in no great hurry. His answer was a chilly hand kneading Isaac's guts like wet dough. "I have other games in mind for the rest of you."

It was clear that this wasn't simply a matter of clinical retribution; this was an obscene and savage scheme concocted by a truly disturbed mind.

"You're fucking insane." Isaac tried to break free and was immediately checked by the hot sting of the cattle prod.

Jensen returned the bolt gun to the surgical tray. "Mr. Roach, I have some special guests I'm sure you'll be quite distressed to see."

Roach's stomach felt as though it was being sucked down an oily drain, hollowing him out completely. He already knew who his guests were. Who else would it be to satisfy this sick bastard's revenge? 'No…" His voice was a raspy whisper. "If you've laid a finger on any of them, I'm going to play with your guts!" Roach exploded, his tied wrists stealing his righteous thunder.

Isaac was breathing heavily from his rocketing pulse, but one of Roach's words sank in. "Them'? He looked at Roach in confusion. Who else had been dragged into this? His ex, Diane? Who else?

"I haven't touched them." Jensen gave him a contemptuous sneer. "I don't harm innocents to make my bread." He gesticulated toward Colquitt. "My associates here, on the other hand, are getting paid good money for services rendered. You can take it up with them very shortly. And if it's any consolation, I had the same plan for Mr. Reid and Mr. Wyndorf, too. But their situations being what they are…" He shrugged apologetically, leaning against the steel gate. "I have been forced to tailor their own bespoke punishments. So don't take this personally."

Colquitt snapped his fingers and the two storm trooper pigs manhandled Roach back along the bridge and out of the pen. Roach was thrashing like a netted rhino until a short, sharp shock turned him limp. Isaac tried to fight back, and the voltage bit once more, making him sag against the railing. He watched hopelessly as the friend who was a brother to him in every way bar blood was dragged away, and knew he would do absolutely anything to keep his final link to the world in one piece, no matter what the cost.

Jensen grabbed a handful of Wyndorf's hair and wrenched his head back violently. "Somebody throw this one in the barn with those other two. I'll be taking my time with him later." Jensen released Wyndorf, wiping his hand on his coat. "Now, Isaac, I understand you and Mr. Roach were very good friends." Jensen pointed at him like he was a bag of luggage to be hauled off, and Colquitt did the honors by straightening him up. "I'd like you personally to watch the entertainment."

Regretfully, Isaac wasn't sure what upset him most: being pulled away from Wyndorf or being an imminent spectator to what awaited Roach. "Don't you go anywhere," he barked at Wyndorf.

"Wouldn't dream of it," Wyndorf assured. His index finger continued to rub small circles around the healed incision on his thumb. The major's insurance policy better be worth it.

Show Time

The grass was cold and springy under Roach's shoes. The dew in the air hinted at the possible coming of a fog he doubted he would get a chance to see. He hadn't noticed them earlier, but in the distance there were floodlights erected around the ramshackle farmhouse, unlit and cold against the backdrop. With the exception of the crickets and ghostly taunts on the breeze, the death march was quiet. He knew Isaac was being guided along behind him at a distance, and tried to look back, maybe clock what might be the last time he ever saw him, but one of the lackeys shoved him on.

The abandoned farmhouse would have been beautiful back in the day, before it went out of business or succumbed to whichever tragic fate had befallen it. Now it was only impressive in its fall from grace. The stone walls and timber awnings looked like they absorbed frost to keep the wraiths within in good spirits. The large windows had been designed to provide gorgeous views of the open landscape and lots of light; now they were wrapped up in dark and dusty curtains.

Roach was led around to the back, where two old cellar doors lay open and waiting, the stone steps leading down to the musty, bulb-lit bowels of the basement.

Jensen stopped him at the top of the steps, an enigmatic look caught somewhere between regret and fanaticism on his roadmap of scars. "It's the feeling of being too helpless to protect them that hurts the most."

It was a vague, unprompted statement, but it made a sinister kind of sense in Roach's head, and he knew then how far gone the wounded man really was. He was about to demand clarification, no, confirmation of the growing dread suppurating in his mind like a wound, when the duo of pigs prepared him for the trial down below. One trained a gun on him and the other untied his wrists, prompting him to descend into the basement alone. After the first tentative step, he added a bit more haste.

It's the feeling of being too helpless to protect them that really hurts, came the echo. At the base of the stairs was a scuffed and dinged metal door, cold to the touch. Ripping it open, he found himself in a freezing cold tomb of bare concrete blocks. Huddled together in one corner, face streaked with tears, were Diane and their twin eight-year-olds, Peter and Vicky. Roach's knees almost buckled, and the fear and anguish on their faces made his breathing hitch. The door slammed shut behind him, locks sliding into place.

"Diane!" He raced for her and the kids, not caring about the pending divorce, about any ill will that existed between them. Right now all he cared about was making sure they were okay. Then what? They practically collided in their tight embrace, then Roach squatted down and kissed Vicky and Peter on the tops of their heads. "Are you guys okay?"

Fresh tears started down Peter's chubby cheeks. "I'm scared, Dad."

Roach pulled him and Vicky in closer, trying to be their rock. He had never felt so weak. The sheer frailty on display made him want to dismiss the inchoate guilt he felt for Jensen. Kidnapping his children, his wife, in a slow-cooking retaliation put that bastard on an even footing. He wanted to cut Jensen's balls off for this.

"What happened?" he asked Diane.

She sniffed back her tears and ran a shaking hand through her blonde hair. "These … men broke into our home a few nights ago. They won't tell us anything." She pointed to the camera mounted in the corner of the room, next to a small speaker. "They haven't hurt us. All we've been told is that this is temporary." A small flicker of her old, wounded trust and anger flashed in her blue eyes. "Is this something to do with"—she went to say any number of despicable things but remembered Peter and Vicky were there—"your work?"

What could he say? There was no point in lying. His silence provided her with an answer. Still she wanted more, needing to know what the hell he had done to have her and her two children snatched from a new home and a new life 240 miles away.

"A past mistake," he added lamely.

Isaac was forced to stop at the front of the farmhouse, but he kept his eyes on Roach's back, watching him round the corner with Jensen and his escort. Colquitt led him up the creaky porch steps, which sounded fit to break, and into the foyer. The cavernous hallway was almost chillier than the night, increased tenfold by the sinking feeling in Isaac's gut, occupying all interstitial space like frozen water. The interior was very similar to the exterior, so much wasted potential. Hardwood floors, no paintings, ornaments, trinkets or homely possessions of any kind. Just some disquieting doorways branching off from the foyer and an uninviting grand staircase leading up into further darkness. Isaac wondered if Jensen had purchased this property. He tried to imagine him living bare, drifting about in the gloom and the harsh labors of memory and thought.

Colquitt flicked a wall switch. At least there was power. The old wall sconces were coated with who knew how many years' worth of dust and webbing, adding a dull hue to their glow.

"Where's Roach going?"

Colquitt led him through the living room, their every step sounding far too loud on the solid boards. "You're about to find out."

The only furniture in the room was a fold-out table with a laptop on it. Colquitt showed him the camera feed that was live on the computer's screen. Roach was hugging Diane and, Isaac was shocked and saddened to see, two little kids. Curtis had kept quiet about exactly how much he had lost during their separation. The omission nicked a small wound in Isaac until he accepted it was he who had wanted the clean break and distance, reducing family to nothing more than former business associates. It didn't matter now. They were all in the hands of a madman they had unwittingly helped create.

Isaac could barely find his voice. "His family is innocent."

"So was mine." Jensen had crept in, quiet as a spider, approaching the laptop and not even deigning to give Isaac a passing glance.

Isaac watched Roach embracing his family on the screen, wishing he was still able to hold Maggie and Will. "This can all end with us, right here and now. This won't fix anything, Jensen. You don't want an innocent woman and two children on your conscience."

Jensen went to speak, but paused as if he had forgotten his words, his fist clenched in thought. He slammed the table top, rocking the image of Roach and his family. "Death isn't enough. I don't want to kill him. Not yet. I need him to know how it feels to have his loved ones murdered in front of him. I have spent every day and every night thinking about subjecting each of you to the hell you put me through."

Isaac's voice was low and dangerous. "I know exactly how it feels. I just went through it."

"Yes, you did. But I was robbed of that catharsis. So you can watch this instead."

"This is beyond vengeance, you know that? It's insane." Isaac looked from Jensen's dead features to the robotic and emotionless expression on Colquitt's face.

"Don't look at me. This is just a paycheque," the mercenary grumbled.

"You want to get even, I get that. I don't blame you. But don't let your anger take innocent lives. It won't fix what's broken. Look…" Isaac's eyes reached out to whatever shred of warmth and humanity clung to Jensen's skin-grafted soul. "I know the hurt. And I know you don't give a shit about my misery, or need a preacher right now, but since that unforgivable scene at yours, I've been trying to stay between the lines. Thinking I could find a little redemption, maybe finally do right by a family I didn't deserve. Then these last few days passed like a blur, and the only thing that's got me through is the thought of all the horrible shit I would do to the guy who took my family. It was a nasty little fantasy I needed to push me forward, to keep what was left of my sanity glued together. I needed someone to hate, and blame, and shoulder my rage. And I started to see how it was the only thing I had left to hold on to. I know killing him isn't going to change anything, won't undo the harm he's done to me. Maggie and Will are still in the ground. And what would I have left? With him dead, what would I do without my anger?"

Isaac's posture relaxed slightly, spent at the unburdening of his dark and hollow passion. "So trust me when I say I understand exactly what you're feeling. And it's no consolation, but know that Roach and I did try to stop that psycho from doing what he did that night. So if you need to see your anger through, and need to get even, all I'm asking is please don't punish his family for a mistake we made. Don't let Wyndorf make you into what he is."

Silence smothered them for a moment.

"Do I look like I can be saved?" Jensen said with hopeless finality.

In those words Isaac heard shallow-grave dirt being padded down with shovels, or more likely, the grunt of belly-distended pigs satisfied. It was dumb and reactionary, yet Isaac was operating on panic and instinct. Forgetting that his hands were bound behind his back, he charged at Jensen. Colquitt was a spring-loaded trap, slamming his fist into Isaac's solar plexus, collapsing him into a wheezing, nauseous heap. Jensen paid him no mind, switching on the small microphone for the wall speaker in Roach's prison. Jensen gave Colquitt a nod.

Colquitt removed a walkie-talkie from his belt. "Game time."

The tinny speaker in the corner of the cinder-block cell squawked like nails on a chalkboard then settled into a snake's hiss. "Curtis Roach. I am giving you the same fighting chance I was given. For your family's sake, make it count." The speaker went dead and there was a sound of deadbolts scraping back from the door.

"What's he talking about? Who is this?" Diane demanded, hysteria rising to a sharp pitch.

Roach crowded Diane, Vicky and Peter into the corner, shielding them from what was coming in. Three of them entered. Still in suits, still in pig masks. Two appeared to be unarmed but the third carried a butcher knife. Diane and the kids were wide-eyed and on the verge of full-blown panic attacks, and Roach was right behind them. The coursing adrenaline didn't whitewash the fact that he was essentially one-handed, unarmed and outnumbered. He didn't trust his aching right fist not to shatter on the first blow. On the balls of his feet, left fist clenched and severely inadequate in this situation, his blood ran high with stress.

"Get the fuck back!" he roared, taking the smallest of steps toward the silent, patient killers, too scared to leave his family unguarded.

The trio fanned out, intending to overwhelm him. Doubt and terror were proving too much for his challenging bravado. They were all going to die. He was going to fail them. Diane, Peter, Vicky, they were all going to die bleeding out in the middle of nowhere, surrounded by agents of a harsh karma. The guard to Roach's right was shuffling closer, hands up defensively, weary of him but moving like he was enjoying himself. Roach was almost paralysed by fear at the thought of stepping toward him in case one of the others got around him, that knife meeting the soft flesh of a loved one. But he couldn't stand there and do nothing. He stepped forward half a foot and snapped out a stiff jab toward the jaw of the guy on his right. Being an ex-soldier, or whoever the hell he was, the attacker bobbed his head backward, so that Roach's knuckles missed his chin. The middle guy with the knife had paused in his advance, allowing the others to close the gap in a pincer movement. Roach stomped out at the left-hand guy, his sole coming up short and merely brushing dry mud across his suit jacket. Behind him he could hear Vicky stifling tears, scared by the shouting, cursing and brewing violence.

The unscrupulous animal on the right suddenly rushed in, popping out a quick jab of his own which caught Roach on the cheek. It rattled him, his wild eyes flitting back and forth between both flanking attackers like a pendulum, but his head cleared quickly, just in time to catch sight of the left guy, the largest of the swine passel, making an attempt. The pig stepped in with a left hook which Roach managed to duck under. Coming up out of his roll, Roach grabbed the puncher's tie with his left hand and slammed his right palm heel into the rotting ichor-tinged snout of the mask. Without letting go, he used the tie to drag the pig in closer, smashing him again and again, wanting to use him as a possible shield against the attacker on his right and, most importantly, the watching knifeman. A quick blur of movement and a shrill cry of 'Dad!" allowed Roach to haul the semi-conscious punching bag by the tie and lapel into the swift and eager right-hand attacker, slamming both their bodies together against the wall in an exclamation of groans.

"Curt!" Diane screamed. The knifeman was quick, darting forward and opening a burning slice along Roach's ribs.

Gasping in shock, Roach pulled away from the blade, blood running freely through his right fingers and palm. He thrust his left hand out, fingers closed, to ward off the blade. One of the downed attackers reached up and seized Roach's right leg, pinning it in place and clobbering him in the stomach. With the breath racing out of his lungs, Roach managed a blind swing, hitting the kneeling guard somewhere along the side of his rubberised skull. It wasn't a satisfying shot, though; it barely clipped him. With an unbearable sinking feeling, Roach felt his knees and thighs burning with the strain of opposing the two punch-drunk lackeys latched onto his legs, beating him until he was finally pulled down to the floor. Through the torrential rain of fists and snarls, Roach screamed out as Diane, Peter and Vicky huddled together helplessly with the knifeman slowly bearing down on them, the 14-inch carbon steel blade mirroring the sterile electric light. Roach was pulled to his knees, his arms pinned behind him at sharp angles, almost to breaking point. He hocked up a thick coating of rusty sinus blood and let it fly, spattering the shoe of the big one holding his right arm.

Diane leaned over the crouching, shaking forms of her children, watching the knife dance in flares of blinding light. Roach thrashed about, unable to break free and fight off the strength-sapping grapplers holding him tight. He screamed their names. He screamed for the killer's mercy. He screamed how much he loved Diane, Peter and Vicky, and how sorry he was.

The pig raised his knife and let it fall.

Isaac had a few bruises of his own. When he'd refused to watch the imminent execution of his friend and his family, Colquitt had decided it would be prudent to slap him about into submission. Now, with Colquitt's vice-like grip on his jaw and the back of his skull, he was forced to watch the nightmare unfolding on the grainy camera feed. Jensen had become a statue in his viewing, his gaze expressing no more life than that of any dull sculpture. Isaac had expected him to be enjoying this more. On the screen, Roach was on his knees, quietly begging and demanding in equal parts, wrath and compromise at war. The butcher brought his ruthless cutting tool up, ready to plunge and turn the concrete room into an abattoir, when Jensen snapped from his deep freeze, hands scrabbling for the microphone.

"Stop," he demanded. The would-be executioner obeyed without fuss. "Leave them. Lock up and leave them."

The knifeman quietly retreated to the doorway. The two roughed-up mercenaries were true professionals, relinquishing their sparring partner without further harm and making a quick exit.

Colquitt brought his walkie-talkie up, selecting the proper channel. "Return to the perimeter." On screen, the knifeman acknowledged the command and closed the door behind him. The bolts were thrown home.

Isaac didn't thank Jensen, or try to convince him that they were both part of some secret and exclusive survivors' club. In truth, as grateful as he was for this unexpected act of clemency, he feared what came next. And how far could this leniency really go? Would Jensen blindfold Roach's family and drop them off somewhere safe and sound?

Jensen swiped the laptop off the table with a ferocious outburst, cracking the screen and reducing it to a useless heap of plastic and chips. "I can't cross that line," he said to himself breathlessly, leaning over the table in bleak contemplation.

Colquitt released his painful grip on Isaac's head and jaw and took a step back, carefully rolling his shoulder under his blood-crusted bandage. After a few moments, Jensen looked up from studying the table top in what, Isaac thought, resembled a look of guidance.

Isaac had to say something; the moment seemed frozen, snagged on this silent cue. "You're not Wyndorf. You're better than him. This is the proof. The world doesn't need another monster. You still have that rage, though, right?" Jensen watched him silently, his own thoughts twisted and lost in the barren landscape of his mind, the beacon fires of vengeance and hatred not fully suppressed. "And you need to put it somewhere. Well, I'm still here. Wyndorf's still here. Do the right thing, Jensen. Let everyone else go." Jensen considered this with a withering stare.

Colquitt remained disengaged, the perfect hired gun. Outside, the rural quiet was suddenly broken by the mechanical chatter of rapid gunfire.

Colquitt's walkie-talkie crackled into urgent life. "Sir, we have an unknown number of hostiles moving in from the west and east sides of the property." The rumble of overlapping burst fire was edging closer like thunder on the horizon.

Colquitt wore a fleeting look of confusion, then gave Isaac an intimidating snarl. "Friends of yours?"

Isaac shrugged, looking unconcerned about the possibility of being flanked by two opposing sides with a common objective of murdering him. "Not mine. Must be Wyndorf's."

"That asshole with the machine gun," Colquitt said through gritted teeth. "Mr. Jensen, stay here and keep your head down until I return."

Isaac looked toward the flimsy wood nailed over the large picture window. "This place screams secure."

Colquitt looked as though he would have enjoyed slapping the wise-ass out of Isaac if time wasn't a factor. "This was a short-term assignment. We didn't anticipate guarding against an attempted siege."

"What are your numbers?" Isaac asked. "The nine from the convoy, plus you?"

Colquitt hesitated.

Isaac assumed he was right. He looked at Jensen, their eyes magnetised. "I still have my rage too. If there's any chance of a last request, let me help you kill Wyndorf."

WEEKEND WARRIORS

Garland leaked through the moonlit woodland north of the farm like spilled ink on a black canvas. The night vision goggles painted his vision in a palette of emerald and white. As expected, one of the strung-out toy soldiers in the westward squad had thought this was paintball or some goddamn game, and sprayed lead at the first target they found, probably an old wheelbarrow or the side of a shed. That was fine. As to be expected. It would create a confusing shitstorm which would pit the itchy triggers against Wyndorf's captors, and allow him and his handful of good men to opportunistically pick off any oxygen wasters during their hunt for Wyndorf. Up ahead, a few disused grain silos were illuminated like squat jade towers.

A pig-masked perimeter guard in a dark windbreaker was listening to the squelch of a walkie-talkie, his frame becoming rigid with alertness. Even without the radio contact, it was impossible to mishear the rampaging Xbox army going off to the east. Garland watched how the enemy guard moved, alert, focused, bringing up his suppressed sub-machine gun and about to join the fray. Garland wished he had a camp full of such sharply honed troops. Though he could do without the strange masks.

A whistling blur raced across Garland's vision, right to left, the arrow piercing deep into the guard's back, flooding his lungs with blood. The dark array of structures was suddenly lit up in a harsh, retina-scalding wash of electric light. Garland ripped his night vision goggles up to his scalp, letting his pupils constrict and adapt to the surprise blaze of the spotlights arranged around the farm buildings. Looking to his right, he saw Schecter, the silent assassin, lowering his takedown bow and removing his own set of Night Owl Tactical Night Vision Binoculars. They made him look like some creepy alien insectoid hunting human flesh.

More sporadic gunfire thundered through the trees and clearing, bouncing off the barns, sheds and buildings to create a confusing din.

Garland's squad moved forth from tree to tree in silence, deftly side-stepping loose branches and dry leaves. Garland made it to the duo of silos first, Schecter, Kershaw and Higgins covering him. An explosion went off somewhere in the thick of it. That had to be that redneck Bruhl and his pet M32 MGL, a six-shot grenade launcher with rotating barrel. It had only ever been a matter of time before that armchair soldier decided to indulge in his Schwarzenegger delusion. Garland shook his head at how easily this was falling into place. He gave it five minutes before Bruhl committed his first act of friendly fire.

"Stupid bastards are going to bring S.W.A.T. down on us," Kershaw admonished, running over and crouching down beside Garland.

"By the time they get here, we'll be long gone."

Schecter swept up beside him, keeping an arrow nocked against his recurve bow. "You think the major's still spitting lead?"

"Crazy old bastard has one eye and a case of the shakes," Kershaw answered. "I'd be impressed if he made it from the drop-off point."

Garland checked Wyndorf's GPS on his phone. The signal placed him a bit further south-east. Right in the thick of it. Garland surveyed the clearing between their position and a large hay barn, the nearest perimeter lights shining on the peeling paint of the tall structure. Raising Shauna, Garland rattled off a short burst at the lighting rig, dropping the area into a concealing gloom. The four of them paced across the open ground in a squat-run.

Halfway across the open ground, Higgins went down, peppered with a few erratic shots to the chest and neck. Something else blew up near the eastern edge of the farm, the explosion rocking the world, spewing flame and hot light high enough to reach over the barn's roof and sketch long shadows behind the three men. Higgins' killer blind-fired from behind the barn again, punching up nothing but dirt this time, his shots barely audible over the ear-rattling of another blast. Garland caught sight of the muzzle flash and let Shauna chew through the aged wood, spraying a fine pink mist into the background shades of fire and electric light. The body went limp and fell away from the cover. Another dead pig.

Kershaw grabbed Higgins' legs and Garland grabbed his arms, Schecter covered them as they raced for the cover of the barn. Another of the distant lighting rigs sparked out into darkness as they lowered the young soldier's body. Kershaw knew the man was dead even before they lowered him. The bullets to the body had hit his Kevlar, but the slug in his throat had turned him into a cardinal garden hose.

Garland heard the thumping tread of shoes on grass-clumped soil rushing toward them from around the side of the building. His Ka-Bar knife was out and ready with a fluid snap. Moving like an oil slick, his massive frame swept around the side of the splintered wall and dispatched the speeding enemy with a savage slice to his carotid. He locked eyes with his opponent. It was one of Thurman's, a jittery liability named Carson, and from the looks of things he was running scared. Abandoning his alleged brothers in the middle of a pitched battle. Setting aside the group's ethos for a debilitating drug addiction was bad enough, but to desert your comrades was cause for execution in Garland's opinion. Garland let him drop in a gasping slump and wiped the blood from the blade, allowing his large hands to caress the cold beauty of Shauna again.

Kershaw sighed in frustration and lowered Higgins, avoiding his blank, staring eyes. Garland dropped a hand on Kershaw's shoulder, bringing the man back to a stand. They had to keep moving.

With their backs against the barn wall, they carefully moved around to the tall doors, the sound and fury of the theatre giving them momentum. They counted to three and swept into the barn, weapons high. It was vacant and lifeless: nothing but old hay bales and cobwebs. Schecter placed a finger to his lips and pointed up to a concealed shooter in the loft, taking down troopers from the window. The archer scurried light-footed across the barn floor, creeping up the ladder, keeping his weight away from the middle of each rung for fear of them creaking in stress. Ducking low, he came up on the sniper and momentarily paused. The vista before him was absolute chaos, the scene validating Garland's strategy. It was a massacre. Although they had the greater numbers, the raw, green Joes of the Midnight Frontiers were getting neatly picked off by superior shooters. Most of Thurman's loyalists were already kissing the dirt. The floodlights had all been shattered, leaving the wide open grounds swathed in oily black smoke and bathed in warm firelight.

A hundred yards in the distance, sheltering behind a low stone wall which was quickly becoming rubble, sat Bruhl, giggling like he had gone apeshit, his M32 braced against his Kevlar. About two hundred yards opposite him was a large farmhouse, controlled burst fire leaping out from the shadows of the porch's front entrance, each shot getting closer and closer to tearing down the cover of the wild man with the grenade launcher. Five feet from Schecter, the sniper was waiting to get a bead on the top of Bruhl's head.

Bruhl boldly sprang up. Thunk. The launcher's revolver-style barrel spun, the grenade trailing over the yard and blasting above the double doors of the farmhouse. Stone slabs and granite chips poured down, sealing the entrance.

The sharpshooter was about to return the favor, his finger slowly squeezing the trigger. Schecter could easily get close and kill Bruhl when the time came, but right now this crazy bastard and his heavy ordnance could come in handy. Pulling a ludicrously large hunting knife from the sheath on his belt, he lunged forward and skewered the prone sniper through the top of his thoracic vertebrae, just as the man pulled the trigger. The bullet veered crazily and disappeared somewhere in the dark tree line.

Elsewhere, the salvos, though greatly diminished, continued sporadically. Peering out of the hay barn's cover, Garland checked his

GPS signal and tried to gauge which building Wyndorf was in. The run-down farmhouse seemed to be too close, but beyond that was what appeared to be a livestock shelter and an enormous airplane hangar. Now the three of them just had to get by an unknown number of well-concealed enemy combatants hidden amongst the smoke and the rusting hulks of long-abandoned agricultural machinery.

Within the farmhouse, the blast threw Colquitt backward down the hallway in a plume of smoke and dust. Coughing his lungs up, he fumbled to his knees and hurried back into the empty lounge, panting and agitated.

The blast didn't even cause Jensen to flinch. "Colquitt, if you want the rest of your payment, do not let them free that bastard." His voice was querulous.

Colquitt let the Heckler & Koch MP5 hang at his side, and boomed into the walkie-talkie, "Secure the pen, they're coming for Wyndorf."

It took a blood-chilling moment for a voice to finally reply. "Rossbach and I got him covered." The responding voice, a merc called Olivetti, sounded terse. "But I can't raise anyone else. I think this swarm of fuckers took out Jordan, Wells and Chase."

Colquitt squeezed the talkie so tight his knuckles bulged like bleached pebbles. "Just hold the position. I'm on my way."

Isaac, the kneeling supplicant, sucked back blood from his torn lip. "Sounds like you need all the help you can get." He raised his tied wrists. "Roach and I might even the odds."

Jensen still looked conflicted at the idea, but the sounds of war were beginning to fade away, along with any hope of keeping Wyndorf in his grip.

Seething but level-headed, Colquitt looked to his employer, hating the idea but lacking a better alternative.

"Bigger picture, Jensen." Isaac pulled his hands as far apart as the wire would allow.

Jensen quietly agonised over it for a taut second, then gave Colquitt a nod.

Grinding his teeth, Colquitt snapped open a wicked, short blade and sliced the black zip tie around Isaac's wrists and ankles. Then he gave Isaac the knife. "Don't do nothing stupid."

Isaac kept the blade close and roughly shoulder-checked Colquitt on the way past. "Is there a back door out of here?"

"Kitchen. Let's go," Jensen commanded, leading the way.

"You're not going anywhere." Colquitt stalled him. "You die, I don't get paid,"

"I lose my chance to kill Wyndorf, you don't get paid," Jensen rephrased.

"Fuck!" Colquitt kicked the fold-out table across the room. "Doc, keep your damn head down and stay the fuck behind me." He hurried past them toward the empty kitchen. "Wait here a minute. In case you didn't hear it, there's a guy out there knocking on the front door with a grenade launcher." He peered through a glass pane in the kitchen door, only able to make out ember-gilded shadows. Then he gently opened the door, his gun leading him out carefully on to the macadam step. The fire-lit fields were clear, as was the eastern side of the large house. Colquitt nudged his head to the pair of them, his attentive eyes constantly scanning for the invader.

Jensen touched down on the gravel path, tasting the cold, smoky air. "We need to hurry," he yelped, speeding toward the basement prison to the north of the property.

Isaac grabbed his shoulder and pulled him back. "Careful."

Jensen shrugged his hand off imperiously, about to retort when a silhouette marched out from the southern corner of the house, backlit by a burning tree. The gangly figure, garbed in Kevlar and camouflage, had a weapon with a big rotund drum at its core.

Colquitt pegged it for an M32 grenade launcher as quickly as it took the shock to kick in. So here was the guy arcing fireballs all about the property like a drunken fire imp, stalking the place for pockets of resistance.

Bruhl's launcher swung down at them in a tight arc, the last payload ready to reduce the group to chunks of cooked gore and bone. Unlike Bruhl, Colquitt didn't have the shakes. As sideways as this assignment had gone, it was just another day on the job. He double-tapped Bruhl with his MP5, the second shot coating the gravel behind him in a fine spray. Bruhl's dead finger spasm tugged the trigger, his limp arms dragging his aim down toward the crunching path before him. The grenade made its familiar tinnitus-inducing boom and propelled Bruhl's shredded body backward ten feet in a shower of tamped soil and gravel.

The topside crescendo had the Roach family flinching from shock and exhaustion, the quartet huddled for warmth in the corner of the musty, empty cellar. After checking to make sure the knife wound wasn't too deep, Diane rested her head on Curtis' shoulder, his coat giving off a faint whiff of countryside. Their son and daughter had gone quiet, and both parents were hoping they might be sleeping it off. If there was any justice, maybe they could get through whatever this nightmare had left without waking to experience it.

"You were right to get as far away from me as possible." Roach broke the silence, taking Diane by surprise. "You did everything for me. You were so patient. But I couldn't turn it around. I just couldn't. It's hard to admit this, but as much as I loved you, and I did, please believe me, I couldn't put you before Isaac. You know how it is … how it was. I thought me and him would be sticking through thick and thin until the end. After he went away, seeing how he chose Maggie, and a future that didn't involve all this bullshit, you'd think that would have been my wake-up call. If anything, I resented him for doing that. Turning his back on me. So I walled myself up, pushed you further away, brought the bottle closer." Diane lifted her head up, brushing a blonde strand away from her cheek, trying not to get angry. "You did everything you could to save us, and I threw it all right back in your face. I was a shitty dad, shitty husband … and now my mistake is going to get us all killed."

"Stop with the self-pity. I don't want to spend my final moments hearing you whine about past mistakes." Her eyes were tough, protective, no-nonsense. "Whatever's happening outside sounds bad. We should save our strength. And you weren't a shitty dad, they both love you."

Roach's smile was exhausted. "And you?"

She didn't answer.

"If we make it out of here, I'm done with this life. I'm going to grab hold of a second chance and not let go. We can start—"

There came the shriek of bolts sliding out of their rusting locks. Roach pushed away from the wall, his tired kids cuddling him for warmth. He gently moved them aside and looked at Diane, his eyes so full of love hardening into hate. Wincing at the shallow slice in his flank, he stood protectively over his family and readied himself to die fighting.

Isaac stepped inside, Colquitt and Jensen hanging back beyond the threshold, listening to the rattle and roar of the few remaining machine guns. Roach was speechless at this bizarre union.

"Some assholes are trying to spring Wyndorf. We stop them, then"—Isaac threw a doubtful look at his other enemies at his back—"we see where we go from there."

Roach couldn't believe his ears. "Sounds like a full-scale NRA invasion out there, and you have a knife. What do I get to take to this gunfight, a shovel?" Roach glanced down at his palm, tacky with blood, turned to his family in the corner, and shook his head, baffled. He brought his harsh stare up to Jensen and Colquitt. "And what's stopping you from killing us?"

"There's no olive branch being extended here," Jensen answered. "No trust to be gained. I realised the bark of my demons exceeds their bite. I don't care what happens to the rest of you after this, so long as Wyndorf doesn't slip the noose."

Roach pondered it for a whole two seconds. "My family, they stay hidden in here."

"Fine," Jensen answered quickly, keen to get back to the barn and ensure Wyndorf was still in place.

Roach kissed Peter and Vicky, squeezing them tight. "Daddy needs to go help take care of something, but I'll be right back."

The twins clung tightly to his coat, begging him to stay with them, their weeping, defenceless eyes wrenching his heart from his chest. He struggled to keep his own tears back and soothed the pair of them with words he hoped carried some weight.

What must it feel like, Isaac wondered, to have loved ones to come back to.

Colquitt paid no mind to the touching scene, while Jensen watched with the glazed expression of a PTSD sufferer.

Roach held Diane's hand and pulled her close, whispering into her ear, "When everything goes quiet, you all sneak out of here. Find the road and don't stop until you get to safety." He paused, a word stuck to his tongue. "I love you." He almost didn't say it, didn't think he still had the right to. "I'm sorry."

Diane looked brave for her children, for herself too, afraid that if she lost it now she might not regain it. "I love you. Promise me you'll be careful out there." They embraced tightly, keeping it quick.

Roach hurried over to Isaac, noticing how his attention was on Peter and Vicky, and realising how surprised he must be. "I didn't know how to bring it up, man. We don't exactly have BBQs on the weekend."

Isaac wasn't offended. "Cute kids, must get it from Diane." He exchanged a quick look with her, glad she was safe but not exactly in the moment to play catch-up. He let his pitch drop, wanting to speak discreetly without giving Jensen or Colquitt cause for concern. "This was my idea, I told them we could both help stop this breakout, but seeing you here with them…" He shook his head. "You're leaving with Di and the kids, now. The three of us will stop Wyndorf."

"No, we all need this closure," Roach countered.

"Let's go," Colquitt thundered.

Isaac knew Roach had made up his mind and gave him a friendly punch on the shoulder. He barged past Jensen and his unleashed wolf, racing for the hellish night above.

Roach sidled up to the frail, scarred man, noticing Colquitt tense, probably sweating over his purse. "Ludlow was like my pops." Jensen possessed no fear, holding Roach's glare like he was ready to die. "But we've all done enough damage to each other." He pointed at his family. "This was some unforgivable shit, but you spared them. My not killing you here and now is me being generous." Roach turned, holding a hand up to his family. "I'll see you soon. I love you." Without another word he ran up to where Isaac crouched at the top of the stone stairs, knife locked tightly in his fist.

Jensen spared a brief look at Diane and her babies, surprising her with a tenderness that was utterly incongruous with his violent features and terrifying actions. "God forgive me." He closed them in but left the door unlocked.

"Stay behind me at all times. Hear me?" Colquitt secured his walking bank balance. They both joined Isaac and Roach, ready to brave what sounded like the death rattle of the apocalypse.

SLAUGHTERHOUSE

Garland could feel eyes on the back of his head, a sensation which prickled his spine like sheet ice. He, Schecter and Kershaw were fifty yards from the livestock enclosures, and were expecting to be scalped by a rifle bullet at any moment. They passed an upturned graveyard of Thurman's cannon fodder, who had been attentive and enthusiastic in their fighting but too erratic, their skills dulled by a crippling ratio of narcotics to training. Identification was difficult for several of them: one missing half his head from a heavy-calibre shot, another cocooned in fire besides a blasted tractor on its side. Garland could almost feel himself being transported to another time and place. The moon dust of Afghanistan, an M1 Abrams tank smouldering in the cold desert night with a company of corpses. The heavy losses of these unsuitable men did hurt Garland, yet he couldn't help but view this as a pragmatic act, a necessary cull. And at the end of this bloody night, he knew the souls of the perished would take the matter up with Major Thurman.

They hadn't crossed any other fallen hostiles. Either there were some up ahead or it was a clear case of quality over quantity. They paused besides a low wall, the sound of crackling bonfires making Schecter think of his melted skin.

Garland tried to raise Thurman on his comm channel, checking to see if the old warhorse was still galloping about somewhere on his demented rescue. "Major, I'm approaching the collection point. What's your SITREP?" All he got back was silence. He shared a look with Schecter and Kershaw, part sympathy, part relief that they might have been spared the act of shooting their once-revered leader like a rabid mongrel. The three of them removed the looped wire earbuds from their ears. "Okay, let's finish this."

Garland took point, leading them the last dozen yards in a careful jog. He split up Schecter and Kershaw so they could surround the livestock enclosure, anticipating some final push back from the enemy. Garland climbed over the metal gate, finger poised to put down any combatants, but the only sounds in the night were the fiery snapping of the charring bodies and trees engulfed by grenade flame.

Inside the pen, he found the bodies of two more of the suited men in pig masks, and three more of Thurman's meth-addled mercs, face down in old hay and dirt. Crouching low, he cautiously swept down the central avenue, paranoid of shooters hiding behind the wooden roof supports or bent low in the long parallel rows of pens. The quiet rush of his pumping blood eased when he spotted Schecter and Kershaw enter from the opposite end of the brick enclosure, moving down to meet him midway.

Mixed voices stopped the three of them dead in their tracks. Tones of elation merging with aggression. Garland rounded a mesh-covered fencepost and found Thurman in one of the central pens on his right, panting and smeared in greasy soot and beaded with sweat, his eyepatch looking like the empty hollow of his skull beneath the fading strip light. He was standing victoriously over a grinning Wyndorf, about to cut his cuffs.

Isaac and Roach followed Colquitt around the side of the farmhouse, with a skittish Jensen at their tail. The mad schemer was untroubled by the death in the stilled air. His main worries were that Wyndorf might get away with the help of well-armed assailants, and, of course, even if they caught him in time, that Isaac or Roach might steal the kill for their own gratification.

Rounding the house's charred and devastated south corner, the four of them got their first glimpse of the Valkyrie buffet laid before them in the smoky, flaming farmyard. The soil rich with spilled blood. Across the infernal meadow they spied a trio of killers hurriedly marching into the hostage pens. Colquitt's knife wound seemed to scream out in righteous retribution when he laid eyes on the great hulking soldier leading the rescue.

Roach stooped down beside the corpse of some whack job in camouflage fatigues and a skull jawbone neck scarf. He dragged the sub-machine gun from the man's dead hands, an HK UMP, another German number. He checked the magazine, about twelve rounds, half-full, then slapped it home again. A short, strangled cry escaped him as a hand seized his ankle. The downed soldier still had a little fight in him. His other hand swung his pistol up at Roach. Roach roughly kicked the hand away, the handgun flailing off into the grass, then smoothly placed a single round into the combatant's chest. Taking a calming breath, he looked up and saw Colquitt had stopped moving, gun trained on him, fire reflected in his eyes and burning him with a warning. Threat shimmered like heat between the pair of them until Colquitt was forced to keep up with the undeterred surgeon, but he was keeping one eye firmly on Roach.

Isaac could sense the anxiety coming off Roach in waves. Clearly he was wanting to get back to his family in one piece, and praying for their safe passage from this nightmare. Isaac, in contrast, had never felt so calm. Unshackled, knife in hand, his only true purpose minutes away from him, ready for his blade. He imagined Maggie, discouraging his blood lust, begging him to turn the other cheek and get out of there whilst he still could. At the moment, though, he turned a deaf ear to his ghosts.

Garland couldn't believe the major was still alive. He was well beyond his prime for the physical rigors of combat. These were his twilight years as a tactician and surely the hard effects of methamphetamine had clouded the stars of his painfully accrued wisdom.

And yet here he was, a broken-down trained killer forged in the steaming jungle, a frosty, carnivorous grin on his seamed face. Garland paid only scant attention to the other two people cinched tight in the pen, a big husky guy and a young woman, both with bound ankles and wrists. They looked like the ones who'd been caught in the shootout on the street earlier.

"Major." Garland hid his disappointment. "Did you lose your earbud? We thought you were dead."

Thurman's expression was one of pure need, and he looked almost reverentially at his cackling speed-king savior. "Some close moments," he admitted. He sawed through both sets of plastic cuffs on Wyndorf. "Come on, soldier. Let's get you back to the DMZ."

Wyndorf was almost grooving on the spot, a drunk office-party employee revelling in the violence in the air, and gave Garland a sneer. "Hey, meathead, I didn't know you cared enough to go through all this trouble for li'l ole me." Schecter and Kershaw were stock still, bow and rifle just waiting for the command to follow through and settle this. Wyndorf got to his feet. "First things first, I need to find a few fellas who I'm kinda hopin' are still very much alive. I'll skin them quick as you please, then we can put this shit-show behind us and get back to business."

Garland cocked his pistol. It sounded like the world's largest rat trap getting sprung, the big silver barrel gleaming in the electric light.

Thurman's one dark piercing eye, white phosphorus burning in a copper-stained swamp, settled on Garland. "What in Christ's name are you doing, son?" the major snapped incredulously, his vile mouth like a sewer manhole spewing forth undesirable materials.

"Sticking to our mission, sir. It's been an honor." He squeezed the trigger. The bullet sped through Thurman's eyeball, splashing gray matter and bone splinters out the back of his gray crew-cut, some of it splashing on Fitzy and Grace. The disgraced and rusty cog of the government collapsed as if his wires had been snipped.

"Is this about our disagreement on business models?" Wyndorf's gaze was a black hole, its immense gravity drawing in all warmth and life, nullifying it, corroding it into nothingness. He faced his death without care.

Garland trained the gun on Wyndorf, trying to absorb as much joy out of this as quickly as possible. He started to squeeze. For one bizarre second he thought he had somehow squeezed too tightly, as he heard the single whip-crack of a handgun. It took a second or two to realise it came from the killing field outside.

That second or two was all it took to rob Garland of his chance. He turned back, ready to finish the objective. He didn't feel the bullet crash through his left cheekbone with a wet snap, altering the structure of his eye socket like a cracked and concave eggshell before continuing out the back of his head, didn't get to process the sight of Wyndorf on one knee with a feral snarl and Thurman's smoking service 9mm in his hand.

Isaac raced the last of the distance, through the gate of the perimeter fence and straight for the livestock pen with his soul collapsing into deepest, blackest despair. Each pounding footstep hammered an image of Wyndorf with a gunshot to his cranium, maybe caught in the crossfire of his backup and Colquitt's final guards, departing this rotten world without staring up into the satisfaction of Isaac's face as his final act. Although Isaac paid him little thought, Jensen, now stumbling and wheezing to keep up with the other three, was brimming with an almost identical distress.

They entered at the exact moment it turned into a shooting gallery. Isaac hopped behind a thick wooden support column, the knife in his hand feeling more ludicrous than ever before. Roach slid behind an old wheelbarrow opposite him, the HK's stock wedged into his shoulder. Colquitt charged in and had to leap over the body of Rossbach, or maybe it was Olivetti, their bodies and those of their killers littered about the doorway in splashes of blood.

To Isaac's surprise, the bullets were not being aimed at them. From his split-second appraisal of the scene, it looked as though

the two soldiers—who shot the third behemoth?—were target-
ing Wyndorf as he dived for cover behind a flaky concrete wall,
several shots puffing up powdered stone. Isaac poked his head
around the splintery column, seeing Wyndorf pop up and fire a
few shots at a burned guy who snatched a steel-tipped arrow from
the quiver on his back, smoothly drawing it back and locking on
to his target with machine-like precision. As Wyndorf's bullets
bored past him through the pen's wall, the archer composed himself and loosed the arrow, his keen eye watching the thin, razor-
pointed shaft whistle through the air. Isaac's heart froze, time
slowing down. Wyndorf flinched, twisting his body to one side,
the arrow skimming past his center mass and embedding itself
deep into the post behind him. Isaac had a wild notion to throw
caution to the wind and just sprint down the center aisle, past
the soldiers and straight at Wyndorf. He would most likely take a
bullet or two, but as long as they didn't prevent him from sticking
his knife in Wyndorf's heart, he could live with that. Or not, as
the case may be.

Schecter traded a couple of arrows with Wyndorf's taunts and
bullets, as Kershaw raised his rifle to drill a couple of bursts toward
Colquitt and Roach, the triplet bursts chiselling the concrete wall
and pinging off the metal wheelbarrow. Roach returned fire, his
bullets sparking off the filthy concrete floor and kicking up damp,
rotten hay. Isaac was getting antsy: he needed to find a way to get
out of this pointless three-way holding pattern of spent brass and
stainless steel arrow tips. He crawled away from the barn's aisle,
shimmying under the metal bars of the nearest pen, and quickly
and quietly moved on his elbows across the thick, damp carpet of
yellowish-brown hay, the noise of heavy calibres tearing up the scen-
ery and Wyndorf's sick taunts mocking the archer about his burns.
Isaac got the impression the two of them had history. In between
exchanges, he heard Grace and Fitzy talking in urgent, hushed
tones. They were a few more pens further in, and scrabbling about,
probably trapped by plastic restraints. Isaac figured the knife could
actually come in handy.

Kershaw was slowly backing away from his cautiously advancing opponents, moving and firing, moving and firing. He paused behind a wooden pillar, knowing his ammo was running perilously low. Good job he picked up that pipe bomb from Buckley's corpse. Kershaw observed Schecter's position, the archer nocking another arrow and moving from cover to cover, carefully pursuing Wyndorf as he vaulted over another of the enclosure's partition gates, getting steadily closer to the building's exit. Kershaw pulled out a box of waterproof matches from his belt, striking the head against the rough wooden support and kissing it to the short fuse in a sizzling display of hissing sparks. Pipe bomb in hand, he had only just pulled his arm back to launch the homemade explosive when Roach's last bullet burned through his midsection, right through his large intestine. Kershaw gasped in shock, numbness temporarily shielding him from the white-hot agony, his wide eyes spotting Roach nestled in the shadowy cover of the former hostage pen. With a last-ditch attempt, Kershaw tried to summon the strength to toss the bomb toward him. As his pain-wracked body awoke with a start from its cottony warmth of adrenalised oblivion, he fumbled the throw and dropped it only a few feet in front of him.

It was a mercy killing compared to the gut shot. The building almost left its foundations with the devilish eruption, the sound, fury, light and heat rattling the timber rafters and making every swinging strip light shudder like a weather vane in a hurricane, shattering many of them like sugar glass and setting the surrounding blast-weakened wooden columns alight. The staunch support post Kershaw had been using in his final moments was split in half with a hungry groan like that of a giant awakening from a deep slumber. The nearby supports voiced their own displeasure.

Isaac was in the act of cutting through Grace's ankle cuffs when the whole world unexpectedly exploded. With the slippery sensation that his goal was becoming more and more unattainable, he went at the cuffs, Fitzy's too, like he was expecting the roof to buckle and drop on them at any second, another obstacle to interfere with his atonement. Roach was suddenly right there at his side, pulling

Fitzy to his feet as Grace quickly swept her eyes about the barn, getting her bearings on what she had missed whilst lamely writhing like a worm across the floor on her knees, struggling to stand up.

"I thought these guys were his friends?"

"I only met that dickhead tonight and I already want to slap the shit out of him." Fitzy ducked a little lower, listening to the high, screeching creak of another damaged roof support beginning to struggle in its purpose.

Through the glow of the barn's smoky blaze, Grace saw the crazy stitch-faced surgeon keeping pace with his undomesticated pet wolf, both in pursuit of the Robin Hood fan and Wyndorf. "What's the play? Find some weapons and kill all these freaks?"

Roach pulled Grace and Fitzy down into a squat, mindful of catching a stray bullet or, somehow more unpleasantly, an arrow. He watched Colquitt and Jensen trot past their pen, the doctor's enforcer still peppering single shots at the archer's back, trying to put him down before he made it out into the open. Roach issued an order which left no room for compromise. "No, I have something more important for you two. My kids and my wife are here, in the basement of the farmhouse, around the back. Get them and the nearest car you can find, and get the hell out of here."

"And you?" Fitzy asked.

Isaac was squeezing his knife with restless pumps like a heavy beating heart, and watching Wyndorf slip out of the enclosure into the dark field. He could barely take his eyes off the ongoing feud to address Roach. "Last chance to leave. No sense in getting yourself killed. Kids need their dad."

Roach held his solicitous stare, challenging him. "We both kicked this hornet's nest. I need to see this through to the end, too."

Isaac didn't argue. He vaulted over the pen's railing and went into the billowing smoke cloud after Colquitt and Jensen.

Grace nodded once, but clearly didn't like bailing on Roach, even if it was for a good cause. "You watch your ass. I won't be there to keep it from getting kicked."

Roach tried to smile but it felt incongruous. "If my family get hurt, it'll be me kicking your ass. Now go."

Grace and Fitzy did as they were told, sprinting away from the hungry flames of the burning livestock barn, briefly stopping to collect a machine gun apiece from the grouping of bodies near the entrance, then back out to the battleground. Roach patted down Thurman's corpse, hoping to find another gun, but if the gnarled gun-nut had been carrying another it was now lost to the blood-soaked farmyard. He checked Garland's body instead, and as luck would have it, he found a 9mm sidearm with a full clip. The stench of smoke was stinging his eyes, the black tendrils pressing to his nose, suffocating him. He bolted from the pen, squinting through the fumes, catching up to the swift and fearless form of Isaac, who was carefully pushing forth beyond the spreading walls of flame. They were both knuckling hot, drifting grit from their watery eyes and trying to stare through the smoke when the archer spun on his boot heel and released an arrow behind him like he was attempting to slay the burning heart of the fiery beast. The arrow was set on a fatal trajectory toward Colquitt, yet he managed to dodge his fate, dropping to one knee, and thereby sealed the fate of another. Over the loud, hungry crackling of flame and groaning timber came a sharp gasp and the awkward tumble of a body collapsing to the floor. Jensen had been hit in the right shoulder, stuck clean through whilst in the middle of turning away from the speeding arrow.

Enraged, not from any sense of friendship or loyalty, but from a cold-hearted professionalism and the near-miss of his pending 50% payment, Colquitt fired off two more single shots, managing to take Schecter in the left lung and heart. The last of Chicago's true-blooded Midnight Frontiers was dead before his knees hit the concrete aisle.

Colquitt had never had the thirst to heal: his former black-ops career was purely carnivorous, dismantling the human condition rather than mending it. Right now he cursed his skilful death-dealing. With some cursory examination, he was relieved to find that the arrow poking out of Jensen's shoulder had cleared the top of his lung. It would hurt like hell but it wasn't an immediately fatal wound.

"Dammit, Jensen. I told you, you should have stayed back at the house."

Jensen was biting his lip into a white bloodless maggot, fighting back his searing agony. "No." His eyes were feverish with lunacy. "It has to be me. I have to be the one to kill him. It's all I have. Then I can die."

Colquitt heard footsteps pounding through the heat haze and roiling black smoke. Isaac and Roach sped past the both of them without a word or thought, chasing down Wyndorf.

"Help me up," Jensen demanded, a scorching spear of pain lancing through his shoulder. "He can't have gotten far."

Colquitt briefly considered forcing his employer to cough up the final instalment of his fee by brute savagery, then putting him out of his twisted misery. Alas, he was a professional. Scooping him up with one hand under his left armpit, Colquitt steadied him on his feet and hurriedly dragged him out of the conflagration, and not a moment too soon. A large section of the roof collapsed in with a demonic bellow, casting sparks and lung-coating poisonous carbon after them on a hot breeze. Up ahead, Colquitt, hampered by hobbling Jensen along, watched the blaze-borne silhouettes of Isaac and Roach trekking across the combat-ravaged field toward the vast structure of the pig polytunnel. He was going to call after them, make them wait under the guise of camaraderie, but really he was primarily concerned with preventing them from offing Wyndorf and costing him a much-needed wage.

"Hurry," Jensen croaked, removing himself from Colquitt's care.

The pair of them hastily continued across the grounds, mindful of the occasional dead soldier littering the blast-ruptured and scorched plots of land, heading for the cavernous tunnel.

Night Drive

Grace and Fitzy were knotted around Roach's family as if they were impersonating secret service agents, their guns pointed at the ground but ready to spring up and put down any lingering threats. Grace had draped her denim jacket over the small frames of Vicky and Peter, winking at them and doing her best to play the superhero who will chase away any nasty evil wanting to snatch them back. Unable to find any cars around the house, Fitzy at least got them to the gravel farm path and away from the carnage, using the silvery moonlight to guide them to the property's south gate.

Diane had resisted the rescue effort at first, telling Grace and Fitzy to take her kids far away from here. Their marriage may be over, but she needed to know Curtis was okay. At least for some form of closure, just in case the worst happened to him. The dilemma only worsened when Fitzy quietly took her aside and judiciously mentioned that the last thing she or Roach would really want was to separate two scared kids from their parents. She conceded his point after a moment, and they left that snuff room behind.

Grace wished she had her phone so she could find out which peckerwood backwoods-ass farm they were on. The nearest neighbor was probably miles away. She'd never thought she would miss that big, wonderful city as much as she did right now.

"Up ahead." Fitzy's voice jumped with a tremor of relief. At the other end of the dark, crunching path was a gathering of midnight black bulks. He instantly identified the sleek bodies of the Audis, but also the robust solitude of a van and a 4x4, both of which looked a bit rugged and incongruous. Maybe they belonged to the survivalists. A single short, sharp crack skittered the gravel in front of Fitzy, but there was no muzzle flash. The sound was the ricochet of a silenced projectile clashing with the hard white chips.

"Down!" Fitzy shouted, using his bulky body to block as much of Diane and the kids as he could.

The cars were only a short jog away. The alternative was to turn back and risk a shot in the back.

Crouching low enough that their chins were practically resting on the floor, Grace looked to Fitzy. "We making a run for it?"

"We can make it." He sounded like he was trying to convince himself.

Grace was up and blasting. She had no clear target, so she fired indiscriminately in a fan-spray toward the parked queue of cars whilst Fitzy made a chain of hands with Diane, Vicky and Peter, dragging them behind him as he too took up arms against the darkness. They made it to the cover of the first Audi, a sliver of moonlight bouncing off the contours.

"Did you get him?" Diane asked, trying to keep calm for her children.

They hadn't heard any returning fire hitting the cars during their sprint, but now wasn't the time for risky assumptions.

Fitzy shrugged, then turned to Grace. "You out?"

Grace was already in the process of reloading. "Nah."

"I need to start this thing up." He patted the hood of the car. "Cover me."

"Hurry up."

Keeping the driver's side between him and the night-concealed killers, Fitzy smashed the window, the glittering gems of glass dusting the black leather seat. He popped the lock and slid into the seat, mindful of the crunching glass, and set about hot-wiring their escape. More glass shards rained down on top of him, singing musically off the brim of his Celtics cap, another shot having punched through the rear window. Grace was returning fire, her gunplay providing enough ephemeral light to catch snatches of their enemies. Out of left field, a brief swirl of memories inspired Fitzy, harking back to his adolescence, when boosting cars was a knee-trembling, sweaty-palmed business. Twice in one night he had performed his best work whilst under duress. If only his young self could see him now, he seemed to smile at the delirious thought, just waiting to feel that first bullet punch into him.

The erratic back-and-forth exchange ceased with a cry of anguish, and a quiet personal celebration from Grace. "Got that motherfucker."

The gunman had been caught running from the south gate's stone wall toward the phalanx of cars, trying to get around to a better angle in order to hit Grace or maybe the Audi's tyres.

Fitzy finished up, the car awakening with a triumphant, powerful purr. "Get in," he blurted.

Grace pulled open the rear door and bundled Diane and the children in. As she slid over the hood to the passenger side, her ass clenched when several more shots aerated her door. She dived into her seat and Fitzy aggressively swung the car out in a hairpin turn with a spray of gravel, almost tossing Grace back out of her open door.

Keeping the headlights off, not relishing the thought of attracting any further attention, he used the diminishing glow of the cloud-obscured moon to thread his way down the farm road. Grace pulled her door closed and looked up in time to feel the car bounce over the wounded shooter she'd dropped. Two starbursts exploded out of the dark treeline, cutting through the air toward the sound of the droning engine.

"Stay down," Fitzy yelled at his backseat charges, the bullets stitching across the hood and spiderwebbing the windshield.

Grace took aim at one of the flashing targets, took a breath, and squeezed the trigger out of her window. Several rifle shots went wide, the bullet wounding if not killing one of the paired shooters. Fitzy barrelled the car straight down the lane. One final gunman stood between them and freedom. The stars flashed in the darkness like Morse code, the bullets tracing toward them like amphetamine-charged fireflies, collapsing what remained of the windshield. Grace emptied her magazine, her final shots coming up short along their bumpy ride. Fitzy stamped down on the accelerator, gunning straight for their determined killer. He popped his headlights on at the last second, the retina-burning full beams stabbing the survivalist through his night vision goggles.

"Hold on," Fitzy shouted to the back seat, and yanked on the handbrake. He lurched the vehicle into a violent whip, the rear left side of the car pulverising the hip and femur of the psychopath, flipping him over the roof where he landed in a bone-jarring heap on the grassy lane.

Waiting there, immobile for an unbearable moment, expecting more gunfire to take them apart like fish in a well-lit barrel, Grace listened to the sobs of the children and the ticking of the stationary engine. She looked at Fitzy like he was slow. "The fuck we waiting for? Go!"

Fitzy took three shallow, labored breaths. "You'll have to take the wheel, pal. I'm done."

In the sparse backwash of the headlights, Grace watched as Fitzy placed a hand to his torso and brought it away wet and dark as engine oil. Grace couldn't get her mouth to work.

"C'mon," he gasped and bubbled up some flecks of blood. "Help me out of this seat. You get them somewhere safe. Don't want Roach kicking our asses, right?" His smile would have looked wan and deathly if not for the poor light.

Grace punched the dashboard twice. "Sonuvabitch, Fitz."

"It's not that bad ... I cashed out behind the wheel." With those final words, the lifelong getaway driver seemed to leave his body, growing limp, eyes closing.

"Dammit," Grace whispered. She heard the sobs and muffled whimpers of the children in the empty silence, expecting their trauma to escalate into a shrill, haunting scream. She quickly checked on Diane and the little ones, asking if they were hurt, but luckily they were all unmarked. Unlike Fitz. Grace wanted to shout and pointlessly smash her empty rifle against the dash until her arms tired, but she wouldn't dare do anything to frighten Vicky and

Peter any further. "Don't worry, I'm not going anywhere. Just keep your heads down, okay?"

Grace switched off the headlights and their whole world drowned in the inky depths of a bottomless ocean, the patchy cloud banks smothering the moon like a chloroform rag, making that giant silvery stone slumber. Her front of protective calm felt as fragile as papier-mâché as they sat there in the naked, isolated danger. Moving as quickly and quietly as she could, she slithered out of her open window, not wanting the car's courtesy lights to become a beacon, and used the awful, agonised gasps to guide her around the side of the Swiss-cheese car to the bundled ragdoll. Her eyes had dilated to their maximum circumference and yet she could still make out very little, letting her ears and hands explore the Stygian wilderness, an ill perspiration bubbling from her pores in anticipation of some unseen killer lining up her helpless form in his sights. Her searching hands found the hardened exterior of an armored vest, but the anatomy of this crash test dummy felt all kinds of wrong. The man wept in shock and core-deep physical torment. Grace reached for his head, finding goggles plastered to his sweaty, groaning face. She ripped them off in an awkward, vicious snatch and laid them over her own poor sight. The world turned toxic green. She spotted the soldier's dropped rifle several feet away and scrambled over to it, spinning in a full circle, ready to cut down any newcomers. The meadows and copses were deserted. Slowly, she lowered her rifle and heard the paralysed man sputter something about 'Help' and 'Sorry', "Please' and 'I'm begging you'. Grace looked down at the blind man in disgust and thought about her dead friend in the driver's seat. She didn't waste the bullet. She stamped down on the beggar's throat with a sick cartilaginous crunch, listening to him choke to death as she removed the goggles. Then she walked back to the passenger seat and opened the door, the interior light highlighting the strain on all of their faces.

Diane was shaking from the adrenaline dump. "I'm sorry for your friend. He saved our lives. You both did."

Grace waved it off, feeling those same shaky effects of dicing with death and far too pissed to accept any gratitude. She was about to climb out of the car and deal with the morbid process of switching seats with a dead friend when Diane, stroking the heads of Vicky and Peter, stopped her.

"We're safe now, right? Can we just wait here for Curtis?"

"There's just been a whole lot of ruckus, and I may not know where we are but there's a chance the cops are on the way. And I ain't exactly a ghost to those guys, y'know. They'll see a sister with a record, on a farm that looks like they've been growing corpses, with a mom and her two scared kids in the back seat, and another known felon dead in the passenger seat. Not a smart play." She lowered her voice for the sake of propriety, but knew it was redundant under the circumstances. The kids couldn't help but hear what she said next. "And Roach ain't no saint, neither."

"This is different. No matter what you've done in the past, we're all victims here. It was self-defence. The police will put that together themselves."

"Yeah, maybe." Grace intentionally sounded cynical. "Look, we can't go anywhere driving this thing. Bit suspect, wouldn't ya say? We'll go back and see if we can find the keys to another set of wheels on one of those dudes, then I'll drop you off at the nearest police station. Cool?"

Diane was digging her heels in, and not entirely sure why. Their relationship was over but she didn't want Curt to die here in all this madness. Didn't want their son and daughter to lose their father because she hightailed it out of there and left him.

Nevertheless, Diane considered the plan for a minute, and accepted.

Grace nodded like her head was on a spring, gearing herself up for what she had to do next. "I just need to move the body of my friend."

SHOWDOWN

Isaac reached the mouth of the forty-foot-wide tunnel, the aluminium central staircase making him think of a large, lolling metal tongue. The sounds of the fat, agitated boars could be heard behind the walls of that giant warren network. The fire in the livestock enclosure had ended up destroying the shared junction box, robbing the tunnel of electric light, but Jensen had shrewdly topped up the backup diesel generator for his big night, turning the large structure into a channel of blood-red shadow. Isaac felt like pig chow in the making. Or maybe Wyndorf would eat him instead, put him in a sausage skin and cook him for fun.

He kept left, walking past the stairs that led up to the high central walkway—or as he now thought of it, a giant pirate plank—and down the maintenance passage between the tunnel and pen walls. Roach vigilantly crept along to Isaac's right, his rifle stock still in his large hands. Fight-or-flight hormones had numbed him to his knife-slash, reducing it to a distant calling, losing out to the tidal smash of his head-pounding pulse. Isaac was moving on autopilot, his self-preservation now well and truly a long lost practice. He was a kamikaze pilot ready to crash and burn against the rocks of Michael Wyndorf. Maggie, his LeConte's sparrow, and Will, their chick, fluttering after him in the slipstream, begging him to stop and turn back now, warning him not to seek gratification through vengeance. No matter what voice his subconscious trickster used to try to dissuade him, it was quickly hushed, silenced by graphic thoughts of Maggie and Will lying dead in their beds, being zipped up in body bags and going cold on some morgue chopping block.

The impolite grunts grew steadily louder somewhere over the wall, the fleshy scoffers sensing another meal.

Colquitt and Jensen had caught up, entering the opposite maintenance passage to the right of the stairs, hoping to run down Wyndorf before Isaac and Roach stole the kill. Colquitt's patience with his severely wounded benefactor was razor thin: he kept having to hold Jensen back from flinging himself ahead down the murky passage into a possible ambush. But Jensen's footsteps were starting to falter, and every third or fourth step he needed to post his arm out to the walls of the pen just to help push him on. He had to keep going, he was so close now. He took steadying breaths to try to muffle the mania screaming in his warped brain, and began his well-rehearsed litany of control, remembering his dominance over his fear, pushing his swinophobia back down deep into the cellar of his primal responses. He slowly exhaled, slowly inhaled, and tried not to think about the cold hard fact that along with the bloated and cruelly starved beasts in there was also the very aetiology of his stomach-churning dread. The violent nemesis who had shaken his life to bits and pieces like a demented child thrashing a matchstick house. He was getting woozy from the pain now, the arrow still protruding through his shoulder like some extreme tribal decoration, but he kept pace with Colquitt.

Isaac and Roach were about halfway through the tunnel when a huge thud came from the wall panel to their right. Roach spun and almost chewed the thick wooden siding to sawdust with his rifle. Isaac brought his knife up and nearly flung himself at the wall. A disgruntled oink followed. It was only one of the boars bungling into the confines of the shelter. They hadn't moved more than three feet away when another soft thud, this one with an added shoe scuffle, came from behind them. Roach turned just in time to glimpse the pipe thwacking against the side of his head with a dull, sickening clink. He dropped like a safe had just fallen on him.

Wyndorf howled in delight, his tightly combed hair now a raven's nest of wild black straw, a crazed refugee from hell. "Like cracking an egg. C'mon, Zack!" Wyndorf kept hold of the leftover scaffold piping, and with the cat-footed grace befitting a sneaky cutthroat, he sped back toward the pen's wall and used one toe to spring himself up and over, back into the pigs' domain. "Come and get some bacon to go with all that runny yolk," his exhilarated voice challenged.

Isaac rushed to check on Roach but couldn't get a good look at the severity of the head wound through the tangles of sweaty hair. He felt for a pulse. It was slow but steady. Wyndorf continued to cackle, the glass-cutting pitch threading through the brewing commotion of excited wild boars. Isaac didn't hesitate. He bit down on the blade and leapt against the high fence, throwing himself over into the thick shrouds of darkness. The red generator lighting was even weaker in here, and Isaac briefly wondered if he would even see his death coming. Tentative steps took him further from the safety of the wall, deeper into the pen's tunnel offshoots. Thoughts of Maggie and Will now mingled with those of Ludlow being torn apart by charging hairy monsters. Somewhere, in one of the maze tunnels, Wyndorf giggled in fright, the humorous japing one makes when almost hurting oneself through folly. One of the pigs nearly running him down?

"Think about how much you want to stick me with that teensy little blade of yours. You could drag my death out for hours with that li'l pig-sticker. Be real mean about it. I really was generous with that bitch and runt of yours. I used a muhhh-uch bigger blade on them. Made it too quick. I guess I got excited."

Isaac tuned him out, worried his words would distract him from a rampaging bulk of teeth and tusks. He could make out a T-intersection up ahead. Palm sweat itched against the wooden knife handle. He approached the intersection slowly, constantly checking to make sure a boar wasn't lumbering toward his rear.

He was about to enter the potentially disastrous fork in the road when a figure sprang from the shadow-swaddled corner of the wide pen, moving with the speed of an ejector seat, a terrifying shriek of merriment scaring the life out of Isaac. Wyndorf swung wildly with the pipe, aiming to separate Isaac's bottom jaw. Isaac backpedalled, the whoosh of the piping caressing his face with a cool breeze, the scent of damp steel in the air. But he stepped back in quickly, his slashing knife only shredding the filthy white cotton of Wyndorf's work shirt. Wyndorf tried again with a backhand swing, tenderising Isaac's right upper arm with a flash of bright electrical agony. The pain was extraordinary, yet at the same time it made his arm feel limp and like a phantom limb. He changed hands with the knife until the sensation returned to his dead arm, thrusting and arcing the blade toward Wyndorf who danced around the strikes, taunting him and enjoying himself.

A wet, steaming grunt stole their fierce, blood-lusting attention. One of the hungry monsters stood at the mouth of the T-section, owning the tunnel with unchallenged territoriality. The pair of them became frozen in amber for a stretched moment, waiting for the clock to restart their survival instincts. Wyndorf, giddy as a schoolboy on the first day of summer, tried for a departing swing, aiming to bash Isaac's kneecap, then sprinted away from the massive pig. Isaac barely managed to hop back from the knee strike, and was about to try to climb back over the fence into the maintenance passage when he realised his arm was still a buzzing wet string. Hearing the fleshy tractor with a mouth pounding the mud-sloppy floor behind him, he turned and fled down Wyndorf's route.

Just up ahead, Wyndorf's sense of gamesmanship was flipped on its head when the second of the boars angled out of another of the corridors, tossing him over its huge, powerful flank. It quickly ambled around to muscle itself into a dominant position over its catch, intending to turn him into a human trough. Its warm breath was like a fine mist on Wyndorf's face and arms. It was about to chow down. Then it stopped, its gluttonous eyes absorbing the other possible meal hurrying toward it.

Isaac skidded on the slippery ground and almost lost his footing, mortified at the thought that the second behemoth might change its mind about Wyndorf and choose him instead, trapping him between two charging garbage disposals. In that brief window between life and death, Wyndorf clambered back to his feet and used the pipe to fend off the grotesque thing guarding him, aiming for its face but clobbering its battering-ram shoulders. Isaac moved like the wind through the dingy, dank pen complex, the beating trotters at his back never too far away. Behind him, Wyndorf clobbered the relentlessly aggressive creature, only serving to make it mad. He ran for the fence and hurled himself at the horizontal struts, climbing it better than any scared squirrel or cat.

Isaac watched the annoyed hog turn from its lost meal, and felt his bladder tighten. It was settling for him instead, even if it would be sharing him with the one breathing down his neck. His right arm was beginning to feel like something resembling functional, and not a moment too soon. A bit further up in the pig hotel, the third resident stomped out of its den, an equally huge silhouette slamming about the place, stirred up by the meddlesome intruders.

With the three pigs converging on him from different angles and cutting off any alternative escapes, Isaac shook his arm out and went at top speed toward the high fencing. He slipped in something wet, dropping him onto his back and knocking the wind out of him like a sledgehammer to the stomach. Alarm bells rang inside his head, and he sensed his death piling in, smothering him in filthy, blood-drenched fur and flesh-chomping, bone-mashing teeth. Somehow, he was up again, moving without the need to breathe, a distant part of his heightened state filling in the blank of what he'd slipped in. It wasn't mud or excrement: it was the pool of Ludlow's leftover gore. He shut the fact out and tried again for the fence, feeling a dozen small aches waiting to bloom into tender grievances. He made it to the top of the reinforced fence as the hungry prisoners skidded into an inelegant pile-up, their collective impact almost bucking him from the top of the wooden panel.

Isaac realised he had dropped his knife in the muck just as he heard Wyndorf say, "Glad you made it. Let's finish this." Wyndorf had used the fence to jump and reach for the aluminium walkway suspended over the pen network. He was leaning almost casually against the handrail, the light turning him into a red-skinned devil taunting one of his hell-sent subjects as they attempted to climb up out of the pit.

Isaac could hear Jensen panicking somewhere over on the opposite side of the tunnel, seriously wounded but still adamant in his endeavors. Isaac gingerly stepped up onto the fence, fearful of it wobbling and dropping him back onto the menu below. He carefully leaned forwards, letting his hands catch the cold, clammy bars of the walkway, hoisting himself through the bridge's guard rail. Wyndorf moved in before Isaac was even standing, swinging the pipe down like an axe splitting a log. Isaac half-rolled, half-fumbled out of the way, the weapon clanging against the walkway with a bright clash, reverberating all the way up to Wyndorf's shoulders. Using the bars, Isaac quickly pulled himself upright before Wyndorf took a second cheap swing. Isaac fired a brief glance to his right, hoping to use his elevated position to catch a glance of Jensen and Colquitt behind the wooden perimeter. He spotted them twisting back to catch the display up on the bridge, and shifting back toward the steps located at the bridge's midpoint.

Wyndorf was acting like a trapped animal, soon to be pressed in from both sides of the walkway. He lunged in at Isaac, big crazy swings, sapping his energy with every two-handed swipe. Isaac was hobbling backward, the pipe clinking off the guard rails or swooshing through the air, when he hip-checked the metal trolley positioned behind him near the gap in the railings. Something heavy landed on the walkway with a deep resonating clang. He realised it was the captive bolt gun. Wyndorf was panting like a sprinter nearing the finish line, so great was his determination to take Isaac's head off, and didn't notice the possible shift in his fortunes.

Isaac swooped down to grab the strange-looking combination of DIY drill and high-tech pistol. Upon seeing Wyndorf's fatalist smile and arms arcing backward for another overhead chop, he urgently moved in low and jammed the muzzle against Wyndorf's knee. He squeezed the trigger and the gunpowder cartridge launched the .22-calibre steel rod like a piston, shattering the center of Wyndorf's patella.

With an ungodly howl, Wyndorf forgot about his killing stroke, and the steel pipe bounced and rattled onto the walkway before jouncing off into the pigpen below. He fell on to the walkway stiffly and awkwardly, somewhere between backward and sideways –any way which would keep his destroyed kneecap from attempting to flex. Lying on his side, he grunted and slobbered through the pain, then segued into wet, insane tittering and hollering.

Jensen finally made it to the top of the steps with tremendous effort, looking like death warmed up, and brushed past Colquitt. Isaac still had a few moments to finish this here and now before Jensen demanded Colquitt remove him from the equation. He straddled Wyndorf's weak, struggling form and wrapped his hands around his throat, his thumbs sinking into the man's Adam's apple, poised to crush it inwards like firm cardboard. Wyndorf's eyes bulged in his red-lit face, his choke increasing the hot hue of his cheeks and veined forehead, his tongue thrashing about in his silent mouth like some grotesque, muscular deep-sea leech. Isaac realised his eyes were watering, the tears tickling down his cheeks as they sluiced away from his pained and desolate snarl. Would Maggie and Will know he was doing this? Watching him fail in his vow to be a better man? Isaac imagined he could hear her voice, soft and musical but firm, beseeching him not to add more sorrow and rage to the cycle by making this violent choice.

Was killing him necessary? He had already caught him and beat him, and was now holding his life in his hands. It felt like such an empty and worthless victory, a runner-up prize. But couldn't that still provide some thin semblance of justice? Of gratification? Then it all fell into place for him. The taunting, the crazed enjoyment— Wyndorf wanted this. His little showdown between the two of them, no matter who walked away afterward. Isaac wasn't going to give him the satisfaction. The denial made him feel a little lighter. He removed his vice grip from Wyndorf's throat and watched him sputter and gag away from the verge of death.

Jensen was only ten feet away now, each step more laborious than the last, his hands holding on to the rails for dear life. Isaac saw the great void in his eyes, one which rivalled his own, and a thick, sharp sliver of guilt reopened that festering wound: he had been culpable in the utter, irrevocable ruination of this man's life and psyche. The poor tormented soul didn't have a chance of a better tomorrow. The least Isaac could do was give him the ending he craved. He climbed off Wyndorf.

"He's all yours."

Jensen looked at Isaac with an unreadable expression. It certainly wasn't gratitude, but it was something.

With heaving breaths, Wyndorf screamed at Isaac, pouring out deepest, blackest chagrin. "YOU FUCKING PUSSY! FINISH IT! FINISH IT THE WAY I FINISHED YOUR WIFE! YOUR BOY!"

Isaac backed away, watching Jensen step over Wyndorf, who was now using one hand to lamely flail at the surgeon's ankles.

Before turning his back on Isaac to lord himself over Wyndorf, Jensen said one thing. "Axillary artery."

Isaac wasn't a doctor but he figured the puncture wound, in addition to all the moving and wriggling about Jensen had stoically undertaken, had created some rapid and deadly repercussions. The ravaged surgeon lowered himself painfully to his knees, adopting the same sacrificial position Isaac had been in a moment before, and dropped his body weight, arrowhead first, into Wyndorf's neck. Jensen's slumped body prevented Isaac from enjoying the dying light in Wyndorf's frantic eyes, but the wet choking of him drowning in his own vile blood made up for it. With his final dregs of strength, Jensen pushed himself up, removing the spear from Wyndorf's throat, and kept tight hold of Wyndorf's shirt as he leaned toward the gap in the guard rail.

"JENSEN!" Colquitt saw what his financier was doing, but it was too late. "Transfer me the second half of my fee, RIGHT FUCKING

NOW!" Jensen had lost so much blood that he looked vacant. All he seemed to know was that he and the soft, writhing man spitting blood bubbles belonged below in the tenebrous pit. "JENSEN! Pick up your phone and transfer the fucking money!" Colquitt raised his rifle, knowing how futile the gesture was even as he did it. As mercenary jobs went, this one had gone sideways in quite remarkable fashion.

With one final heave, Jensen pulled himself and Wyndorf down into hell. A delight of scoffs, slurps and wet smacks rose from the depths.

"Looks like there are no winners today," Isaac said to Colquitt.

Colquitt burned holes through him with his stare. "This was never personal." He lowered his automatic. "But before I change my mind, you better get the f—" Colquitt's sentence broke off with two thunderous bangs, the bullets throwing him backward a step before he gripped the railing. Falling to one knee, he looked about for his executioner in confusion.

Roach was leaning his smoking and depleted HK barrel against the railing of the opposite flight of steps. "That's for my family. For Robert Ludlow. For Monahan. And it was personal." Colquitt tried to respond but only managed to flap his mouth like a fish before banging face first to the walkway.

Isaac was riding a disorientating wave of shock, fatigue and a whole concoction of grief, relief and anger. He looked at Roach with an almost unperturbed air. "So you can still walk and talk."

Roach dropped the gun, slowly taking the last couple of steps up to the walkway. "Always had a hard head. You okay?"

"In time," he answered after some cursory consideration. He gave a last glance at their surroundings, staring out of the long tunnel and seeing the distant firelight still crackling away in the fully engulfed livestock enclosure. "Let's go see if your guys got your family out of here."

The walk was slow going for Roach, who was still a little wobbly from the head blow, but they reached the parked cars eventually, not entirely sure if the walk had taken minutes or hours.

"I still can't believe you didn't tell me you had kids," Isaac said, cracking the fatigued silence.

"I wanted to. But it was about finding the right time. Busy day."

Isaac almost laughed but was afraid he wouldn't be able to stop if he did.

"After all this," continued Roach, "I'm understanding the appeal of the quiet life."

"You already own a bar. That's a decent way of making an honest living, right?"

"I've toyed with the idea of opening a second. Maybe have a chain going by the time I'm a fat old man."

Isaac liked the sound of that. "Ludlow, Monahan … they each had a good inning, but their work got the best of them in the end. One way or another. I don't think many bar owners find themselves getting targeted by psychopaths and mercenaries."

They walked on in silence for a short distance, then Roach had to ask, "So what are you going to do now?"

Isaac mulled it over. "Depends. You need a bartender?"

Roach smiled sleepily, wanting to make sure his family were okay before spending three days in bed. "I'm always looking for reliable staff."

They stopped before the cars when it dawned on them that the keys would be in the pockets of the scattered corpses back where they came from.

"Shit." Isaac slapped his palm on the Audi's roof, then decided to check the van on the off chance that fortune was smiling upon them. It wasn't. They must have exhausted their quotient of fortune by pulling through this ordeal with their skins intact.

They both heard the sounds of an approaching vehicle, the headlights glowing as it rounded a bend in the lane. It was hard to discern these new arrivals in the deep shades of early morning navy blue, so they both ducked behind the van, bone tired, unarmed and unprepared for reinforcements or whatever other fresh hell was arriving on the scene. The Audi slowed to a dying stop. It looked like it had been used for ballistics testing, but Roach almost left the ground in excitement when he saw Grace climb out of the driver's seat and help Diane, Peter and Vicky out of the back. He called out to them and lumbered over, almost scaring Grace into shooting him where he stood.

Isaac stayed behind by the van, the volume of their reunion dialled down by distance and the first of the early morning birds waking up with joyous chirps. He watched Roach hug Diane and the kids, their past familial difficulties forgotten for the moment, and imagined how it might have been to have Maggie and Will waiting for him at home. He would never know that comfort again, but at least he could carry their memories. They would always be a family in the quiet vignettes of his daily thoughts. Listening to the birdsong, he allowed himself to believe that a LeConte or two were singing exuberantly in that early pre-dawn choir. Swallowing a bitter lump, he smiled at Roach's happiness, and remembered that he still had some family left after all.

ABOUT THE AUTHOR

Daniel James is an English author (not his fault, and he voted Remain) from Liverpool. A lifelong geek, he was raised on a diet of horror novels, action and martial arts movies, comic books, and punk and heavy metal music. It was during his dissertation year at Liverpool Hope University that he decided, for no discernible reason, to have a crack at writing a novel. Since earning his Bachelors of Science in Health, Nutrition & Fitness, he has been steadily putting in hours at the keyboard. Having dabbled in kickboxing and bass playing in bands in the past, it was getting his ideas down on paper that really took hold as a passionate outlet and hobby. When not writing, he has the great misfortune of working as a hackney taxi driver.

About the Publisher

This book is published on behalf of the author by the Ethan Ellenberg Literary Agency.
https://ethanellenberg.com
Email: agent@ethanellenberg.com

www.ingramcontent.com/pod-product-compliance
Lightning Source LLC
Chambersburg PA
CBHW070646100726
47907CB00007B/2116